THE BRIDE HE STOLE

ROGUES OF MULL
BOOK TWO

JAYNE CASTEL

WINTER MIST PRESS

All characters and situations in this publication are fictitious, and any resemblance to living persons is purely coincidental.

The Bride He Stole, by Jayne Castel

Copyright © 2024 by Jayne Castel. All rights reserved. No part of this publication may be reproduced, stored in a retrieval system, or transmitted in any form or by any means—electronic, mechanical, recording, or otherwise—without the prior written permission of the author.

Published by Winter Mist Press

ISBN: 978-1-991280-04-6 (paperback)

Edited by Tim Burton
Cover design by Winter Mist Press
Cover image generated by Midjourney

Visit Jayne's website: www.jaynecastel.com

He stole her to hurt his enemy. He never
planned to fall for her. A vengeful warrior
abducts the proud daughter of the man who
murdered his father—only to discover she is his
soulmate. Vengeance and epic love collide on
Medieval Isle of Mull.

**Jack Maclean wants revenge against the man
who butchered his father**. He's waited long enough
to claim it, but now he has a plan: he's going to hit
Kendric Mackinnon where it hurts and steal his lovely
daughter.

Tara Mackinnon is doggedly loyal to her clan.
She'll do what she can to help her father gain the edge
over their enemies—the Macleans—including marrying
to secure a powerful alliance.

**But when a stranger abducts her, Tara is thrown
into another life, full of danger and unexpected
passion.** Dragged into the wilds of the Isle of Mull, she
finds herself inexplicably drawn to the warrior who has
stolen her.

And it doesn't take Jack long before he makes a soul-
shattering discovery.

**He should hate the woman he's stolen … but why
does it feel like he's been looking for her his
entire life?**

*THE BRIDE HE STOLE is Book Two of an exciting new
trilogy by Jayne Castel—full of flawed yet irresistible
Highland warriors and determined Scottish lasses!*

***
To my wonderful readers.
Thank you for loving the worlds I create.

***

*All my wrong turns became
the right ones when they led me to you.*
—J. Střelou

BOOK ONE: CAPTURED

1: THE SMIRKING STRANGER

Tobermory
Isle of Mull, Scotland

March 1315

THE MAN DREW her eye.

Tara wasn't one to stare—for her handmaid had always counseled her against such bold behavior—however, as she walked along the bustling pier, this stranger was striking enough to make her look away from where fishermen hauled in their catch of live crabs, winged skate, and silvery mackerel.

The man weaving his way through the crowd was tall and broad-shouldered, with a thick head of rich auburn hair that brushed the collar of the fine quilted gambeson he wore. He walked with the confident swagger of a warrior, a dirk swinging at his hip.

Tara's gaze narrowed. There was something familiar about him, and she wondered if they'd met before.

As he drew close, she scrutinized him. His eyes were an unusual shade of green. It wasn't dark like pine, bright emerald, or moss—but an earthier fern-green. He had proud, aquiline features and full lips that looked as if they smiled easily.

Aye, she had seen him somewhere, yet she couldn't remember when or where.

Marking her stare, the stranger looked at Tara then, those sensual lips curving, not into a smile, but a knowing smirk.

Heat rolled over her, and she immediately cut her gaze away.

The Saints forgive her, it had been a mistake to observe him so frankly.

Tara quickened her stride, relieved when she'd passed the smirking stranger by. Aye, he was handsome enough to make a lass lose her wits, yet he was clearly a knave. She didn't know when their paths had crossed before, but she hoped she wouldn't see him again.

Glancing over her shoulder, Tara focused instead upon the heavyset woman with a red face who followed a short distance behind with three warriors at her heel. "This way, Orla," she ordered briskly.

"Aye, I'm right behind ye, Lady Tara," her loyal maid puffed, quickening her step.

Sighing, Tara tried to swallow the irritation that now tugged at her.

Orla was a good woman, who'd been with her since childhood, but Tara often felt smothered by her presence. She wished she could have made this trip to Tobermory with just her guards in tow. They'd taken her father's birlinn the short distance east along Mull's northern coast from his fortress of Dùn Ara, for she wanted to pick up some red ribbon to finish off her wedding surcote.

Can't I have just one day to myself before the wedding?

A new life awaited her, and although she was keen to do her father proud, there was a part of her that quailed at leaving everything she knew behind. Today, she wanted to indulge her love for shopping a little and forget she'd soon be Callum MacDonald's wife.

At the thought of the gruff young man whom she barely knew, Tara's mouth thinned. A moment later, she checked herself. *Daft lass. This marriage is an honor ... never forget it!*

Tara was about to forge an alliance between two powerful clans. She'd also tip the delicate balance that existed upon the Isle of Mull in favor of the Mackinnons. Those traitorous Macleans had recently broken faith with her father, and understandably, he was keen to make them pay. Although she'd privately thought Astrid Maclean was a poor choice of bride for him, she'd witnessed over the past months how bitterly disappointed he was that the Maclean clan-chief had broken off the betrothal.

However, Tara's upcoming marriage to Aonghas MacDonald of Sleat's eldest would give her clan the edge her father needed against the man he now named his enemy.

"Aren't we heading for the shop on the front?" Orla called out then.

"No … I hear there's another merchant that sells ribbons on Little Brae," Tara replied.

"Isn't that a squalid back alley?"

With a dismissive snort, Tara turned right, away from the docks, where women haggled with the fishermen over the fresh fish. Excited voices rose high into the damp morning air.

Tobermory wasn't a rough port, although her maid was a nervous woman who often worried about safety.

Tara headed toward a row of stone buildings with turf roofs that lined the waterfront, skirting an ox pulling a cart full of turnips, and made for one of the narrow lanes that led up between two buildings. Aynsley, one of the lasses who worked in the kitchens at Dùn Ara, had told her where to find Little Brae—in between *The Bonnie Badger* inn, and an apothecary—and she'd assured her the merchant sold the loveliest ribbons in Scotland.

It was quite a claim, and Tara was excited to see for herself. She loved pretty things and wanted her wedding gown to be special.

Nonetheless, when she entered the alleyway, the overpowering stench of stale urine made her eyes water. Drying washing festooned the lane, creating an obstacle course. Stepping over the rotting corpse of a large rat, Tara murmured an oath under her breath.

Maybe Orla had a point.

Relief swept over her when she found the shop halfway up Little Brae. She then waited for her maid and guards to catch her up.

"Ye can all wait here," she informed her escort.

"Don't ye want me to accompany ye, Lady Tara?" Orla asked hopefully.

Tara shook her head. "It'll be cramped inside ... don't worry, I won't be long." In truth, she intended to take her time over choosing the ribbons—on her own.

Orla nodded, although her expression clouded.

Shoving aside a stab of guilt, for she knew that Orla loved shopping as much as she did, Tara pushed her way indoors. A bell chimed as she stepped into a shadowy, musty-smelling space. A few moments later, a lanky man with thinning dark hair emerged from behind a curtain.

"Good morning, my good lady." He gave Tara an obsequious smile. "How may I be of assistance?"

"Good morning." Tara straightened her shoulders and favored him with a haughty look in return. "I wish to purchase some red ribbon."

The ribbon merchant bowed his head, gaze gleaming. "Aye ... we have plenty of red ribbon. However, ye must make yerself plainer as to the shade ye require. We have crimson, cherry, rose, wine, berry, currant, garnet ... and blood."

Tara's brow furrowed. "I'm not exactly sure..."

He smiled once more, gesturing to the curtain behind him. "This way then, my lady."

Tara followed the owner into a long narrow room with an open window. Tables lined the edges, and upon them sat wooden boxes. "I display my wares in here," the man explained. "For customers like to see the ribbons in daylight ... candlelight fools the eye."

"Indeed, it does," Tara agreed, following him down the room.

He halted at the far end of the room, where a small table sat against the wall, and flipped the lid on a box— and inside were a myriad of ribbons, all in various shades of red.

Tara's breathing caught at their beauty. The scullery maid hadn't lied: these were far more splendid than any she'd seen elsewhere. Some of the ribbons were even embroidered with patterns.

"See something ye like?"

She glanced up, unease tickling the back of her neck. She hadn't warmed to the ribbon merchant at all. She didn't like the oiliness in his voice or the slyness of his smile.

"I'm not sure as yet," she replied, her tone cooling. "I will need to take a proper look."

He ducked his head and stepped back, still smiling. "But of course ... I shall leave ye for a few moments."

Relief washed over Tara as she watched him depart, pushing aside the curtain and returning to the shop front. She'd need to watch herself with that slimy fellow when she haggled over a price with him.

Alone, she turned back to the box of ribbons and picked up one. It was a bright cherry-red—pretty, but not the shade she was looking for. She wanted something darker, richer.

Rifling through the ribbons, Tara plucked another out and held it up to the daylight streaming in through the open window. It was a deep red with hints of brown in it. "What shade is this called, I wonder?" she murmured.

"Blood," a low male voice drawled from behind her. "The perfect choice, Vixen."

Tara froze, the ribbon slipping from her fingers and fluttering down into the box.

That wasn't the ribbon merchant. She hadn't heard the doorbell chime either. There shouldn't have been anyone else in here, yet there was.

Swallowing, she turned, her gaze alighting on the tall man with wavy auburn hair standing a few feet behind her.

Tara's heart leaped into her throat, and she lurched back, colliding with the edge of the table.

The smirking stranger from the docks was in front of her—and he was holding an unsheathed dirk.

2: TIME TO GO

A HEARTBEAT PASSED and then another.

Tara opened her mouth to scream.

"I wouldn't do that," the stranger said softly. "Or this blade will meet yer tender throat."

Tara's lips snapped closed.

The glint in his green eyes warned her he'd do just that. "What do ye want?" she whispered.

With his free hand, he patted a slender coil of rope that hung at his belt.

Tara's heart slammed against her ribs.

For a few instants, she froze. This couldn't be happening. The whole situation felt unreal. No one would be insane enough to attack the Mackinnon's daughter, surely?

But it *was* real. God's blood, this brute was going to bind her wrists—and then, Lord knew what plans he had for her.

Suddenly, stomach-churning terror pierced her shock. An instant later, perhaps realizing that she would indeed scream for help, the stranger lunged at her.

His body slammed up against hers, and his free hand clamped over her mouth. "Careful," he growled. Their faces were now so close, she could see the different shades of green that flecked the irises of his eyes. "Let's not do anything hasty."

Tara tried to shout, yet his palm muffled the noise. Lifting her hands, she shoved him hard in the chest. But it was like trying to move a stone wall; he didn't budge an inch. Not giving up, Tara balled her hands into fists and struck at him in a frenzy, not caring where she hit.

One of her blows connected with his chiseled jaw, and, with a murmured oath, her assailant sheathed his dagger and used that hand to grab hold of her right wrist. "Enough of that."

The next thing Tara knew, he'd whipped her around and shoved her against the table. She started to struggle, yet he held her fast.

Surely, he'd need two hands to bind her wrists and would have to remove his hand from her mouth—and when he did, she intended to scream the roof down.

However, the bastard was cannier than that. Instead of binding her wrists, and allowing her to scream, he deftly gagged her with a length of linen instead. He tied it firmly while she flailed against the table, her hands scrabbling for something she could use as a weapon. The boxes of ribbons went flying, their contents fluttering to the ground.

A moment later, he pulled Tara's arms behind her and bound her wrists.

Terror beat like a raven's wings in her chest as she squirmed and twisted in his grip. Tara managed to land a vicious kick to his shins and heard his sharp intake of breath. The weather had been rainy of late, and so she'd worn her winter boots for this shopping trip, rather than the pretty slippers she favored in the summer months.

Vindication arrowed through her, and she kicked him again.

In response, Tara's attacker pushed her forward toward the open window. "Out ye go," he said, his breath feathering against her ear. Tara shook her head and dug her heels into the wooden floor. However, he merely picked her up and shoved her, feet first, outside.

Tara's feet hit mossy stones, and her right ankle twisted, collapsing under her. She cried out, although the gag muffled the sound, and fell to her knees. Her assailant had dropped her into a damp, cramped courtyard behind the shop. Surrounded by high walls on

all sides, the yard had a narrow gateway just a few feet
away.

Gritting her teeth against the pain in her ankle, Tara
lunged toward the closed gate, limping as she reached it.
A sprained ankle or not, she'd run.

But when she scrabbled to release the rusted latch, it
jammed.

Eyes stinging with tears, as panic caught her by the
throat, she turned to face her attacker.

He'd climbed through the window after her and now
closed the distance between them. Although he hadn't
drawn his dirk again, the look on his face made her quail
inside.

Hate glittered in his eyes—and yet he was a stranger.

Recognition tugged at Tara once more. Curse it, she
had met him. But where?

There was no time to ponder the question, for he
reached her then, his hand fastening firmly around her
arm. "Time to go," he said roughly.

Yanking the latch free, he opened the gate and towed
her down a narrow path between two buildings—so
narrow, in fact, that their shoulders brushed against
mossy stone—and into a larger courtyard, where a
saddled bay courser awaited them. Tara limped heavily,
and her captor cast her a sharp look, as if he thought she
was using her twisted ankle as a ruse.

Tara ignored him. She was too focused on the sight of
the horse. It made this villain's intentions clear. This was
indeed an abduction. Of course, her father was a wealthy
man. Would he try and blackmail him?

How dare he?

Fury pounded through her, and she began to struggle
once more in her captor's iron grip. She tried to shout,
yet the gag made it impossible.

No one messed with 'The Butcher of Dùn Ara'. Aye,
she knew her father's moniker, and how that name
struck fear into the hearts of his enemies. He'd cut this
knave into fish-bait once he got his hands on him. He'd
show him no mercy, and neither would she.

But despite the outrage that made her strong, and even though she twisted and squirmed like an eel in his arms, her abductor managed to wrestle her across to his horse.

He then threw her, face first, across the horse's withers. Tara's breath rushed out of her. Gasping, she tried to push herself forward, so that she slid to the ground. Yet with her arms twisted behind her and her wrists bound, she couldn't manage it. The stranger then vaulted up onto the saddle behind her and hauled Tara up so that she was sitting astride the horse, her bound wrists pressing against his belly.

Hot mortification flushed through Tara at the intimacy of the position.

However, propriety was now the least of her worries, as her abductor urged his mount forward, sending it clattering across the empty courtyard and under an archway.

Tara hoped they might emerge onto a busy street, but he'd taken her into another one of Tobermory's fetid back alleyways, where only a stray dog witnessed their passing. The thin hound stopped scratching its fleas to watch the man and woman astride a leggy courser canter up the hill and out of town.

Sitting rigid in the saddle, her gaze cutting from left to right for the sign of anyone who might be able to help her, Tara's chest heaved.

Panic surged up then, eclipsing her anger momentarily.

The bastard was going to get away with this!

Desperation pummeled into her with cruel fists, making it hard to draw breath, especially with her mouth gagged. She began to fight him again, but her captor held her fast within the cage of his arms. Dizziness swept over Tara then as the lack of air started to affect her.

Halting her attempts to free herself, she concentrated instead on remaining conscious.

3: SWEET VENGEANCE

JACK COULDN'T BELIEVE it. He was finally getting what he craved. Vengeance. How sweet it was—especially after fifteen long years of waiting. He wasn't done yet though. Merely stealing his enemy's daughter wasn't enough.

He had to *ruin* her.

His shin throbbed as he urged his horse faster up the hill outside Tobermory.

Mackinnon's daughter had a mean punch and a vicious kick. His jaw still ached from where her fist had caught him, and he'd have livid bruises the next morning from the toe of her boot.

A hard smile curved Jack's mouth then, and he tightened his grip a little around the torso of the woman seated in front of him. Tara had stopped struggling for the moment. All the same, he didn't trust her. The lass's courage had surprised him. She had fire in her belly.

Jack's smile turned into a grimace then. For a few moments, he'd thought things might go awry.

He'd drawn his dirk merely as a means of scaring the woman. Despite his threat, he hadn't intended to cut her. Instead, he'd expected her to quail at the sight of his dagger, for the blood to rush from her face. He'd even thought she might swoon.

But instead, she'd drawn in a deep breath and readied herself to scream.

Fortunately, he'd moved quickly, and just as well too, for the lass had fought him every step of the way. She appeared to have twisted her ankle, which was unfortunate. Jack hadn't meant to dump her so unceremoniously through the window. Nonetheless, even injured, she fought him like a feral cat.

Tobermory was behind them now, although Jack cast a quick look over his shoulder to ensure no one was following.

Upon seeing the way behind them was clear, relief and then vindication spiked through him once more.

Choke on this, Mackinnon.

No, the abduction hadn't gone as smoothly as he'd hoped, but at least no one had spied them leave. Nonetheless, it wouldn't be long before one of Lady Tara's escort ventured into the ribbon shop to see why the clan-chief's daughter was taking so long over her purchase.

A nervous, jittery sensation swept over Jack then, and he tensed in the saddle. There had been so much to organize, so many details to remember. He just hoped he hadn't forgotten anything vital—something that might unravel his carefully laid plans.

He'd paid the ribbon merchant well to aid him—an obscene amount of silver. Nearly all of Jack's savings, but it had been worth it. Nonetheless, the man was taking a risk on his behalf. When the guards eventually entered, Declan would be sitting calmly just inside the shop entrance, as they'd discussed, pretending to work on his accounts. He'd send them into the back of the shop to fetch Lady Tara and feign complete ignorance when they couldn't find her.

The window was open, after all.

The lady might have decided she didn't want to wed Callum MacDonald and taken flight.

Jack's gut tensed then, anxiety flooding through him once more. He just hoped that Declan had gone in and tidied up the scattered ribbons, or it would be clear a struggle had taken place.

Pushing aside his worries—for he was sure the man he'd hired would look after things, as it was his neck at stake too—Jack focused his attention southwest.

Now, he just had to get his captive across the isle, to complete his revenge against his enemy. Kendric Mackinnon would suffer as he searched in vain for his precious daughter. And then despair would claim The Butcher when it dawned on him that he'd never see her again.

The same despair Jack felt the day he learned his beloved father was dead.

The same grief that drained all color from the world.

Aye, Mackinnon would taste it all.

They crested the hill then and rode down a rocky slope, jumping the trickling burn at the bottom. And all the while, his captive sat as rigid as a plank of wood in Jack's arms.

He didn't fail to notice the softness of her body though, pressed hard against him, or the scent of rose that kept tickling his nose.

Irritated by his awareness of the woman, Jack kicked Mòine—so named for his dark coat was the color of peat—into a flat gallop. A sense of urgency swept over him. Only a fool would let complacency lower his guard.

Soon enough, Mackinnon's men would come after them—and he wanted to hold onto the advantage he'd gained.

They rode for a couple of hours before Tara's abductor drew up his horse for a rest in a shallow glen.

"It's safe to remove this now," he announced as he reached up and untied the strip of linen that gagged her. "Out here, if ye shout … no one will hear."

"Foul dog," Tara choked out, the moment she could speak. "How dare ye?"

"On second thoughts, maybe I should keep ye gagged," he growled. "I was enjoying the peace."

Hot fury pulsed through Tara. Despite her bound hands, she drove her elbow back, jabbing him in the ribs.

He grunted before grabbing her arms to prevent her from repeating the move. "No, ye don't."

Tara snarled another insult, but her captor merely swung down from his horse. A moment later, he pulled her down after him.

Balancing on her uninjured ankle, Tara whipped around to face him.

The cur met her glare boldly, with an arrogance that made her want to punch him in the mouth. She clenched her teeth and balled her hands into fists. They were useless, bound behind her. How she wished she was quick enough—and skilled enough—to knee this man in the cods.

However, remembering the dangerous glint in his eyes back at the ribbon shop when he'd pulled a dirk on her, she held her rage in check. "Where are ye taking me?" she demanded, her voice rough with anger.

He didn't answer.

"My father will tear out yer guts for this. And I will enjoy watching."

The villain gave a dismissive snort. Then he stepped back and retrieved a skin of ale from behind the saddle. Unstoppering it, he took a couple of gulps before handing it to Tara. "Thirsty?"

"Go to the devil!"

Shrugging, her captor replaced the stopper and moved around Tara, leading his mount toward the burn that cut through the peaty soil at the bottom of the glen.

"Mull isn't big enough for ye to hide from my father," Tara said hoarsely, silently counting to ten as anger pulsed inside her.

"Lucky for me, I don't have to," he answered, not bothering to even look her way.

The man's supreme confidence was as breathtaking as it was vexing. It was the arrogance of someone born into the ruling class.

Tara's gaze narrowed then, recognition flickering once more. And this time, she was able to retrieve the memory. "I knew I'd seen ye before," she whispered, even as dread crawled across her skin, dousing her anger as if someone had just dumped a pail of water over a smoldering hearth. "We met at Duart Castle last autumn."

The rogue halted and glanced over his shoulder at her, his fern-green eyes widening. "I was wondering if ye'd recall my face."

Tara's blood started to roar in her ears, and suddenly, her knees went weak and shaky. Dear Lord, she was in trouble. "Ye are the Maclean clan-chief's cousin."

"Aye."

"Did he send ye?"

Her abductor favored her with a thin smile. "No."

She didn't believe him.

"Jack Maclean," she said hoarsely. She recalled the introductions then, which had been made just after she and her brother had followed their father into the great hall of Duart Castle. "Ye are Rae Maclean's younger brother."

He stiffened. "God's troth, ye do have a good memory."

"And just as well too." Tara drew herself up, her fingernails biting into her palms as she tried to claw back her outrage. Anger warmed her belly and kept the fear at bay. She felt naked without it. "For my father will need to know yer name."

Jack Maclean's face twisted, violence darkening his eyes. "Ye speak as if ye will see yer old man again," he snarled, "but ye won't."

Tara's heart kicked hard against her ribs at his outburst. "What will ye do with me?" she rasped.

His mouth twisted once more, yet he didn't deign to answer her.

Heart still pounding, bile stinging her throat, Tara continued to stare at him. "So, this is vengeance?" she eventually asked, her voice barely above a whisper now. "For yer father's death?"

"Aye." Maclean turned from her once more and led his horse over to the burn. His shoulders were rigid now.

His movements were jerky as he loosened the gelding's girth slightly while it drank. "And I've waited a long time to claim it."

He wasn't looking at her as he tended to his horse, yet Tara couldn't take her gaze from him. He appeared in the grip of a strong emotion, and not half as sure of himself as earlier. However, his abrupt change of mood made Tara even more wary of him.

She'd been a bairn of no more than seven when her father had slain the chieftain of Dounarwyse, yet she knew the story. According to her Da, the two men had met in good faith to discuss where the border between their lands should lie. The discussion became heated, and Baird Maclean lost his temper. The argument escalated into violence, and her father ended up killing him.

And this man was his youngest son.

"Surely, if there's any reckoning to be had, that's up to yer elder brother?" she said after a long pause. Discovering who her abductor was made her belly churn. Nonetheless, if she kept him talking, she might learn something that could help her.

Maclean's gaze cut to her. "Rae's priorities are elsewhere," he replied coldly. "It's up to *me* to avenge our father's death... and I shall."

Tara's pulse quickened. His ominous tone chilled her blood.

"Do ye really think this one cruel act will ease yer hatred and bitterness?" she challenged him, raising her chin while she valiantly tried to hide her swelling fear. "Ye should use yer wits, Maclean, and let me go right this instant. It'll only be worse for ye in the end if ye don't."

Maclean glared back at her. "For a woman in peril, ye have a perilously waspish tongue," he muttered. "Leash it, or I shall gag ye again."

4: HEEDING HIS WARNING

TARA HEEDED HER captor's warning.

It galled her to do so—for he deserved to be spat at—but she had no wish to be gagged once more, so she shut her mouth and instead thought hard on what she'd discovered.

Her abductor was Jack Maclean, a man twisted and embittered by his thirst for revenge. He also appeared to be working alone, claiming that neither his clan-chief nor his brother had sent him.

However, the villain was clearly unhinged—and that made him dangerous.

Standing on the slope, Tara watched Maclean finish tending to his horse. His jaw was clenched and his brow deeply followed.

Tara's mouth thinned. The whoreson didn't have the right to be angry. *She* was the one who'd been abducted and hauled across Mull like a sack of oats.

Outrage still vibrated through her as she drew in a deep, steadying breath and took in her surroundings. They were in the middle of nowhere, surrounded by nothing but wind-blasted hills. To the east, the long ridge of Dùn da Ghaoithe rose against a cloudy sky, while to the southwest rose the dark peak of Ben More, Mull's biggest mountain. They'd crossed into Maclean territory now, and Tara didn't know this part of the isle at all.

Nonetheless, despite her sore ankle, she wanted to run. It would be foolish though, for Maclean stood just a few yards away. Without a way of distracting him, she wouldn't get far. No, escape wasn't possible at present, but she'd bide her time and watch her abductor carefully.

He's not going to slit yer throat, she reassured herself then. *He could have done that back in Tobermory, but he wants ye alive.*

A shiver rippled over her then as she reminded herself that he could have worse plans for her. Maclean could be taking her to a hideaway, where he'd rape and torture Tara *before* killing her.

The man was surely unstable enough.

Cold sweat beaded upon her skin at the chilling thought, and her bladder started to tingle.

Lord, how she wished she'd brought her father's men inside the shop with her. Maclean wouldn't have dared attack her then. However, she was relieved that she'd told Orla to stay outside. Her abductor was no doubt ruthless; he might have killed her beloved maid.

Tara's throat tightened as she imagined Orla's panic now. She'd be searching Tobermory for her, desperate. Her father would likely blame Orla for letting his daughter out of her sight.

The full reality of her situation hit Tara then—for the first time in her twenty-two winters, she was utterly alone in the world.

"We're moving on now."

Her abductor had finished watering his horse and was leading the courser up the incline toward her. Tara cut him a simmering glare, one which he ignored. Instead, Maclean pushed her up onto his horse's back and vaulted up behind her.

Tara stiffened, her nostrils flaring as the man's scent enveloped her: pine, leather, horse, and the musk of fresh sweat.

Maclean turned his mount south then, urging it into a brisk canter. Throwing lumps of peaty soil behind them, they continued their journey. As earlier, Tara perched rigidly in front of her abductor, resisting him even though each of their mount's long strides jolted their bodies together. The muscles of her upper arms ached now from being twisted behind her back.

They were sitting so close, she could feel the way his thigh muscles flexed as he guided his horse, feel the heat of his body burning like a furnace behind her. It was far too intimate, and she tried to focus on something else.

Da will be on his way, she reassured herself. *He'll rescue me from this madman.*

Aye, Tara's escort would have raised the alarm by now, although her captor had already carried her far from Tobermory. They were nearing the end of a body of water at present that she presumed was Loch Ba—the long loch that stretched south from the Mackinnon-Maclean border into the middle of the isle.

Leaving the loch behind, the horse carried them into a narrow glen where thickets of hazel and twisted oak grew. They rode through dells carpeted in bluebells. In an attempt to ignore the man sitting behind her, Tara focused instead upon the brightness of the bluebells, their bonnets nodding in the breeze. The morning had started out fine, but now that noon had passed, the light wind carried spots of rain with it.

The horse stumbled, throwing captor and captive together for an instant.

Fear wreathed up, choking Tara. Maclean's body was hard-muscled. He was strong. If he tried to rape her, she wouldn't be able to fight him off.

Don't think about it.

Swallowing down her rising panic, she gazed ahead at where the dark silhouette of Ben More to the southwest marched steadily closer. From a distance, the mountain appeared smooth-sided, its peak still clad in snow, but now she could make out its rocky surface.

She'd never seen the great mountain so close—and the sight of it was a reminder that she was in the heart of Maclean lands.

Jack scowled up at the sky. The weather upon Mull was as fickle as a beautiful woman. That morning, he'd been certain the rain would hold off, yet it hadn't. The wind had grown gusty, and rain drove across the interior of the isle as dusk approached. Drawing his cloak over the lass perched in front of him, Jack urged Mòine down the narrow gully toward their destination.

A remote hunters' bothy.

He just hoped it wasn't occupied, or they'd be sleeping out in the open tonight.

A sheet of rain slashed across the valley. Jack clenched his jaw and urged his gelding from a trot to a canter. Meanwhile, his captive remained silent.

He'd thought Lady Tara wouldn't heed his warning earlier—yet she had.

Indeed, she hadn't uttered a word for the rest of the afternoon.

He didn't trust her though, and he'd kept one arm clamped across her belly, just in case she tried to throw herself from his horse.

Up ahead, through the rain, he spied the sod roof and dark stacked-stone walls of the tiny bothy. Jack slowed Mòine to a walk, his gaze traveling over the hut. He couldn't see smoke wreathing up from the roof or smell cooking.

Good. It looked as if they'd have the bothy to themselves.

A grim sense of satisfaction filtered through Jack then.

He'd been building up to this moment for months now—since learning that Kendric Mackinnon planned to wed his daughter to Callum MacDonald of Sleat. It had taken some work, and a great amount of luck, for things to come together. But they had.

Thanks to Aynsley, the lass who worked in the kitchens of Dùn Ara—whom he'd met at *The Bonnie Badger* a day earlier and who'd been happy to betray her mistress for some coin and a cheeky kiss—he'd learned that Mackinnon's daughter would be visiting the ribbon shop in Little Brae that morning. However, he hadn't been sure how he was going to get her alone. It was likely that her maid, at least, would accompany her into the shop, and Jack had brought enough rope and linen to gag and tie the woman up. Nonetheless, it would have been difficult to keep both Lady Tara and her maid quiet, to prevent them from raising the alarm.

Lady Tara browsing the ribbons on her own had been a boon indeed.

Jack had waited behind the curtain at the back of the shop, listening to her haughty voice as she spoke with Declan. Aye, he'd bided his time until the right moment—and then he'd struck.

Drawing Mòine up before the shelter, Jack dismounted and pulled Tara down after him. He then motioned to the low doorway. "Get inside."

In response, Lady Tara flashed him a venomous look yet didn't move. Anger brought a flush to her face, emphasized her high cheekbones, and darkened her eyes.

"Off ye go," he growled.

Mouth compressed, as if swallowing a curse, his captive finally obeyed, disappearing inside the bothy.

Jack didn't linger outdoors, for the weather was worsening now. The rain had turned to hail, and it stung his face. There was no lean-to next to the bothy. However, a hardy pine provided shelter for his horse. He unsaddled Mòine, rubbed the gelding down, and gave him a nosebag of oats.

"Good lad," he murmured, ruffling the horse's forelock. Mòine had been a gift from Loch, along with the role of marshal at Duart. He'd appreciated his cousin's generosity and would have enjoyed his return to Mull more—if the thirst for revenge hadn't consumed his every waking thought.

Jack's pulse quickened then as his thoughts turned to his reckoning.

'The Butcher' must pay.

He hadn't slept well for months now. It hadn't taken long, after returning to Mull, for food to turn to ash in his mouth and ale to taste like dishwater. A decade of war against the English had distracted him, but being back here had reignited the rage that tore him asunder after his father's murder.

And he'd been unable to cut himself free of it. There was only one answer: to claim the reckoning his soul cried out for.

However, recalling everything Loch had done for him made Jack's stomach clench. His cousin would be wondering where his marshal had gotten to. The clan-chief had dispatched him to Dounarwyse a few days earlier. Jack had delivered the news to Rae that the Mackinnon had sent Loch a threatening missive. He'd declared his intention to reclaim the lands he'd recently given back on their border and threatened to lay siege to Dounarwyse Castle itself.

Kendric Mackinnon's aggression had spurred Jack into action—although not the kind either his clan-chief or Jack's brother would have expected. Aye, Jack had delivered the message to Rae, but he'd only remained at Dounarwyse for an hour or two before riding north into Mackinnon lands.

Loch would be expecting him back. But he couldn't return to Duart—not until he'd avenged his father. He couldn't go on like this. The need to get even was consuming him.

The light was fading fast now, and Jack slapped Mòine on the rump, picked up his saddle bag, and ducked inside the bothy. Blinking as his eyes adjusted to the gloom, he spied a figure sitting hunched by the cold hearth.

Lady Tara's gaze gleamed. Her hate stabbed at him across the fire pit.

"Christ's bones, it's cold in here," Jack muttered, fumbling for the flint he carried in a pouch on his waist. He opened the saddle bag and withdrew a handful of dry tinder. He then knelt before the hearth and got to work lighting a fire. It didn't take him long, for it was a skill he'd honed over long years of war against the English— weeks of campaigning, in all weathers, when he'd often struggled to light a fire in the pouring rain.

In comparison, this was easy. Even so, a glow of accomplishment sparked inside him as he sat back on his heels and watched the flames devour the tinder and the dry pieces of wood he'd just added. As the fire grew, it cast a golden light over the interior of the bothy, illuminating a stack of wood and peat against one wall—the hunters who used this hut were a considerate lot.

His attention shifted then to where Lady Tara sat. She was shivering in her damp woolen cloak, and her fiery hair curled in tendrils around her face.

Meeting his eye, she cut him another glare. However, when she spoke, there was a slight quaver in her voice, betraying her fear. "Please ... I must know what ye are going to do with me?"

5: EVERY MAN HAS HIS PRICE

"YE WILL FIND out soon enough." Jack approached his captive, hunkering down to untie her wrists from behind her back.

Lady Tara sighed with relief and rolled her shoulders before rubbing at her chafed wrists. However, Jack didn't leave her hands unbound. Instead, he moved around to her front and retied her wrists once more—in front of her this time.

His captive muttered an oath. "Do ye think I'll try to escape?"

"Aye."

"At least tell me what lies in store for me."

"No."

"Why not?"

"Because I don't owe ye anything," he replied curtly. "Don't talk to me like I'm one of yer servants."

Jack then reached toward her once more. His captive flinched, yet he ignored her reaction, instead removing her damp cloak from around her shoulders. Although he intended to keep his plans for Mackinnon's daughter to himself, they didn't include this lass catching a chill.

Underneath her cloak, the lady wore a fine plum-colored surcoat over a wine-red kirtle. The necklines of both her surcote and kirtle were low, showing off her milky skin and the lush upper curve of her breasts.

Aye, the lass was a high and mighty Mackinnon—but she was also lovely. It was hard not to stare.

Averting his gaze, Jack moved away and hung up her cloak on a peg upon the wall before removing his own and draping it next to hers. He then sat down, cross-legged, before the fire, and pulled out something wrapped in oiled cloth.

Unwrapping the hunk of cheese and coarse oaten bread, he broke them both in half and held out some to her.

"Keep yer food," she ground out. "I hope ye choke on it."

Jack shrugged and took a bite of bread. "Suit yerself."

The fire was crackling nicely now, suffusing the interior of the bothy with warmth. But as Jack ate his supper, he was aware that his captive's gaze never left him. Eventually, he glanced over at her. "I know I've a handsome face, lass," he growled. "But didn't yer mother tell ye it's rude to stare so?"

"What will it take for ye to release me?" she asked.

"The knowledge that yer father is a broken man," he replied without hesitation. He then flashed her a bloodthirsty grin. "Better yet, that he's taken a dirk to his own throat."

"And ye think abducting me will make him that desperate?"

Jack held her eye, even as his belly clenched. Lord, how he wanted his enemy to suffer. "Aye."

Lady Tara swallowed, her slender throat bobbing. "That can't be the only thing ye want," she said, her voice lowering. "Every man has his price … name yers."

Tara couldn't believe it. The rogue smirked.

Her fingers curled into fists, her nails biting into her palms. "Do I amuse ye?"

Maclean snorted. "Aye … ye have some nerve, asking me such a thing." He then took a bite of cheese and chewed slowly.

Tara glowered at him. She hadn't lied earlier—she did hope he choked on his supper. She'd then find a way to cut the rope binding her wrists and escape on his horse.

But it was a vain hope, for few folk ever choked to death on bread and cheese.

"So, ye can't be bought then?"

His mouth curved once more. "No. Not by *ye*, anyway."

"*I* didn't kill yer father, Maclean," she pointed out. "Why are ye punishing me for my father's crime?"

His green eyes, dark in the firelight, narrowed. "Because as heartless as Mackinnon is ... I hear that he *loves* his bonnie daughter."

Apprehension clenched her chest.

God's blood, the man was insane.

"Yer act will start a blood feud between our clans," Tara pointed out after a pause. "Is that what ye want?"

Maclean reached into his saddle bag and withdrew a skin of ale. "What I want, lass, is for Kendric Mackinnon to pay for taking my father from me. If it takes bloodshed to achieve that end, so be it." He unstoppered the skin and drank deeply before holding it out to her. "Thirsty?"

Tara was. Her throat was dry and her mouth gummy. Nonetheless, she wouldn't take anything this bastard offered.

"Ye'll never best my father," she growled. "All ye'll do is enrage him." She drew herself up as fire ignited in her belly. "He'll crush yer clan ... and will end up sitting upon Loch Maclean's seat at Duart Castle."

Her captor's face turned to stone. "That shall never come to pass. My cousin will tear down his castle, stone by stone, rather than let Mackinnon take it."

Tara leaned forward, her gaze spearing his. "Well, prepare yerself for that day, *whoreson* ... for it's coming."

Their stares locked, the moment drawing out.

Tension crackled across the space between them.

And to Tara's vindication, Maclean looked away first, fury burning in his green eyes. She'd won that round, and victory rushed through her.

However, it was short-lived.

She wasn't hungry—this ordeal had robbed her of appetite—yet thirst nagged at her now. She wouldn't ask him for something to drink though. No, she'd just suffer.

Dropping her gaze to her lap, Tara leashed her temper. There was little point in raging at her abductor or provoking him. She was in a vulnerable position here.

A dull gleam to her left caught Tara's eye then, and her breathing hitched.

A small boning knife, its blade partially rusted, sat on the dirt floor next to her sheepskin, within easy reach. She hadn't noticed it earlier, for there hadn't been enough light. But now that the fire crackled merrily in the hearth before her, she did.

Her heart started to pound, and she quickly averted her gaze, glancing up at Maclean.

He wasn't looking her way. Instead, the man was scowling at the fire.

Her captor was a tormented soul; she could see that much. His father had died by her father's hand many years earlier, yet he talked as if it had just happened the day before. The need to get even was like a sickness within him. And that made him dangerous indeed.

She had to get free of this lunatic—and she'd just spied her chance.

Moving casually, as if her legs were stiff and she needed to stretch them, Tara shifted position, uncurling her legs, and extending them to the left, crossing her booted feet at the ankles.

Now she'd covered the knife from view should he approach her.

Silence stretched out between them, the crackle of the fire and the whine of the wind outdoors the only sounds. Tara didn't speak. Instead, she bided her time. A plan had formed in her mind, and she was eager to execute it.

Meanwhile, Maclean's expression had become morose. A muscle flexed in his jaw as he ruminated. Tara wondered if the excitement of stealing her away was ebbing now, and the reality of what he'd done was sinking in.

After a spell, her captor roused himself from his brooding and turned from the fire. He rose to his feet and crossed to fetch a lump of peat from against the wall.

Tara seized her chance. Grabbing hold of the small knife, she deftly slid it into her boot.

When Maclean returned to the fire, she sat demurely once more, hands folded upon her lap.

Maclean added the lump of peat to the hearth and poked at the glowing embers with a stick, sending sparks spitting high into the air like a cloud of fireflies.

Tara cleared her throat, even as nervousness fluttered in her belly. The man's mood was mercurial. His instability made her wary of how he might respond to her.

Maclean cut her an irritated look. "What?"

Feigning embarrassment, Tara lowered her gaze. "I … need to … relieve myself," she murmured.

"Now?"

"Aye."

"But it's howling a gale outdoors."

Tara kept her head bowed so he wouldn't see the lie in her eyes. "It's … urgent."

"Satan's cods," he growled, pushing himself up off the sheepskin he'd been sitting on. "Get up then."

Swallowing a smile, Tara rose to her feet and followed him to the door. Her right ankle was a little tender. She hoped it would hold up. The ceiling was low in here, so they both had to bend double to avoid cracking their heads on the beams overhead and the low stone lintel at the door.

Halting, Maclean pulled their cloaks off the hooks and shoved Tara's at her.

His gesture was ungracious, but Tara didn't care. Aye, she would need her cloak—for she wouldn't be coming back indoors tonight.

Her belly tightened then, excitement curling inside her.

Not long now.

They might be in the midst of the wilderness out here, but it was dark outdoors, and if her plan worked, she'd get a goodly head start on her captor.

As Tara stepped outdoors, a vicious gust of wind smacked her in the face, followed by a volley of needle-like hailstones.

Satan's fiends, it *was* a foul night.

A little of her excitement faded then before she rallied. Aye, the wind and hail would make for an unpleasant escape, but her father would still be looking for her. She would go to him.

It was hard to see out here too, for they had no lantern with them. However, after a few moments, Tara's eyesight adjusted, and she was able to make out the shapes of the pine trees surrounding the bothy, under which her abductor's horse sheltered.

Tara's pulse quickened. She needed that horse but knew that it would be too risky to try and steal it. When she fled, her feet would have to carry her to safety.

"Go and relieve yerself behind that tree," Maclean ordered, gesturing to where a gnarled pine sat to their left.

Wordlessly, Tara moved toward it, limping slightly and with head bowed against the rain that angled down the gully.

Slipping behind the tree, she quickly glanced around, noting that there was a growth of ferns at her back, which she would flee through.

All she had to do now was cut the ropes that bound her wrists.

Crouching down, Tara withdrew the knife and wedged its handle between the toes of her boots. Then, carefully, for she couldn't see what she was doing and was wary of cutting herself, she lowered her wrists to its rusted edge. Working by feel, she started to saw at the rope. It wasn't easy, for her hands trembled slightly with nerves, yet she persevered.

Time passed, and then Maclean muttered a curse. "God's teeth, woman. What's taking ye so long?"

"Nearly done," Tara called out.

And she was, for at that moment, the binding around her wrists finally gave way. Heart pounding, she palmed

the knife—as it was her only weapon—and turned,
slipping through the ferns and into the stormy night.

6: NOT BEATEN YET

TARA WAS HALFWAY through the carpet of the ferns when the ground angled suddenly and she slipped, traveling the rest of the way down the slope on her backside.

Swallowing an oath, she scrambled to her feet, wincing as her right ankle protested. Tara squinted into the gloom as she tried to make out her surroundings. Hades, it was difficult to keep her sense of direction. There was a full moon out tonight, yet the roiling storm clouds overhead obscured it.

She was fleeing blind.

Tara set her jaw and started moving, in what she hoped was the direction they'd arrived from. It didn't matter she couldn't see a foot in front of her face, flee she would.

It was hard going. She stumbled and tripped her way along the rocky gully, colliding with prickly bushes and the sharp edges of boulders as she went. Yet all the while, Tara reminded herself that she was running toward safety.

Da will be out here, somewhere. He'll find me.

Kendric Mackinnon wouldn't let darkness and foul weather prevent him from tracking her down. Maclean was right about one thing—the Mackinnon clan-chief adored his daughter.

And his wrath would be terrible when he caught her abductor.

Jack Maclean would wish he'd never been born.

Tara limped on, intent on widening the distance between her and Maclean. Urgency pushed her forward, even as she kept stealing nervous glances over her shoulder. Her hunter was out there somewhere. She had to make sure he never caught her.

At least the hail had ceased now, although the seeking wind tugged mercilessly at her clothing, driving under her wet cloak. The rain had plastered Tara's hair to her scalp, although she barely noticed that she was drenched. The clouds above parted then, allowing moonlight to filter across the gully. She caught a glimpse of a tangle of stunted pines before her that climbed the steep rocky sides of the gully.

Panic surged up, clawing at Tara's chest. She didn't remember seeing this view when they'd ridden in at dusk. Maybe she'd run in the wrong direction, after all.

The clouds rolled over the moon once more then, throwing the world into darkness.

Tara gamely limped on, sweat trickling down her back. Her breathing was ragged as fear and exertion took their toll. When she tried to clamber up a rocky slope through the trees, her sore ankle gave a sharp twinge. Hissing an oath, she didn't heed its warning. She couldn't. Desperation surged up, lodging like a plum in her throat. She had to keep going.

Rocks dug into her hands and branches clawed at her clothing as she climbed, the resinous scent of pine filling her lungs. Soon she was crawling, yet she didn't stop.

And all the while, her ears strained for the sound of pursuit. It was difficult to hear anything though, above the pounding of her heart and the roar of the wind.

Reaching the top of the rocky slope, Tara slithered down the other side, swallowing a cry as the way grew so steep that she lost her footing. Suddenly, she was tumbling, her hands flailing as she tried to catch hold of the branches that thwacked her in the face.

She landed at the bottom hard on her belly, the air rushing out of her lungs.

For a few moments, she lay there, gasping. And then, when she was able to breathe, Tara rolled gingerly over onto her back. Curse it. If she'd broken a limb, she was done for.

However, despite that her body now felt bruised and her ankle throbbed, her legs and arms all worked fine.

She realized then that during the fall she'd dropped her precious knife. A sob rose up, but she choked it down.

Get ahold of yerself, lass. Ye're not beaten yet.

Pushing herself to her feet, she looked about her. Her belly clenched. Where was her father? Maybe he was farther north, beyond these rocky, wood-clad foothills.

She had to get to him.

Tara staggered forward. Dark shapes hemmed her in on all sides—tall trees that rose toward the inky sky. The ground beneath her feet was softer now, a bed of pine needles.

Relief barreled into her. Finally, she'd left the rough terrain behind. Now, she could put some distance between her and Maclean. The soft ground made it easier on her ankle too, although she was limping heavily. Once the moon showed its friendly face again, she'd find herself a stick to help her walk.

Tara had only covered a few yards when something heavy crashed into her back.

Crying out, she fell forward, sprawling upon the pine-needle-strewn ground.

"A good effort," a male voice growled into her ear. "But not good enough."

Snarling, Tara twisted around and brought her knee up. She'd been aiming for Jack Maclean's cods. Instead, she kneed him in the stomach.

He grunted at the blow, caught her flailing hands, and pinned them at her sides. And then, to prevent her from kneeing him once more, he lay his body down over hers, pressing her to the ground.

Fear exploded in Tara's chest, and she went wild, squirming against him with no care for whether she hurt herself or not. She just wanted this beast off her.

He didn't move. And the harder she struggled, the heavier he leaned upon her, until Tara finally collapsed, panting, her strength giving out.

"That's better," Maclean muttered, his voice strained. "Ye've got guts, I'll give ye that … but where did ye think ye were going?"

"My father will be tracking us, Maclean," she choked out. "And when he finds us, ye are a dead man!"

He didn't answer.

The clouds above parted once more, and moonlight filtered over the pinewood, illuminating the sharp planes of her captor's face and the glint of his eyes.

And upon seeing him, something inside Tara quailed.

Maclean looked as if he wanted to grab ahold of her throat and throttle her.

Tara stiffened, waiting for him to do just that. But moments passed, and he didn't.

However, he didn't remove his weight from her either. A hot, prickling wave of mortification swept over Tara then at the realization that, in her struggles, her legs had parted, and her skirts had ridden up. The cold night air bit into her exposed flesh. Their hips were now pressed close, his groin nestled against hers.

"Get. Off. Me," she ground out, horrified to find herself in such an intimate position with her captor—a foul Maclean.

"Aye, once ye promise to behave yerself."

Tara wheezed a curse. She'd do no such thing.

Maclean's features tightened, his mouth a dark slash across his face. "We're heading back to the bothy now," he said, his voice lowering dangerously. "And ye *will* heed me."

Tara didn't reply.

A moment later, Maclean rolled off her, and with disconcerting strength and speed, hauled Tara to her feet. He then pushed her ahead of him.

Tara obeyed, even if hatred pulsed through her with every limping step. Her ankle now throbbed like toothache.

"I'm not surprised ye are lame, Vixen," Maclean growled. "Yer ankle isn't up to such ill-treatment."

"Don't call me that," she snarled.

"I'll do what I want … *Vixen*."

"I shall enjoy watching my father drive his dirk into yer guts," she replied hoarsely. "I hope ye have a slow, *painful* death."

"The next time I come face-to-face with yer Da, *I'll* be the one doing the killing," he shot back, his temper splintering. "Now leash yer tongue and walk."

It took them a while to return to the bothy. It was hard going, scrambling up over rocks covered in bramble and blackthorn, with spiky pine branches grazing their faces.

And now that Tara wasn't fleeing, fueled by determination and fear, her body seemed clumsier.

Her right ankle was hurting piteously, causing her to grit her teeth whenever she was forced to put her full weight upon it.

But her injury was nothing compared to the despair that sat upon her chest. Her crushing sense of failure eclipsed everything else.

How she wished she hadn't lost that knife. She could have stabbed Jack Maclean in the throat with it. But instead, she was his captive once more.

Tears stung Tara's eyes as she crested the top of the incline she'd tumbled down earlier, grabbing hold of a pine branch to pull herself up. The wind was still howling, although the rain and hail mercifully continued to hold off.

She glanced over her shoulder into the impenetrable darkness then. *Where are ye, Da?*

Kendric Mackinnon had to be nearby. She couldn't understand why he hadn't yet found her. Surely, he'd catch up with them with the dawn?

Her breathing grew shallow, and panic crested once more. What if his men hadn't picked up their trail? They had to hurry or Maclean would get away with this.

Find me, Da, she silently implored. *I promise I will make Callum MacDonald the finest of wives ... I will forge an unbreakable alliance between our clans that will make ye proud. Ye will then crush yer enemies.*

Heat ignited in the pit of her belly, causing the panic to subside. Aye, they would. Her animosity toward the Macleans had once been abstract. But now she had a real reason to hate them.

Eventually, Tara and her captor climbed the last incline and emerged before the bothy. The clouds had parted once more, moonlight frosting the squat, turf-roofed hut and surrounding pines. However, as they drew closer, Maclean spat a curse, the hand that clasped her upper arm tightening its grip.

Fear slammed into Tara. Her abductor had proven to have a mercurial temper. She'd expected him to hurt her earlier for running away, yet he hadn't. Perhaps he was waiting until they returned to the bothy.

But Maclean wasn't focused on her. When she glanced his way, she saw he was glaring toward the trees where he'd tied his horse up overnight.

Only, when Tara peered into the shadows, she couldn't see the large courser.

His horse had gone.

Wordlessly, Maclean pushed her ahead of him toward the bothy. However, when they ducked inside, he snarled another salty curse.

In the light of the fire, which had now burned down to glowing embers, Tara could see the interior clearly enough. The saddle bag he'd brought inside earlier was missing.

There was a thief at large.

Tara glanced around as if expecting to see someone lurking in the shadows. Hope sparked for a moment that it might be her father. However, he wouldn't steal Maclean's horse and saddle bag.

Disappointment settled like a stone in her belly.

No, Kendric Mackinnon wasn't the sort to hide from his foes. It didn't look like anyone was coming to her rescue tonight.

7: THE DELICIOUS DREAM

JACK TOOK A deep breath and tried to keep his rage banked.

Curse the harpy to Hades. Tara Mackinnon was quickly becoming a bur up his arse. She was to blame for this. If he hadn't been chasing her through the darkness, the thief wouldn't have had such an easy time of it.

Having his saddle bag stolen was an annoyance to be sure—although he still had his dirk at his side and a purse with his dwindling coin upon his belt—but the real blow was losing Mòine. Not only had he developed a bond with the courser over the past months, but he needed his horse right now.

And as Tara had helpfully pointed out earlier, her father would be hunting them. If he tracked them down, they couldn't outrun him on foot.

Jack's gut clenched.

Satan's cods, his plans were quickly unraveling. He didn't even know how the woman had managed to remove the rope around her wrists. By the time he'd gone after her, she'd gotten a good head start too.

When Jack had caught up with Tara, he'd been incensed. The urge to throttle her had surged up as she'd struggled under him, yet he hadn't given in to it. He had a volatile temper, yet he'd never raised a hand to a woman, even when sorely provoked.

His temper had simmered all the way back to the bothy, and upon discovering some light-fingered, shit-eating bastard had stolen his horse, his mood turned black indeed.

As if sensing he was on the edge, Tara now held her tongue.

The lass was looking far less defiant than she had earlier. Wet and bedraggled, with twigs and foliage in her hair, her slender shoulders sagged with exhaustion.

However, when her silvery eyes met his, they hardened. No, she wasn't beaten yet.

Jack had to hand it to her; his captive was no willing victim. Had he not been so furious with her, he'd have admired her pluck, her cleverness. She'd grown up surrounded by servants, having her every need catered to, yet for a coddled lass, she was a formidable opponent.

Their stare drew out, and to Jack's surprise, his breathing quickened. Aye, she had fire in her belly.

He stepped closer, deliberately not breaking eye contact. "I can wait ye out all night," he murmured. "If ye wish to continue this staring contest, so will I."

A flush crept over Tara's high cheekbones. "Ye are a vile turd," she ground out.

"Aye." Jack reached up and brushed a bright-russet curl off her cheek. "And don't ye forget it."

Tara jerked back from him, but he gave a dismissive snort and moved toward the door.

Enough of this nonsense.

Closing the door, he drew the wooden bar across, locking them inside. It wasn't just to help prevent his captive from making another attempt to flee, but to protect them both, in case the thief still lingered nearby and decided to return.

Jack would keep his dirk close while he slept.

He then collected a large lump of peat and some logs of pine and set about rousing the fire. Now that he was cooling after retrieving his captive, the cold and damp drilled into his bones.

Glancing up, he noted that Tara was observing him with a veiled look he didn't trust. The lady was wily, but he wouldn't give her another chance to escape.

"It's time for bed." Jack motioned then to the sheepskin that lay between them. "Lie down."

Indeed, they'd rise with the first blush of dawn the following day. Their destination was still some way off, and it would be a day's journey to reach it on foot. Jack had arranged to be there by a certain time and didn't want to be late.

Flashing him a look of simmering hate, Tara wrapped her cloak about her and moved forward. She then lowered herself to the ground.

A moment later, Jack joined his captive and stretched out on his side behind her. He then reached out, his hand curving over her belly, and pulled her back against him.

Tara squealed and elbowed him hard in the ribs.

Jack sucked in a sharp breath but didn't slacken his hold. "Don't bother fighting me on this," he growled in her ear. "After yer earlier behavior, I'm not letting ye out of my sight again."

"I can't sleep like this," she choked, struggling in his grip.

"Too bad." He slung a leg over hers then, trapping them against the sheepskin. "Because *this* is where ye are staying until dawn."

Locked in the cage of his leg and arm, and pressed up against his front, his captive's body trembled with outrage.

"Don't worry," he added after a pause. "Yer virtue will be safe with me."

"I don't believe ye," she gasped, her voice choked with panic.

"I'm not a ravisher; I give ye my word."

"The promise of a Maclean means nothing to me."

Jack tightened his grip on her as she struggled once more. "Well then, looks like ye are going to have a long night."

Tara muttered an oath—a coarse one too—yet Jack chose not to reply. It had been a tiring day, and his body was bruised and wary. It was comfortable here, lying on his side, basking in the fire's warmth.

His captive's body was warm too. He liked how supple and soft she felt in his arms.

He'd keep his word to her though. Although he wasn't averse to abducting a woman, to get him the revenge he craved, he was no rapist. There was no pleasure to be had in taking a lass against her will.

Bitterness soured Jack's mouth then. As lovely as his captive was, she was also the fruit of Kendric Mackinnon's loins. That alone was enough of an incentive to keep lustful thoughts at bay.

Jack rolled his hips against the woman's firm backside, his rod stiffening.

God's teeth, it had been a while since he'd had a tumble. His bollocks were so tight they ached. He hadn't meant to abstain for so long. However, what with the end of the war, and his return to Mull, he'd been focused on other things. The months had slid by, and now it was over a year since he'd lain with a lass.

The woman in his bed had a lovely body. His hand slid up her long coltish leg, enjoying the lush swell of her hip and bottom, and the curve of her back. And she smelled just as good: of sweet woman and musky rose. She filled his senses, drove back reality—with its bitterness, pain, and insatiable need for reckoning—and made him believe in miracles.

Right now, he didn't care about making his enemy suffer. He just wanted to lose himself in pleasure.

His mouth traced his lover's warm neck, and he grazed his teeth against her skin.

In response, she gave a soft, breathy gasp.

Encouraged, Jack rolled his hips once more, his rod straining to reach her through the layers of clothing that separated them.

Why were they both wearing so many clothes in bed?

The thought was fleeting, evaporating like morning mist as the lass moved, unwittingly pressing her delicious backside against his rock-hard erection.

A moan rumbled up Jack's throat. Aye, he needed her. Badly.

His hand slid over her hip, traveling up her midriff to where her cloak had parted, revealing the low neckline of her surcote.

A surcote? Why was the comely serving lass he'd brought upstairs wearing a lady's garb?

His fingertips traced the swell of her breast then before he pulled her gown off her shoulder, sliding it down her upper arm. He leaned into her, his lips trailing over silky skin. He nipped her sweet skin with his teeth, and she gasped once more.

Heat flared in Jack's belly.

Lord help him, she was lovely. He ached to strip her naked, to taste all of her.

He stroked the lass's breast then. It was small and soft, and filled his hand perfectly, while her nipple—as hard as an acorn—pressed against his palm.

Tara was trying to escape a dungeon cell.

It was a dank and fetid hole with rats scurrying in the corners, and she had no intention of staying there. She was getting free, no matter what.

Indeed, she'd climbed up to the window—how she wasn't quite sure—and was attempting to squeeze herself through the narrow gap.

Freedom was so close now—she could feel a soft, fresh breeze feathering across her face, beckoning her.

Tara scrabbled upward, trying to find purchase, and then stopped. Curse it, she was stuck. A sob caught in her throat. *So close!*

She struggled and twisted, her vision blurring with tears—and then, suddenly, strong hands fastened around her waist, helping her up. Tara gasped with relief. How gallant of someone to assist her. When she got free, she would thank him.

However, she was halfway through the window when one of the hands slid up from her waist and cupped her breast.

Tara stiffened. *What is he doing?*

An instant later, a hot mouth slid down her neck to her shoulder. Teeth then nipped her skin, the sting making her gasp once more. Murmuring an endearment in her ear, the individual, who'd turned from helping to groping her, gently squeezed the breast he was cupping.

Confused, Tara's gaze lowered to where a man's long fingers played with her exposed nipple.

What had happened to her clothing?

The boundaries between sleep and wakefulness separated then like a ripping curtain—and Tara jolted out of her dream.

She wasn't escaping a dungeon cell and being molested by the man assisting her.

Instead, she was in a hunter's bothy under the shadow of Ben More, the captive of Jack Maclean.

And he was fondling her naked breast.

8: A SPECTER AT DAWN

"GET YER HANDS off me!"

The woman's angry voice shattered Jack's dream into fragments, jolting him from the haze of pleasure and gathering hunger.

One moment, he'd been lying with his lover in a chamber above an alehouse somewhere, anticipating the moment when he'd roll her onto her back and swive her. And the next, he was on the floor in a drafty bothy.

Blinking, Jack rolled back.

Meanwhile, Tara pushed herself upright, both small round breasts popping out of her gown.

Face flushed, she cursed and hauled her surcote up, covering herself.

Jack gaped, coldness rolling over him.

He hadn't been about to tumble a willing serving lass, but a woman he despised.

A woman he'd promised not to touch.

"Christ," he muttered, raising his hands in supplication as she scooted away, her eyes wild with panic. "I'm sorry, lass."

"Beast!" Tara was pressed up against the wall now and had yanked her cloak tightly around her. "How dare ye?"

"It was a mistake."

"Aye!"

"I was dreaming. I thought ye were ... someone else."

Her lip curled at his excuse, even if her body now trembled with fear.

Jack moved over to the fire. It had almost gone out, and the air inside the bothy had an unpleasant chill. Placing a pine log upon the glowing embers, he noted that his hands shook slightly. Horror stole over him, chilling his blood. God's holy rood. What had he done? He was an animal.

Drawing in a deep breath, Jack watched the log as it caught alight. Meanwhile, he attempted to gather his wits.

His rod was still bone-hard, and his balls were throbbing piteously.

He couldn't believe he'd had such a lewd dream, or that he'd mistaken his Mackinnon captive for a lover. Aye, it had clearly been far too long since he'd had a woman. Holding Tara Mackinnon in his arms overnight had been a mistake.

Her nearness—her warmth, her scent, and the softness of her body—tricked his senses.

Earlier, he hadn't thought he'd be able to sleep, especially since he couldn't trust his captive not to try and escape again. But eventually, he had. And when sleep claimed him, it had pulled him deep into its clutches.

"I won't touch ye like that again," he said roughly, even as his belly twisted—for his traitorous body rebelled against his words. "I swear."

"Save yer breath," she snarled.

A brittle silence fell then. Jack clenched his jaw so tightly that his ears started to ache. He couldn't blame the lass for not believing him. He'd taken liberties with her while she slept, fondling her body as if she'd given herself to him freely. And after he'd told her that he wasn't a ravisher, his behavior made him look like a filthy liar.

Jack checked himself then. *I'm worse than that ... far worse.*

The reminder made his gut curdle.

Tara Mackinnon didn't realize so now, but her opinion of him would sink even lower in the days ahead.

A murky, misty dawn crept across the land, chasing away the long wet night. As soon as the first rays of light touched the world, Maclean ushered Tara outdoors, clearly impatient to move on.

Using a branch as a makeshift crutch to take the weight off her twisted ankle, Tara limped ahead of her captor down the gully, away from the bothy. Ghostly tendrils of mist wreathed through the surrounding pines like a crone's hair. Dank, cold air feathered across her skin, although she barely noticed it. She was already chilled to the marrow, and a lump of ice sat in her stomach.

Maclean had fondled her while she slept. What would have happened if she hadn't woken up when she did?

She shuddered to think.

Maclean had looked as shocked as her though. Although she'd accused him of lying, there hadn't been any guile in his wide green eyes. Just horror. His reaction surprised her, although she made a note of it. The man did have a moral compass, after all.

"I should bind that ankle," Maclean said gruffly then, rousing Tara from her brooding. "We're walking far today … and must reach the coast by nightfall."

Tara ignored him, keeping her gaze firmly ahead.

"Did ye hear me?" he demanded, his voice hardening. "I won't have ye slow us down."

Tara's mouth pursed. Of course, that was the only thing the rogue cared about. She'd caught the impatience in his tone and wondered if he had a meeting arranged at their destination. Her pulse quickened at the thought, for it wouldn't be a rendezvous that she'd likely enjoy.

Maclean fell silent after these words, although his heavy tread behind her warned Tara that he'd be her shadow today.

Mercifully, he hadn't bound her wrists this morning. It was clear that with her sprained ankle, she wouldn't get far if she tried to run off again, and she couldn't use a stick to walk with her hands tied.

They still traveled under the long shadow of Ben More. The sun rose from the east, behind them, and the light was gloomy, the mist ethereal. Wet ground squelched underfoot, and with each step, Tara's ankle let its presence be known.

Maclean was probably right; she should bind it. However, she didn't carry any wrapping, and she wasn't going to heed anything he said.

More than her sore ankle, it was thirst that bothered her the most this morning. Her tongue felt swollen and her throat raw. She might have given in and asked her captor for a drink from the skin he carried—if it hadn't been stolen, along with everything else in his saddle bag, the night before. Hunger started to gnaw at her now too, although the need for food wasn't half as pressing as that for water.

The gorge widened to a glen before them, the trees falling back to reveal scrubby hills studded with boulders.

But they'd only walked a few more yards when the drum of hoofbeats intruded.

Tara abruptly halted, causing Maclean to walk into her back. She paid him no mind, glancing around instead, desperate to see what direction the sound of an approaching rider was coming from.

Relief swelled like a spring tide in her breast. Had her father finally caught up with them?

Wordlessly, Maclean took hold of her arm and pulled her back against him. The scrape of steel on leather followed as he drew the dirk at his side.

Tara tensed. The light was still murky, for the sun had yet to clear the edges of Ben More, but through the swirling mist, she caught the outline of a horse and rider, cresting the hill to the north and descending into the glen at a flat gallop.

The thunder of hoofbeats now shattered the dawn.

A shaft of worry pierced Tara's relief. Just one horse? Surely, her father wouldn't have followed on his own?

Her lips parted as she readied herself to call out, but then Maclean muttered an oath, cutting her off.

Tara frowned, not sure what concerned him, as, to her disappointment, the horse and rider weren't heading in their direction. Indeed, the rider hadn't noticed them at all.

She jolted then, her breath catching.

The Lord strike her down, the rider was *headless*.

Jack watched the black horse gallop across the glen before them, and his heart stuttered.

The figure crouched atop it, wearing a flowing black cloak, bore nothing but a bloodied stump upon its shoulders.

A chill shivered through him, the ice in his blood making his limbs tingle. Just a few months earlier, at Samhuinn, he'd donned the guise of Eoghann a'Chinn Bhig—Ewan of the Little Head. It had been a gruesome costume, and he'd grinned at the frightened squeal of bairns as he strode into the crowd gathered around the bonfire outside the walls of Duart Castle.

But he wasn't grinning now.

"The Headless Horseman," Tara breathed. "I thought it was just a tale for bairns."

Jack's bowels cramped. Curse it, she'd seen it too— the vision before him wasn't merely a figment of his imagination.

His gaze tracked the horse and rider. They'd crossed through the heart of the glen and now climbed the southern side.

Unfortunately, the Headless Horseman wasn't a story made up to scare wee ones. Eoghann a'Chinn Bhig had been a real man who'd fallen in a clan battle at Glen Cainnir many years earlier. The tale went that his soul was so enraged he was denied his chance to be a chieftain, that he was left unable to rest in peace.

But the most chilling thing about the specter was his connection to the Macleans—a connection Jack tried hard not to think about.

Even so, his heart now hammered against his ribs, and sweat slicked his body.

Tara murmured something else under her breath as they both watched the specter disappear over the brow of the hill to the south, but Jack ignored her. He stepped forward then, bringing his captive with him. "Come on," he muttered. "Let's keep moving."

9: FIRE IN YER BLOOD

TARA STUDIED HER captor with interest as she limped along beside him.

Jack Maclean had gone the color of ash. He was sweating too, and deep grooves had etched themselves on either side of his mouth. His reaction was curious. Aye, bearing witness to the infamous specter that was said to haunt these parts of the isle chilled the blood. But her captor appeared as if he might keel over at any moment.

Tara's mouth thinned. With any luck, he would.

Nonetheless, his reaction surprised her. Maclean was superstitious, it seemed. It was another chink in his armor—and Tara made a mental note, as she had noted his horror earlier that morning when he'd realized the liberties he'd taken while they both slept.

Her father had once told her that a wise man tried to understand his enemies. Sage advice, indeed. But apart from Maclean's odd response now, what had her time with him revealed?

The man was driven by vengeance to the point of madness. His bitterness and thirst for reckoning had made him ruthless—yet he wasn't utterly without scruples. Apart from when he'd used his superior strength to quell her struggles, he hadn't been violent toward her. And some men wouldn't have stopped, after realizing he'd been taking advantage of his captive while she slept.

No, what he'd done was villainous, yet knavery wasn't in his blood. She sensed a struggle in him.

Jack Maclean was also deeply emotional—something he hadn't bothered to hide over the past day. Only a man who felt things keenly would have let resentment consume him as he had. It made him shortsighted and reckless. Taking revenge against her father was foolish, for Kendric Mackinnon would be savage in his retribution. Maclean would know that, yet he didn't care.

"Do ye need to stop awhile?" she asked, her gaze still roaming over her captor's sweaty face. Of course, she wasn't concerned about this bastard's wellbeing. But the longer they lingered here, the more time she'd give her father's men to track them into this glen.

"No," he croaked, shaking his head as if to clear it. His grip on her arm tightened a fraction—a warning for her to drop the subject. "Leash yer tongue and walk."

Mouth pursed, Tara looked away from him, focusing on the glen that stretched ahead. The watery sun had broken through behind them, chasing away the last of the dawn mist. She squinted then, catching a glint of something in the distance. "Is that a burn?"

"Aye."

A sigh of relief gusted out of Tara. *Thank the heavens.*

"Thirsty?"

Tara didn't reply.

"I did offer ye some ale *twice* yesterday, if I recall."

"Ye did," she snapped, still not looking his way. "But I'd rather accept a drink from the devil."

"Pride won't help ye now." His voice sharpened with scorn. "It's time ye dropped those airs of yers."

Tara cut Maclean a glare. "I don't have any 'airs'."

His lip curled. "Aye, ye do … yer father clearly brought ye up to believe ye are better than others."

Tara yanked her arm from his. She then leaned heavily on her crutch, swallowing the hot anger that surged through her. "Ye don't have the right to criticize my character." She didn't want to engage with this villain, but his comments made her forget herself. "Not when *yers* is as black as tar."

Maclean gave a derisive snort. "At least I own who I am."

"So, ye admit ye are a man driven mad by the loss of his father?"

His handsome features tightened. "I haven't lost my wits," he growled.

"Aye, ye have … ye are unhinged!"

His eyes darkened as his temper quickened. "Ye might believe that, but since I arrived back on this isle, my purpose has become clear to me. Baird Maclean's death shall, finally, be avenged."

"My father insists that yers attacked him first that day" —she threw the words at him— "after yer Da refused to accept to split the lands around Faing Burn."

Jack Maclean skidded to an abrupt halt, catching her by the arm and swinging her around to face him. "Then yer father is a lying dog!"

"Says who?" she shot back, stabbing at him with her crutch. "Were ye there? Did ye see the incident unfold?"

"No, but my father's captain entered the chamber just moments after, to find Kendric Mackinnon standing over his body, a bloody dirk in his hand."

Tara wrenched her arm free of his grip once more. "Aye, and what does that prove?"

Maclean glared at her for a heartbeat before he snarled a curse and resumed his long stride.

Tara hobbled after him, leaning heavily on her stick. How dare he walk away? She wasn't yet done. "So, that's what ye do when an argument doesn't go yer way, Maclean?" she called out. "Ye just run off, like a baseborn coward?"

He didn't answer, and Tara's heart started to pound in her ears as her temper flared once more. "That's what ye are … a *fazart*!" she shouted. "Ye don't have the balls to face my father, so ye stole his daughter instead."

Maclean whipped around to face her, his jaw clenched. "Enough, woman," he snapped. "Keep heckling me and I shall take pleasure in gagging ye again."

Tara's heart knocked hard against her breastbone. She wanted to continue raging at him, yet the banked anger in his eyes made her check the urge. Instead, silently fuming, she limped off ahead.

Reaching the burn, she descended a pebbly slope to where clear water bubbled over stones. Her captor stepped up next to her then and halted on the edge of the stream, surveying it while Tara sank to her knees at the water's edge, scooping up the cool, crisp water in her hands and drinking greedily.

After a moment, Maclean joined her.

Sitting back on her haunches, Tara cast him a sidewise glance, watching him drink. Once again, she was loath to talk to him, yet curiosity niggled at her. "Why the hesitation?"

He straightened up, wiping his mouth with the back of his hand. "Not all watercourses are good," he replied. "Some will make ye as sick as a dog if ye aren't careful."

Tara tensed. "And this one?"

"It comes down from Ben More, so it should be safe." His gaze glinted as it met hers. "I wouldn't have drunk from it otherwise."

"Aye ... but ye let me?"

His mouth twisted. "I might enjoy watching ye puke yer guts out."

"Bastard," she muttered.

A shadow fell across them then, as if a cloud had just obscured the morning sun. Tara twisted left, toward it, just in time to see a big dark-haired man in well-worn braies and a leather vest club her abductor over the back of the head with a branch.

Tara gasped, reeling back. God's teeth, where had he come from? Just moments earlier, the glen around them had appeared empty. She shifted her attention farther left to see four more men, all similarly clothed, standing a few feet behind him. One of them led a bay horse. Jack Maclean's courser.

Meanwhile, her abductor lay sprawled upon the bank of the burn, out cold.

His attacker stepped forward, rolling him over onto his back with a big booted foot.

Maclean's head lolled back. His breathing was quick and shallow; the blow hadn't killed him.

The newcomer's bearded face then split into a grin. "I don't believe it," he said, his deep voice rumbling through the still morning air. "Look who we have here lads … a boon indeed."

"Isn't that the laird of Duart's cousin?" One of his companions asked.

"Aye, that horse and gear we took last night must have been his."

Recovering from the shock of seeing Maclean dealt with so suddenly, Tara scrambled to her feet. She didn't know who these men were—most definitely thieves, and likely outlaws or livestock rustlers—but they looked like trouble.

Reaching for her makeshift crutch, she edged away. "Thank ye for coming to my assistance," she murmured. "I'll be on my way now."

The big man inclined his head, focusing his dark gaze upon her. "Oh, aye?"

Tara kept moving. Pain shot through her sprained ankle, yet she breathed through it. "That fiend abducted me … but my father is on his way."

"Stop there a moment, lass," the big man rumbled. Meanwhile, his companions moved forward, hemming her in.

Tara complied as trepidation tightened her belly. He was staring at her as if she were a tasty morsel served up for supper.

"What's yer name?" he asked then.

"Tara Mackinnon … the clan-chief's daughter," she replied, lifting her chin as she struggled to rein in her mounting fear. This admission drew murmurs from her rescuers. "This man" —she nodded to Jack's prostrate form— "stole me away from Tobermory."

The individual who'd attacked Maclean nodded, his gaze sharpening. "To what end, lass?"

"To avenge himself against my father." Tara's pulse fluttered then. She'd hoped revealing who she was might intimidate him, but instead, the man wore a thin smile.

"Has he ransomed ye, lass?" Another of his companions asked. He was a small fellow with pinched features.

"No." Tara's voice trailed off here, her skin prickling. All five of them were watching her intently now, hungry expressions upon their faces.

And when one of them licked his lips, her stomach knotted.

God's bones, she was possibly in even bigger trouble than before.

10: SPILLING BLOOD

JACK AWOKE TO find himself being dragged over rough ground by his ankles.

For a few moments, his head felt as if it were filled with wool. He winced then as the bruised back of his neck caught a stone.

Two men hauled him by the ankles with as much care as if he were a felled log.

Jack's breathing grew shallow. Satan's cods, how had he ended up here?

Meanwhile, two other men had Tara by an arm each, even as she struggled against them.

A big man with wild dark hair walked alongside them, leading a fine bay courser.

Mòine. His horse.

Jack's gaze narrowed as he tried to focus through his muddled mind and pounding skull.

Ramsay MacDonald.

His gut clenched as incredulity and then anger swept over him. It had been over six months since he'd last set eyes on the farmer. He'd wondered what had become of him, and now he knew. He'd heard whispers of a group of MacDonald outlaws preying upon travelers and stealing livestock in these parts. But he should have realized it was Ramsay and his friends.

None of them had noted that Jack had awoken.

"Get yer hands off me!" Tara snarled, kicking one of the men grasping her in the shins.

He hissed a curse while Ramsay barked a laugh. "Giving ye some trouble, is she, Malcolm?"

"Little bitch doesn't like her paps being fondled," the man grumbled.

"Aye, well … now isn't the time or place for that," Ramsay replied, his dark brows knitting together. "Let's deal with Maclean first, and then we'll find a nice comfortable … quiet … spot where we can each take our turn with the lass."

Tara's sharp intake of breath followed, and Jack shut his eyes.

This was a right mess.

"We should have just drowned Maclean in the burn, Ramsay," one of the men dragging Jack grumbled. "The whoreson is heavier than a sack of rocks."

"What … and deny ourselves a proper reckoning?" their leader replied, a sneer in his voice. "No, lads … we'll drag these two back to the foothills of Ben More and take our time with them both. I want Maclean begging for his mother by the end … and as for this lovely lass" — Ramsay's voice turned gravelly then— "I intend to be the first to hump her."

Heat washed over Jack at these words, his temper quickening now. He squeezed his eyes shut, trying to douse the protective instinct that made his heart thump out a tattoo against his ribs. What a rank hypocrite he was, to worry over Tara Mackinnon's fate after what he'd done.

"I was the one who found their tracks this morning," the other man who held Tara muttered, oblivious to the battle Jack was waging with himself. "I should go first."

"I'm in charge here, Aodh," Ramsay replied. "So, no one's sticking his spear in her before I do."

"We could just have some fun first though," Aodh whined. "Come here, lass … give us a kiss."

Jack's eyes snapped open to see that the outlaw had stepped into Tara, grabbed her by the hair, and slammed his mouth down over hers.

Red-hot rage slammed into him, yet an instant later, Aodh gave a howl and staggered back, releasing her. "The bitch bit me!"

Rough laughter echoed across the hills. Meanwhile, Aodh wiped his mouth. "She's drawn blood."

Jack's lips compressed into a thin smile. Tara Mackinnon had already taught him that she wasn't helpless. But despite her bravery, she couldn't fend off five brutes on her own.

"Why shouldn't we take her now, lads?" Malcolm, who still grasped Tara by the arm, grinned widely. "The lass clearly wants to play."

"My father will hang, draw, and quarter the lot of ye for this," Tara panted, struggling against the man who still held her.

"Only if he catches us," Aodh growled, dabbing at his injured lower lip. "And since we are far from his lands, he'll never do that."

"No … scream all ye like, lassie," Malcolm added, shoving her onto the ground as he began to fumble with the laces on his trews. "Yer Da won't hear ye."

"Keep yer slug in yer braies, Malcolm," Ramsay barked, throwing Mòine's reins to Aodh. His heavy-featured face was now thunderous. "I told ye … we're waiting to have our fun."

Malcolm growled a curse at Ramsay and continued yanking at his trews.

Meanwhile, the two men dragging Jack halted and turned to watch their companions. "Sounds like old Malcolm is ready to rut," one of them jeered.

"Aye, and I'll kick his ball-sack hard enough to lodge in his throat if he swives this woman before I do," Ramsay replied, striding toward where Malcolm was now on the ground, struggling to yank up Tara's skirts. "Do ye hear me, man?"

Malcolm's face turned florid, yet he minded Ramsay this time, reluctantly heaving himself off Tara and backing away as the bigger man loomed over him.

Meanwhile, Tara had scrambled back over the rocky ground, trying to get away from the outlaws. However, her scuffle with Malcolm had exposed her long legs.

Ramsay stared down at her, his expression slackening. "Ye *are* a bonnie one, aren't ye?" he said hoarsely. "I can see why Malcolm forgot himself." He then started unlacing his braies. "I might dip my wick now, after all."

The men standing in front of Jack chortled before one of them elbowed his friend. "This should be good to watch."

Meanwhile, Jack readied himself to move. Even though the back of his head still throbbed, his mind had cleared, and his limbs had regained their strength. Violence now coiled inside him, ready to be loosed. None of the lust-addled fools were looking his way. He'd never get a better chance than this.

Time to spill some blood.

They'd stripped Jack's dirk from him, and so his first move would be to get himself a blade. Rolling into a crouch, he lunged for the man nearest, yanking his dirk free from its sheath and plunging the long thin blade up under his ribs.

It was a lethal strike—one he'd learned long ago during his first campaign against the English, and only possible when a man wasn't wearing armor—but Jack wasn't in a merciful mood this morning.

He was the angel of death, and these five were corpses.

The outlaw's breath gusted from him, and he let out a rattling wheeze as he crumpled to the ground.

Jack dropped him like a stone, rolled to his feet, and launched himself at the man standing next to him. He'd moved so fast that he took this outlaw by surprise as well, dragging the dirk across his throat.

Shouts rang across the hillside now, for the remaining three *had* noticed him.

Ramsay had stopped unlacing his braies, while both Aodh and Malcolm drew their dirks. In the meantime, Tara had the good sense to scramble to her feet and back away. Her gaze was wide as it flicked between Jack and the three outlaws who now stalked him.

She clearly thought he was done for. However, Jack hadn't survived a decade of war—countless bloody skirmishes and battles—to be cowed by the sight of

Ramsay and his friends. He too was armed. And even though his head throbbed sickeningly, a fury had sharpened his senses.

These three were farmers, violent and brutal men who were good with their fists. But he was a trained warrior. If they had their wits about them, they'd run.

Instead, the fools closed in on him.

Jack widened his stance and bent his knees, holding the dirk loosely in his right hand as he waited for them to come to him. Aye, he could be a hothead with an explosive temper, but his anger was always his ally in battle. Suddenly, it was as if he were watching the scene from above, as if he were playing a game of Ard-ri and calculating where to move his next piece.

Ramsay lunged first, and Jack ducked under his guard, slicing him across the ribs.

Cursing, the big man staggered back. He hadn't expected Jack to be so fast. Malcolm struck at him then, and Jack narrowly avoided a blade to the face before he stepped into his opponent and stabbed his dirk through Malcolm's throat.

Out of the corner of his eye, he caught a flash of bright-red hair.

Ramsay, clutching his bleeding side with one hand, was now heading toward Tara.

To Jack's surprise, instead of trying to run, she scooped up a stone and palmed it, before hurling it at the outlaw.

Her throw was impressive, smacking him hard on the temple.

Ramsay reeled back, but Jack didn't have time to reassure himself that Tara would be all right, for Aodh crashed into him.

The two of them sprawled to the ground, Jack's dirk flying from his hand.

Curse it, he'd let Tara distract him. Yet he quickly recovered. Aodh tried to drive his own weapon into his opponent's eye, but Jack grabbed hold of his wrist and held it tightly, stopping the wicked point just inches from his face.

Then, clenching his jaw, he drove his knee into Aodh's gut.

His opponent grunted, his hold slackening just a little.

Jack seized the opportunity, rolling so that Aodh was under him. A heartbeat later, the outlaw's own blade drove into his throat.

The pounding of hoofbeats intruded then, and Jack whipped around to see Ramsay MacDonald riding away on Mòine, as if the devil himself were on his heels.

And to his surprise, he found Tara Mackinnon standing just a few feet away, another sharp rock in her hand.

Pushing Aodh's twitching corpse aside, Jack rolled to his feet.

His head throbbed viciously then, and he muttered a curse, lifting a hand to cradle the back of his skull.

Tara swung around to face him. "What's wrong?"

Jack swallowed a groan as the anger that had propelled him forward dimmed. "Nothing," he rasped. Hades, it hurt. Nausea washed over him, and bile stung the back of his throat.

"Here." She approached him warily, as if he were a rabid dog. "Let me look."

Her behavior hit Jack in the solar plexus. It surprised him that she'd show concern for him. Frankly, even though he'd saved her from Ramsay and his friends, he didn't deserve it.

Tara hobbled around the four dead men scattered around Jack, casting them a jaundiced eye as she went. Then, moving behind him, she parted the hair at the back of his scalp. The delicate touch of her fingertips against his sore head made Jack's eyelids flutter shut.

"Ye are fortunate," she said after a moment. "Yer hair is thick ... it cushioned the blow."

Jack gave a soft snort. "Aye, luckily I have a thick skull too."

"I'm not disputing that. A wicked bruise is coming up on yer neck though."

Jack's lips thinned. "They'd have done better to kill me right away," he muttered. "That was their first mistake." Opening his eyes, he turned to face her. "Threatening to rape ye was their second."

Tara's gaze shadowed as she stared back at him, her face pale and strained. "Is that any worse than yer plans for me?" she asked huskily.

Jack's chest tightened. He wanted to deny it. God's teeth—that would make him both a hypocrite *and* a liar. "I couldn't let them hurt ye, Tara," he admitted then before catching himself.

Tara.

It was the first time he'd addressed her so.

His captive's gaze snapped wide.

Jack's pulse quickened then. God help him, what was he doing?

Moments passed, and then Tara's full lips pursed. "Don't want me ruined for whatever ye have in store?" she asked, the sudden quaver in her voice betraying her. The lass was tough, but she wasn't invincible—and he shouldn't be staring at her like this either.

Blinking, Jack stepped back from his captive. "Aye, that's right," he answered, pulling himself together. He looked away from her then, instead surveying the men he'd killed. Curse it, he shouldn't have let Ramsay MacDonald escape. He needed Mòine too, for they still had a way to go until they reached the coast. Glancing up at where the sun was now high in the sky, he scowled. This attack had delayed things; they risked being late.

His plans were swiftly unraveling, but he wouldn't let them. No, he'd see this through until the bitter end.

11: A CHIVALROUS ROGUE

PAIN LANCED THROUGH Tara's ankle, and she gasped, stumbling despite the stick she'd been leaning heavily on.

Maclean, who'd been following a few strides behind, stepped up to her side. They'd left the dead behind them and set off southwest once more. Her captor was keen to make up for lost time, and Tara could almost taste his impatience.

His eyes narrowed now as they fixed on her. "We need to bind that ankle."

"I just need to walk slower," Tara snapped.

Maclean shook his head, irritation tightening his features. "We're wasting time."

"I don't care." And she didn't. The slower they walked the better, for it gave her father time to catch up with them.

A muscle flexed in Maclean's jaw. He then gestured to a large flat rock that jutted out of the earth a few yards away. "Sit down."

Tara pulled a face yet didn't move to obey him.

Her captor fixed her with a stare, his frown deepening. "Sit. Down."

Swallowing, Tara reluctantly did as bid, backing up to the rock he'd pointed to and sinking down. Earlier, she'd have told him to go to the devil for using such a tone with her, but in the aftermath of the fight with the outlaws, she was cautious around Jack Maclean, and a little in awe of him too, if she were honest.

Aye, he'd saved his own hide, but he'd also protected her, dispatching four of her would-be rapists with shocking economy. Unlike his opponents, he didn't waste any energy or movement. Instead, each strike had been purposeful, sparing, and deadly. Watching him fight was like watching a skilled dancer.

She still didn't trust the man though—not one bit. And every time she believed she was getting close to understanding how her abductor thought, he surprised her.

Watching him approach, his expression forbidding, Tara assessed her situation. She'd been so sure her father would have caught up with them by now; however, there was still no sign of him. Her breathing quickened at the realization that wherever Maclean was taking her, help wouldn't likely come in time. She needed to save herself.

Could she use this man's sense of chivalry to her advantage? Maybe if she was clever—if she was able to appeal to his protective instinct—she could get him to regret abducting her, and to let her go.

It was devious and manipulative, yet time was running out. She was desperate.

Such a ploy wouldn't work with a lot of men. But there was something about Jack Maclean. She sensed a need in him—to protect and care for others—that contradicted his behavior.

Seemingly unaware of his captive's scheming, Maclean hunkered down in front of her. Lifting the hem of her skirt, he took hold of her booted foot. Then, with surprising gentleness, he pulled the boot free. A groove furrowed between his eyebrows then.

Glancing down, Tara caught her breath. Her ankle was swollen and purple. "Mother Mary," she whispered. "Is it broken?"

"No ... if it was, ye wouldn't be able to walk upon it at all," he replied, even as his frown deepened. "It's a sprain." He glanced up then, his green eyes shadowed as his gaze met hers. "I dumped ye too heavily out of that window, lass."

Tara stared back at him. Her first instinct was to tell him her sprained ankle was the least of his crimes against her. However, there was an apology in his voice, and remonstrating with the rogue wouldn't make him question his behavior.

Shrugging, she consciously lowered her gaze then. "I made it worse by running away."

Maclean huffed and rested her ankle on his knee. Then, reaching up, he grabbed the edge of the lèine she wore under her surcote and kirtle with both hands, ripping a length of it off.

Tara stifled a gasp. "What are ye doing?"

Maclean glanced up. "Making a bandage."

Swallowing the urge to tell him he could have asked first, Tara remembered her goal and favored him with a tremulous smile. Their gazes held for a few moments before her captor jerked himself from his reverie. Jaw tensing, he then started binding her ankle. His movements were deft and sure.

"Ye look like ye've done this before," she observed.

"Aye ... many a time," he replied tersely. "Ye'd be amazed how often warriors turn their ankles in battle."

An awkward pause followed, and Tara cleared her throat. "Ye saved me," she murmured, forcing a meekness that didn't come easily to her. "And I'm ... grateful."

He glanced up again then, his gaze glinting. "Ye were brave back there."

"Was I?" she replied. "In truth, I was terrified."

His mouth curved, his expression warming. "But ye didn't let fear immobilize ye ... that's what true courage is. Do ye think most men go into battle not wanting to shit themselves?"

Tara raised her eyebrows. "I did, actually."

Silence fell between them then as he picked up her boot and gently wedged it back onto her foot.

"That man ... Ramsay," Tara said finally, suppressing a shudder as she recalled the brute. His ravenous look as he'd unlaced his braies still haunted her. "He appeared to have an ax to grind against ye."

"Aye."

"What did ye do to him?"

Her captor sat back on his heels and pulled a face. "I helped the laird defend the virtue of the woman who ran our local inn … around six months ago. Loch dealt with Ramsay MacDonald, while I and two others saw to his friends." He shrugged then. "It seems that Ramsay carries a grudge. He and his friends used to farm run rigs just outside Craignure, but after that incident, Loch cast the five of them from his lands."

Tara inclined her head as she took his explanation in. It seemed Maclean wasn't the only one looking for revenge.

"Aye, well … the woman was fortunate that ye stepped in to help her," she said, deliberately softening her voice, even as her belly clenched. Lord, being civil to this devil was harder than she'd thought.

Maclean's mouth curved, his cheeks dimpling. "The lass in question is now Loch's wife."

"So, the rumors are true then?" she asked. "That yer clan-chief wed a tavern wench?"

That was the wrong thing to say, for her captor's smile slipped, his features hardening. "Loch wed Mairi Macquarie, the *owner* of *The Craignure Inn*," he corrected her. His response made it clear just how loyal he was to both his laird and his bride. Loch Maclean had scandalized the whole isle with his choice of wife, yet his cousin was defensive on his behalf.

"The Maclean could have had any lady he wished," she pointed out, forgetting that she was supposed to be softening him up. "He could have made an alliance that would strengthen his clan. Instead, he chose to wed a woman with no connections, no lands … no dowry. He's also lost the respect of the other clan leaders."

Maclean's mouth curved into a humorless smile. "Loch's never been one to care what others think," he replied, his eyes narrowing in an unspoken challenge. "Loch and Mairi have known each other a long while. It took him a few months to come to his senses, but after returning to Mull, he eventually realized that there would never be anyone else for him … but her.”

Once again, Tara caught the edge to his voice. He wouldn't have anyone criticize Loch and Mairi's actions.

“So, ye believe in 'true love' then?” she teased, unable to prevent herself.

Maclean stilled. Her question had caught him unawares. “Aye,” he admitted after a moment. “It's rare, yet it exists.”

“Well, I haven't seen it.” She looked away, even as her chest tightened.

She felt her abductor's gaze upon her but deliberately didn't meet his eye. Despite her dismissiveness, there was a part of her that *did* want the kind of love that minstrels sang of—although even if someone rescued her, that wouldn't be her fate. She and Callum MacDonald would have a bond based on practicality and mutual advantage.

Orla had assured her that affection would develop once they were wed, and that the strongest marriages were built on mutual respect, not attraction, which often flared hot and then faded. She hoped her maid's words were wise ones.

Maclean stood up abruptly then, severing their fragile connection as he loomed over her. Glancing up, Tara put out her hand so he could help her to her feet.

Her gesture surprised him, and he hesitated. However, a heartbeat later, his sense of chivalry won. Taking her hand in his, Maclean drew Tara to her feet.

Her belly swooped at the shock of their fingers clasping, the strength and warmth of his hand. The sensation was unexpected and discomforting.

And judging by the way his eyes widened, he too had felt it.

Maclean smartly let go of her hand then and gestured for her to move on. Picking up her stick, Tara hobbled off. With her ankle bound, walking was easier. All the same, each step hurt.

She'd only gone a few yards when she stumbled. Gasping, she choked back a cry of pain.

"Doesn't the bandage help?" Maclean asked.

"Not really," she grunted, wincing.

Muttering a curse, her captor stepped up next to her. However, to her surprise, he then lowered himself to a crouch. "Climb on my back."

Tara inhaled sharply. "What?"

"Ye heard me."

"I'm not having ye carry me, Maclean."

He cut her a hard look. "Climb on, or I'll throw ye over my shoulder. Yer choice."

Tara glared back at him, even as heat washed over her. Curse it, she was supposed to be getting him to lower his guard with her, not arguing with the cur. However, she didn't want to touch him again—especially after the reaction she'd just had to grasping his hand.

Don't be a goose, she counseled herself then, choking back her anger. *This is a chance to use yer vulnerability to weaken his defenses, to let doubt and guilt creep in.*

Reminding herself of this, she swallowed her anger, cast aside her walking stick, and climbed onto his back.

12: YE'LL NOT FIND THE ANSWERS YE SEEK

CARRYING THE LASS wasn't the brightest idea he'd ever had.

For one thing, the back of Jack's head still pounded, throbbing with each step. The other problem was that the feel of her soft body pressed flush against his back, her lithe legs slung over the crooks of his arms, was a distraction he didn't need.

And she *was* a distraction.

Their conversation as he'd bound her ankle had knocked him off balance. He was used to the lass spitting at him like an adder—and her anger was easier to deal with—but instead, she'd revealed a vulnerability that unsettled him. Helping Tara to her feet earlier had been a mistake too. The feel of her slender fingers curled around his had made his pulse leap into a canter.

Pushing aside the memory of the response her touch had roused, Jack doggedly walked on, over tussock-covered hills, studded with rocks and intersected by shallow burns. As he walked, he stole the odd glance behind him—just in case Ramsay MacDonald decided to have another go.

He couldn't believe the whoreson had managed to sneak up on him earlier while he'd been drinking at the burn.

Ye know why, a scorn-filled voice intruded then. *It's her. Ye can't concentrate when Tara Mackinnon is near.*

This insight was so shocking that Jack stumbled and nearly went down on his knees.

Tara let out a squeal as he lunged forward. The sound pierced his ear and jolted him back into reality.

"It's all right," he muttered. "I just tripped, that's all."

No, he was mistaken. His captive wasn't distracting him.

Aye, she is. The voice was back, needling him. *Face it, every time ye meet her gaze, ye drown in her eyes. Ye want her.*

Jack clenched his jaw. No, he didn't. He couldn't stand the woman. And this time tomorrow, he'd be rid of her for good.

A pit opened in his stomach then as he looked ahead, and his pulse quickened. There was no need to panic—the rendezvous he'd organized wasn't scheduled to take place until dawn the following day. They'd been delayed, yet they'd make it.

But being late wasn't what bothered him the most. It was the fact that what he'd planned for his captive no longer filled him with a sense of vindictive satisfaction.

Instead, it made him feel sick—at himself.

Is this what I've become?

Aye. To revenge himself against 'The Butcher', he'd needed to become just as ruthless. Just as cunning. Just as cruel. But the truth was that he lacked Kendric Mackinnon's killer instinct. His enemy would have slit the throat of a woman without blinking an eye, if it served his purposes, yet Jack now had to steel himself to go through with his plans.

He started to sweat then, not just because he had been carrying Tara on his back for a while, or because the sun now warmed his face. It was a cold sweat, the same one that had washed over him after he'd spied the Headless Horseman at dawn.

But this time, it wasn't the grim specter that froze his blood.

It was the realization that he now *cared* what happened to Tara Mackinnon.

"Where are we?"

"Fionnphort."

Sliding down from Maclean's back, and wincing as she tested her stiff ankle with her full weight, Tara took this news in.

It made sense, given the direction he'd taken them in. She'd never visited Fionnphort yet knew it was the main port for the Ross of Mull, looking over the narrow stretch of water between this isle and the much smaller one of Iona.

Tara was afraid—as well as tired, hungry, and desperately thirsty—yet she found herself surveying her surroundings and looking for escape routes.

Unfortunately, at first glance, Fionnphort didn't appear to have any.

The scene before her was picturesque, at odds with the hell Tara now inhabited. Of course, this place was ignorant of her predicament. White-washed cottages nestled against the rocky green headland, and a wide silvery beach stretched before them. Wooden fishing boats sat on the sand, where fishermen mended nets and ribbed each other as they prepared themselves to head out at dawn the following day.

Tara thought about calling to them for help yet checked herself. They were a rough-looking crowd, and after her experience with the outlaws earlier in the day, she was apprehensive.

If there had been some women among them, she might have risked it, but it was best to be prudent, or she could end up in a worse mess than she was currently.

Farther down the beach, a sturdy wooden dock thrust out into sparkling sapphire-colored water, where a collection of birlinns bobbed with the tide, while at the end of the pier sat a much bigger vessel.

Tara's gaze narrowed as she studied it. Like the birlinns, the cog was flat-bottomed and single-masted, but it was nearly twice the size of the galleys, with high wooden sides made of clinkered oak. The black-and-white-striped sail was down this evening, but Tara recognized the cog nonetheless.

"Isn't that Logan Black's ship?"

Maclean jolted as if she'd just stuck her elbow into him before whipping around on his heel to face her.

"Aye," he said warily, his gaze roaming her face. "How do ye know that?"

Tara arched an eyebrow, amused by his reaction. "Ye'd have to live under a rock not to know about the fearsome pirate that sails the western isles on a cog with a black-and-white sail."

Maclean snorted. "Black isn't a pirate … he's a mercenary."

"Isn't that the same thing?" Tara's attention flicked back to the cog, frowning once more. "My father has put a price on his head."

"Aye?" Maclean put an arm through hers—as if they were sweethearts, and not captor and captive—expecting Tara to lean on him as he steered her toward the cluster of dwellings that lined the unpaved street at the heart of the tiny village. She reluctantly did as bid, if only to take the pressure off her throbbing ankle.

"Aye … one hundred silver pennies to whoever brings him in alive," she informed him. "Logan Black is a villain. He has raided several Mackinnon birlinns en route to Dùn Ara in recent years, slain the crew, and scuttled the boats afterward."

"That's hardly surprising," Maclean replied. "For yer father's men slew his family." Her captor wasn't looking in her direction now. Instead, he stared straight ahead, his jaw flexing. "It's no coincidence he calls his ship the *Revenge Tide*."

These words made Tara's stomach clench, and she glanced once more out at the cog. She hadn't realized Black had a bone to pick with her clan. He'd carved out a fearsome reputation over the past decade, and the sight of his ship moored so boldly at a port upon the Isle of Mull was a sign he had allies amongst the locals here.

"Are the Blacks kin to the Macleans?" she asked then, swinging her attention back to her companion.

"Aye, they're a sept of our clan."

This news unsettled Tara even further. *What is he up to?*

Falling silent, she let Maclean lead her toward a small tavern halfway down the street. *The Creel Inn* was a squat single-storied cottage with a wing out back for those staying over. Whitewashed with tiny shuttered windows, the lodgings looked as if they'd been built recently. And as they drew near, Tara inhaled the rich aroma of roasting mutton.

Saliva filled her mouth, and she almost forgot her predicament. God's bones, she was *starving*.

"Right ... this is how things will go," Maclean said then, squeezing her arm firmly. "If ye want a full belly and a soft bed for the night, ye will keep yer gaze lowered and yer voice meek. If anyone asks, we are husband and wife."

Tara bristled at his order yet held her tongue. She'd hoped Maclean might develop a conscience over the day, yet upon their arrival at Fionnphort, his manner toward her had hardened once more.

And there was still no sign of her father either.

Time was running out for her, but it was difficult to concentrate when her belly was as hollow as a drum, her throat was parched, and her ankle pulsed with each heartbeat.

She was in desperate need of food, drink, and rest. Once she'd taken care of the necessities, her mind would clear again. And as soon as it did, she'd throw herself at the mercy of the locals. She'd tell them this rogue wasn't her husband but her abductor; someone would surely rescue her.

"And don't think about asking for help from the folk here," Maclean went on as if reading her thoughts. "They're all Macleans ... and most of them have plenty of reason to hate yer father. If ye tell them who ye really are, even *I* won't be able to protect ye from their wrath."

Tara's heart started pounding, and she tried to wrench her arm free of his. "Pig," she hissed. He really was a ruthless bastard.

In response, he favored her with a thin smile.

Tara ate ravenously, stuffing roast mutton and coarse oaten bread into her mouth at the same time, without a care about how it looked. Ladylike behavior be damned—she was famished.

She sat at a small table near the fire in the chamber Maclean had taken for them both. Of course, he hadn't gotten them separate rooms, for it would be too easy for her to escape. Instead, he'd smoothly told the innkeeper that this bonnie lass was his wife, and that they were taking a boat to Iona the following day, where he'd bought land and a small crofter's cottage for them.

Tara had cast Maclean a sharp look at these words.

There was said to be little upon the neighboring small isle, save for a tiny fishing village and an abbey.

She'd wondered fleetingly if he intended to drop her off at the abbey yet dismissed the idea soon after. Iona Abbey wasn't easy to enter. Only the daughters of wealthy men, with hefty dowries, were admitted. And even if she were allowed entry, the moment the abbess discovered who she was and that she'd been brought there against her will, she'd send word to Dùn Ara.

No, Iona was just a ready excuse. Jack Maclean had other plans for her.

Picking up her cup of ale, even as her belly now churned uneasily, Tara took a large gulp before eyeing the man seated opposite her. Curse it, she had to find a way to escape him.

Maclean also ate heartily, although his gaze was narrowed this evening, his handsome features tense. He looked preoccupied.

Hope fluttered in Tara's breast. Were his plans going awry? Maybe their delay in arriving in Fionnphort had complicated things for him. She certainly hoped so.

"There's no point in staring at me, woman," Maclean muttered. "Ye'll not find the answers ye seek."

"No?" Tara straightened up in her seat and bit into another piece of mutton, chewing and swallowing before she continued. "But if it unnerves ye, I shall not stop." Since sweetness didn't seem to work on him, she'd abandon it.

In response, Maclean scowled.

Tara shrugged, helping herself to another chunk of bread. Despite that anxiety squirmed like a sack of eels inside her, she'd enjoyed the meal. And now that her clawing hunger had drawn back, she could think again. "I'm tired," she announced after a brief pause, "and I reek like a sewer rat."

Her captor arched an eyebrow in response.

Tara lifted her chin, meeting his eye squarely. "Are ye going to let me bathe?"

Their stare drew out before he gave a grudging nod. "Ye won't have the large iron tub ye are no doubt used to … but once we're finished here, the innkeeper's wife will bring hot water, soap, and drying cloths."

13: DECENT

JACK WATCHED THE innkeeper's wife set the wash bowl full of steaming water on the table. She then lay down the pile of fresh drying cloths that she'd carried in, draped over one arm, and a block of coarse lye soap. "Here ye are, lass," she said to Tara with a kindly smile.

"Thank ye," Tara replied sweetly. Jack tensed at her tone—he'd already warned his captive not to try and get help from the locals. However, he couldn't trust her to heed him.

The older woman nodded before gathering their dirty dishes and cups from supper. "Please let me know if ye need anything else."

"Thank ye, will we," Jack replied, eager for the innkeeper's wife to leave.

The woman departed their room, the door thudding shut behind her. Jack then turned to his captive.

Tara had dropped her docile expression and was eyeing him warily, as if she wasn't sure what he'd do next.

He didn't blame her, for he hadn't said a word about what he had in store for the lass. Indeed, he'd refused to tell her. A queasy sensation stole over him then.

It's just the greasy mutton, he told himself. *It'll pass.*

"Fear not, I'm not going to stand here and watch ye bathe." He jerked his chin to the door. "I shall wait right outside." He frowned then, injecting a warning edge into his voice as he continued. "Don't think about trying to escape."

Tara's full lips pursed, yet she didn't dignify him with a response.

Their gazes fused for a heartbeat before Jack tore his away. Christ's blood, the woman had a mesmerizing stare. Her eyes were the color of polished steel with a ring of smoke-grey around the edge of the irises.

Without another word—and berating himself for noting such details about his captive—Jack turned on his heel and left the room, pulling the door firmly shut behind him and locking it. Alone in the yard beyond, his gaze traveled over the straw-strewn space to the stalls where three horses had been stabled.

The sight of the horses reminded him of Mòine, and he scowled.

Losing the courser still stung. He'd spent most of his coin on bribing the maid at Dùn Ara and Declan the ribbon merchant. He only had enough in the purse on his belt to pay for accommodation and food.

It matters not, he told himself, leaning against the rough stone wall of their accommodation. *I'm almost done here.*

His pulse kicked hard then, nausea biting at his throat. Jack winced and rubbed at his abdomen. However, this time he didn't blame the mutton. It wasn't the supper that was the problem.

As bent as he was on getting his revenge on Kendric Mackinnon, the reality of it was much harder than he'd imagined. He'd expected to feel vindicated by now. But even when he imagined how desperate the clan-chief would be to retrieve his daughter, and his worry that something awful had befallen her, Jack couldn't rouse any excitement.

Instead, when he thought about what he had planned for his captive, his innards twisted.

It was a lovely evening outdoors. The sun was setting to the west in a blaze of rose, lilac, and gold behind the sod roof of the inn. Jack couldn't see the dock from where he stood but knew that the crew of the *Revenge Tide* would be waiting there, eager for her precious cargo.

Of course, Black had kept his word. He was as intent as Jack was on revenging himself upon 'The Butcher of Dùn Ara'. Mackinnon had earned himself many enemies over the years, and, finally, his reckoning had come.

Aye, his mission had been blighted by trouble from the very beginning, but things were back on course.

Why then, wasn't Jack happier about it?

Leaning his head back against the wall and closing his eyes, Jack winced as the tender skin on the back of his scalp protested. He reached up then and prodded the back of his neck and head, grunting as pain lanced through his skull.

That was quite a knock he'd taken that morning.

The innkeeper's wife had said to ask if there was anything else they needed, and he'd see if she had some ointment for bruising. Tara's ankle could do with some attention as well.

Pushing himself off the wall, Jack cast a look at the door and the shuttered window right next to it. He didn't trust Tara not to try and escape through that window. But she'd think he was still out here, watching and waiting.

As long as he moved quietly, it was safe to duck inside the inn for the moment.

Once she was alone, Tara scoured the room deperately for an escape route. Maclean had taken the large iron key, locking the door behind him. The window was unlocked, but he was now standing outside it.

Curse it, she was trapped.

Muttering an oath under her breath, Tara decided she might as well bathe. Nonetheless, she kept one eye on the door as she quickly stripped off her clothing. Jaw set, she lathered up a washcloth with soap, turned back to the wash bowl, and focused on washing herself. The hot water and soap were welcome indeed, although she'd have to put on her old clothes again afterward.

Her breathing grew shallow, her chest aching as she imagined herself back in Dùn Ara, in her comfortable bedchamber, soaking up to the neck in rose-scented water while Orla bustled around the room, laying out her night-rail and turning down the bed for her.

Tara's eyes stung then. She'd taken her handmaid for granted over the years, and indeed had been irritated the morning before when Orla had accompanied her on that shopping trip to Tobermory.

What she would have done to see the woman now, to be comforted in her arms.

Tara's late mother had been a cold, distant woman who gave neither of her children any time or affection. It was Orla who'd tended Tara's scraped knees as a bairn, who'd sung to her in the evenings, and hugged her when she wept.

Tara's throat tightened. *I'll never see her again.*

The realization stabbed her in the belly. She wanted to deny it, to stay brave. But the truth was that there was no going home. And whenever she thought about the pirate ship moored nearby, fear coiled in her chest.

Maclean hadn't indicated that Logan Black was part of his plans, yet she sensed his presence here was no coincidence. Would she soon be at the mercy of not just one, but two men crazed by vengeance?

Why haven't ye found me yet, Da? Her father had skilled trackers amongst his men. He should have caught up with them by now.

Blinking as tears blinded her, Tara hurriedly finished washing before drying herself off. She'd just wriggled into her clothing once more when a heavy knock came at the door.

"Are ye dressed?"

Turning to the door, Tara considered lying, anything to give herself more time alone. However, there wasn't any point. The bastard had the key.

"Aye," she called out.

A moment later, the grating sound of iron in the lock followed, and the door opened. Maclean entered before closing the door and locking it. He then placed the key in a pouch at his waist. Tara marked the keeping place, although she wasn't sure how she'd ever manage to get

the key off him—or get out of this room without being
caught.

Her chest started to ache cruelly then, despair
catching hold of her. No, she wasn't going to escape this
man.

Crossing to the smoldering fire, Maclean placed a
small clay pot on the mantelpiece.

"What's that?" Tara asked huskily.

"Goatweed ointment," he replied. "I'll see to yer ankle
in a bit ... but for now, I should use that water before it
cools."

Alarm barreled through Tara at these words. He was
going to undress and wash in here—in front of her?

Backing away, she found herself with the backs of her
thighs pressing against the narrow bed.

"Don't look so worried, lass," Maclean muttered with
a frown. "There's no need for ye to look. Just turn away."

Jaw clenched, Tara did just that. She stood facing the
wall, arms folded across her front, while she waited for
her captor to go through his ablutions. She hoped he'd be
quick about it.

The thud of his belt and dirk sheath hitting the floor
made her stiffen, and at the rustle of his braies that
followed, nervousness prickled her skin. She didn't like
the thought of the brute standing behind her naked.

He'd looked horrified after this morning's incident,
yet she didn't trust him not to try something.

Splashing followed then, and Tara closed her eyes
tightly and slowly started to count. The trick worked, and
she managed to soothe her nerves until Maclean finally
declared, "Ye can turn around now ... I'm decent."

Unclenching her jaw, for her ears were now starting
to ache, Tara slowly let out a relieved exhale and turned.

However, she stiffened once more when her gaze
alighted upon Jack Maclean again.

Aye, he was decent, but barely.

He'd donned his braies, yet they sat low, revealing the
narrowness of his hips. Not only that, but he was
currently shirtless as he reached for his lèine. Whorls of
damp auburn curls covered his muscular chest, and his

skin glistened with droplets of water in the ruddy light of the fire.

Jaw clenching again, Tara jerked her gaze away. Climbing onto the bed, she shuffled along so her back was up against the wall. Meanwhile, Maclean pulled on his lèine, loosely tucking it into his braies. He then buckled his belt and strapped his dirk back on. Even within the safety of these walls, the man wasn't going unarmed.

"Did ye sleep with yer weapons on while ye were on campaign?" Tara asked then before clamping her mouth shut. Where had that question come from, and frankly, who cared?

"Aye," he replied with a half-smile. Barefoot, he padded over to the mantelpiece and retrieved the small pot of ointment. "Ye never knew when there would be a midnight raid, or if ye'd have to mobilize in the wee hours. It paid to always be prepared." He approached her then, pulling up a stool next to the bed and lowering himself onto it. "Now, let's have a look at that ankle."

14: ROTTEN TO THE CORE

"I CAN RUB ointment onto it myself," Tara said stiffly. She'd let him bind her ankle earlier in the day as she'd hoped to manipulate him, yet now that it was clear she couldn't, she didn't want him touching her.

He raised an eyebrow. "Aye … but I'll do a better job of massaging it into the bruising." He slapped his knee then. "Come on … don't argue."

Tara glared at him a moment before reminding herself that if she wanted to get anywhere near the key tucked away in that pouch on his belt, she needed to be clever. Aye, she couldn't manipulate him outright, yet maybe she could *distract* him.

Pushing herself forward, she reluctantly let him take hold of her ankle. It was still very tender and did need looking after.

He unwrapped the bandage he'd secured earlier, with surprising gentleness, and examined the swollen joint. He then gave a low whistle. "Aye, that's a pretty sight."

Tara scowled. Of course, it wasn't in the least—the bruise had gone all the colors of the rainbow now, and her ankle was horribly swollen.

Maclean unstoppered the clay pot and scooped out some goatweed ointment. He then gently massaged it into her ankle.

Tara bit her bottom lip. Hades, that hurt—yet at the same time, it was a blessed relief.

The villain had deft fingers that seemed to know where exactly to stroke and where to smooth, and when he caught hold of her heel and gently pulled it toward him, the pressure in her ankle released.

She couldn't help it; a soft moan escaped her then.

Maclean's head snapped up, and their gazes fused.

An instant later, heat flushed across Tara's chest, up her throat, and over her face. Good Lord, what a sound she'd just made. She was relieved, not aroused, yet her moan had sounded almost sensual. "That's enough," she muttered.

She expected her captor to smirk at her then, to make some rakish comment about how he could make any lass groan under his touch. But thankfully, he didn't. Instead, Maclean's expression veiled as he picked up her ankle off his knee and placed it back on the bed. "Ye are welcome," he replied, his tone curt.

Still seated on the stool, he shifted sideways then, scooping out a little more of the ointment. Reaching up, he tentatively massaged his neck. A hiss of pain followed.

Tara watched him for a short while, letting her embarrassment cool. Meanwhile, her mind started to churn. She had to get closer to that key, which meant she needed to find a way to draw his attention elsewhere. "Ye are making a mess of that," she observed finally. "And ye're going to get most of it in yer hair."

"I know," he snapped. "But needs must."

"Here." Tara pushed herself across the bed and stood up. "I'll do it."

The moment Tara's fingers touched his neck, Jack's already rock-hard shaft started to ache.

Curse it, what did the woman think she was doing?

He was already in a state; he didn't need her touching him and making things worse. Earlier, he'd been focused on gently working ointment into her ankle and then had pulled her heel to loosen the swollen joint a little, but when she'd groaned, his wits deserted him.

In an instant, heat ignited in his belly and his rod sprang to attention.

He'd turned away from her, to rub ointment on his neck, and to mask the way the front of his braies tented.

But now she was massaging him, and her touch sent fire through his veins, giving him the most painful erection of his life.

Christ's bones, this was torture.

Utterly oblivious to the effect she had on him—for if she'd known, the lass would have surely shrieked and thrown herself to the opposite end of the room—Tara continued to carefully work the ointment into his neck. She'd pushed up his hair, which brushed the collar of his lèine, and rubbed ointment into his hairline too.

"Ye need to relax yer shoulders and neck a little," Tara said after a little while. "It's like massaging a block of wood."

Jack closed his eyes. This woman had been sent to test him.

Heaving in a deep breath and then slowly releasing it, he did his best to let the tension drain from him. However, the mast in his braies made it almost impossible.

Tara's nimble fingers were digging into the muscles of his upper shoulders now, kneading them expertly.

Jack bit the inside of his cheek as the urge to groan welled up. He didn't want to embarrass himself.

A few moments later, a tug at his belt jerked him out of his reverie.

Forgetting to hide the wood between his thighs, he swiveled around, meeting Tara's eye. "What was that?"

"Nothing," she replied, her gaze widening slightly.

Jack scowled. They both knew she was lying. The minx had seen him put the key away and had tried to grab it. "Aye, well … we're done here," he muttered.

Tara huffed something under her breath and withdrew, scooting back across the bed to sit where she had earlier, with her back against the wall.

Meanwhile, Jack returned to his previous position. Luckily, Tara's gaze hadn't strayed downward—all the same, he couldn't move yet. The moment he stood up, she'd see his erection. Leaning forward, his elbows upon his knees, Jack glanced Tara's way. She was watching him, her silvery eyes veiled.

Jack grew hot under her stare. That gaze stripped him bare. Tara Mackinnon was ferociously sharp; he'd been a fool to let himself be distracted.

"Is something amiss?" Tara asked then, all innocence.

Jack gave a soft snort. "Other than discovering ye are a cunning wench?"

"Not cunning enough," she replied, scowling, "or I'd have that key in my hand now without ye any the wiser."

"Aye, well, ye'd still have to get past me to unlock the door."

"I was going to wait until ye were asleep."

Jack flashed her a rueful look, letting her know that her plan was seriously flawed.

The fight appeared to go out of Tara then, and her shoulders slumped. "Can't ye tell me what tomorrow will bring?" There was a slight tremor in her voice now, betraying her fear.

Jack's gut clenched. She was right to be scared. He hesitated then, considering whether to reveal his plans. He originally hadn't intended to, for it made it easier for him. But did he deserve to have things easy?

"I'm surprised ye haven't guessed already," he said roughly, deciding he didn't. "Since ye spied the *Revenge Tide* the moment we arrived in Fionnphort."

Her face stiffened, her brow furrowing once more as she took his words in. An instant later, understanding sparked in her eyes. "Ye're giving me to *pirates*?" she whispered. She had suspected something like this, yet it still came as a shock.

"Logan Black wants to revenge himself upon yer father too," Jack replied, even as nausea washed over him. This plan had seemed brilliant when he'd hatched it. The ultimate revenge against his father's murderer. But now, it just seemed deranged. Even so, he forced himself on. "He also wants a wife ... and has a liking for fiery redheads. He jumped at my offer."

Tara's full lips parted, and her face drained of color. A moment later, fury sparked in her eyes. "Foul worm!" Jack didn't doubt it was *him* she was referring to, not the mercenary captain. "How much is he paying ye?"

"Nothing," Jack replied, rising to his feet. It was safe to do so now. "Vengeance is payment enough."

"Ye won't get away with this!" Tara launched herself off the bed and struggled to her feet, heedless of her sprained ankle. She then shoved Jack hard in the chest.

Jack grabbed hold of her wrist as she tried to follow up with a slap to the face. She brought her other hand up to hit him, and he caught that one too. However, she wasn't done. "My father will hunt ye to the edges of the world," she shouted in his face. "Ye will spend the rest of yer miserable life looking over yer shoulder!"

"So ye keep saying," he replied coldly. "But where *is* yer precious Da?"

As he'd expected, his response merely vexed her all the more. "Ye'll burn in the fiery pits of hell for this!" she snarled, struggling in his grip.

Jack held her fast, although he was wary of bruising her wrists, for she fought him hard. "Aye, lass … but it'll be worth it."

He let those words hang between them, even as tears filled Tara's eyes. "I thought there was some decency within ye," she rasped, stilling her struggles, "but I was mistaken. Ye are rotten to the core."

Jack stilled at these words. However, a moment later, he shook himself free of their snare. "Aye," he ground out. "And ye have yer dear Da to thank for that."

"No." She shook her head vehemently. "Ye did it to yerself, Maclean. My father might have handed ye the cup, but it is *ye* who willingly sipped poison all these years." Her jaw tightened then, even as tears now ran down her pale cheeks. "Let. Me. Go."

He did, releasing her wrists smartly and stepping back from her.

He thought Tara might leap at him and try to slap him again. This time, he wouldn't stop her. Yet the fight had gone out of his captive. Disgust and sorrow shadowed her eyes.

"I shall take ye to Black at dawn," Jack informed her, careful to keep his voice emotionless.

Tara didn't reply. Instead, she turned from him and climbed onto the bed. Rolling onto her side, she faced the wall, blocking him out.

Jack's gaze settled upon her back for a few moments. He then woodenly walked over to where his cloak hung on the wall. Taking it down from its peg, he wrapped the mantle around his shoulders and lowered himself onto the worn sheepskin that lay before the hearth.

It would be an uncomfortable bed, yet he'd slept rougher.

His gaze flicked then, back to the bed, and the woman who lay, fully clothed, upon it. Tara's back was rigid, although her shoulders shook. She was weeping, doing her best to keep it muffled.

Jaw clenched, Jack rolled onto his back and stared up at the ceiling.

I thought there was some decency in ye ... but I was mistaken.

Her impassioned words, brought forth by anger, surprised him. She'd been paying close attention to her captor, it seemed—and not just marking where he hid the key. At the same time, her comment also revealed something about her character. Aye, Tara was a haughty Mackinnon, yet there was also something sensitive and nurturing about her. She was a woman who'd provide a safe refuge for a man in a violent, cruel world.

A woman he was about to hand over to Logan Black.

15: A HEAD START

TARA AWOKE SLOWLY from a deep and dreamless sleep. She couldn't believe she'd managed to rest. She'd lain there for a while, her tears soaking the straw-stuffed mattress until exhaustion finally claimed her.

Blinking, she let reality slowly sink back in, and with it, the knowledge of where she was and what was about to happen to her.

Closing her eyes, she whispered a silent prayer to the Lord. However, even as she did, despair pulled her down. No one could help her now. If Jack was right and the mercenary held a grudge toward her clan, she was in deep trouble.

"Up ye get."

Tara stiffened at her captor's voice. Pushing herself up, she twisted on the bed, focusing on the man who stood by the hearth. Wearing his cloak and boots, his dirk strapped to his hip, Jack Maclean appeared wide awake and ready to go. But his face told a different story. His handsome features were strained, almost gaunt. His eyes were hollowed, with dark smudges under them, as if he hadn't slept a wink.

"We need to go," he added tersely. "Now."

Something frayed and snapped inside Tara then, like a rope that had been stretched tight over a blade. "Please, Jack," she gasped, desperation choking her. It took everything not to rush to him, fall at his feet and beg. She had no pride now. Tears blurred her vision. "I know ye aren't truly a bad man ... not really."

Maclean's mouth thinned. "Ye know nothing of the kind."

"Don't do this!" Tears scalded her cheeks now.

"Enough talk." He moved toward her then, lifting his hand to show he held the bandage he'd removed from her ankle the evening before. "Time to put this on."

"Don't touch me," Tara snarled, even as she swallowed a sob. She meant it too. She'd scratch his eyes out if he laid a finger on her. Heartless bastard. How could he give her over to a pirate?

Maclean halted midstride, his gaze narrowing. Then, he tossed the bandage to her. "As ye wish."

Tara swallowed the venom that bubbled up inside her, grabbed the bandage, and bent over, doing her best to wind it securely around her ankle—difficult since her hands were now shaking, and tears blinded her.

Maclean waited while she finished her task and pulled on her boots before he passed Tara her cloak.

Rising to her feet, she snatched it from him. "Keen to rid yerself of me?" she rasped, rubbing at her wet cheeks.

Maclean merely grunted. He then made for the door and unlocked it, leaving the iron key in the lock as he swung the door open.

Darkness filtered into the room, along with fresh, salt-laced air.

Tara yanked her cloak about her. The sun still hadn't risen outdoors. Maclean was indeed eager to deliver her to Black. Stepping outside into the yard, she looked up at the sky; the moon had set, yet the stars still twinkled in a milky swathe above her.

Another sob rose in her chest, although she did her best to swallow it down.

This was a waking nightmare. She was desperate to pick up her skirts and flee, yet she already knew how that ended.

"This way." Her captor took her by the arm and led her across the yard to a narrow wooden gate. Although she was limping badly, her ankle stiff and sore despite being rested overnight, Tara tried to twist out of his touch. Nonetheless, Maclean kept a firm hold on her arm. "Lean on me," he ordered tersely. "It'll take the pressure off yer foot."

Tara didn't reply, although, after a few moments, she did as bidden. God's blood, how she hated him, yet she no longer had her makeshift crutch and needed to ease her ankle when walking.

Leaving *The Creel Inn* behind them, they stepped out onto the single narrow street that formed the spine of the tiny village. The shadows surrounding them were long and deep, and there wasn't a soul around.

Tara's gaze shifted right to the dock and the dark bulk of the *Revenge Tide*. The cog's tall mast cut a sharp silhouette against the inky western sky. Her knees wobbled, and if Maclean hadn't been holding onto her, she might have fallen. To her shame, she realized that she was trembling like a frightened fawn. Her pulse now pounded in her ears.

"Easy," Maclean murmured. His voice gentling now. "This way."

He turned her east then, away from the dock, and they began walking. Tara stiffened, cutting him a surprised look, but her captor's face was cast in shadow, and she couldn't see his expression.

Why were they traveling away from the cog and not toward it?

Was Logan Black waiting for them elsewhere?

Sweat slicked Tara's back as she glanced nervously about her. She'd never set eyes on the mercenary, but she'd heard he was a huge, terrifying man with wild dark hair and a merciless gaze that struck fear into the hearts of sailors. She expected him to loom out of the shadows at any moment, but they walked on, and no one appeared from behind any of the nearby dwellings or stone walls.

And soon they'd left Fionnphort behind.

A rutted road led them east, and they walked it for a spell. Then, Maclean turned them northeast so they left the road behind and walked over scrubby hills.

Her captor kept his arm linked through hers, allowing her to put her weight on him instead of her injured ankle, and all the while, Tara's confusion grew. Finally, as the sun rose over the mountains, she couldn't hold her tongue any longer. "Where are we going?"

Maclean glanced her way. His face was still tired and strained, yet his green eyes now glinted. "I was wondering how long it would take for ye to ask that."

Tara scowled back at him. "Just answer me."

"I'm taking ye to Duart Castle."

Tara stumbled before drawing to a halt. She then yanked her arm from his and turned to face him. "What?"

Maclean met her gaze squarely. "Ye heard me." He paused then, his expression turning rueful. "Ye are a free woman, Tara."

Her eyes snapped wide. "Ye mean, I can just walk away?"

"Aye ... although since Logan Black is expecting ye this morning, I'd advise ye to stay with me for the time being, for yer own safety."

"What happened to giving me to the pirate?"

"I changed my mind."

Tara stared at him, her hands clenching at her sides now as a mixture of relief and exasperation pummeled her. "What's yer game, Maclean?"

His gaze never wavered. "There isn't one."

"There clearly is ... for just yestereve, ye told me I was to be Black's wife."

"I did," he admitted, his expression giving nothing away. "But, as I said, I've—"

"Changed yer mind. Aye, but *why*?" she cut him off. He didn't answer, and Tara's mouth thinned, anger gathering like a storm inside her. "Are ye toying with me, is that it? Ye want to see how far ye can push me before I break?"

He shook his head. "No, lass ... I'm done with that."

"I don't believe ye."

Maclean huffed a deep sigh. "Once we get to Duart, I shall organize a boat to take ye back to Dùn Ara."

Tara jolted as if he'd just struck her.

An instant later, her legs did give out under her. And she would have fallen back onto a gorse bush if Maclean hadn't caught her under the arms and hauled her upright.

Sagging in his grip, Tara's vision blurred once more. It was too much. She was brave, but even she had her limits. "Ye are indeed a cruel bastard," she gasped as tears spilled down her cheeks.

"Aye, I'll not deny it," he admitted, his voice roughening now. "But I'm not lying to ye, lass."

Clawing back her self-control, Tara pushed herself away from him and scrubbed at her wet eyes. "Ye still haven't told me why."

"It doesn't matter." Maclean had taken a step back, although his gaze was shadowed as he regarded her.

"Aye, it does."

He shook his head. "We've got a two-day walk ahead of us … let's not waste time arguing." There was a stubborn edge to his tone now. Whatever the cause was for his change of heart, he wasn't willing to talk about it.

Eyeing him warily, for she didn't understand this man's behavior in the slightest, Tara nodded.

Unspeaking, Maclean held out his arm to her, and reluctantly, she took it. They set off again then across the scrubby, pebbly hills. Tara's ankle had benefitted from being rested overnight, but it soon started to protest at the uneven terrain. Despite his help, it wasn't long before she was hobbling. However, she merely set her jaw and pushed on. She had the motivation now. She was no longer a captive and was eager to return home—even so, she worried that Jack Maclean might change his mind on the way to Duart. The man was unpredictable, to say the least. She couldn't trust him.

After a spell, Maclean muttered an oath. "I'm going to have to carry ye again, aren't I?"

"No," she growled. "I can manage."

He gave his head a rueful shake. And then he released his arm and lowered himself onto one knee. "Climb on."

Tara ground her teeth. She didn't want to be carried around like a cripple again—especially by *him*. She'd found the intimacy of the position the day before unsettling and wasn't keen to repeat it.

But their journey to Duart Castle had only just begun, and they still had a long way to walk. The longer she fought with him, the longer it would take for her to be returned to her kin.

Reminding herself of this fact, Tara hobbled over to Maclean and climbed onto his back.

An instant later, he heaved himself to his feet and started walking.

It wouldn't have been easy for him. She wasn't a big lass, yet she was no waif either. Not only that, but Maclean was already fatigued. Nonetheless, he didn't utter a complaint as he marched on, their progress slowing as he navigated a rough slope and a shallow burn at the bottom.

"Surely, it would be easier to take the road," she pointed out.

"Aye ... but I'd rather not."

Tara silently digested these words. It occurred to her then that Logan Black would still be waiting for his prize. When Maclean didn't deliver her, he'd likely come looking for them.

She cast a nervous glance over her shoulder then, surveying the way they'd come. She couldn't see anyone following—for the moment. She now understood why Maclean had insisted they depart so early. He'd wanted a head start.

Turning her attention back to the direction of travel, Tara's thoughts shifted once more to her captor.

What the devil was he up to? The night before, he'd been bent on revenge, and now he was willing to throw it away.

For the life of her, she couldn't understand why.

16: THIS AFFLICTION

A PINK-HUED DUSK settled over southern Mull when they finally halted their journey.

Maclean hadn't been able to carry Tara for the entire duration of the day. However, the respites he had provided had taken the pressure off her sore ankle.

And despite her reluctance to let him bear her, she appreciated the gesture in the end.

As daylight faded, they both collected wood, hazel with some dry gorse and broom mostly. Tara found another stick to use as a crutch too—hopefully, that would allow her to walk without his assistance the following day. Once they'd collected enough fuel, Maclean set about starting a fire, using the flint he carried in the pouch at his waist.

"Is it safe to light a fire?" she asked Maclean as she dumped the last of the wood she'd collected near the hearth he'd made.

Glancing up from where he was trying to coax some smoldering dry grass into tender flames, Maclean pulled a face. "It should be."

"So, ye don't think Black will come after us?"

"No. If he had, we'd have caught sight of him and his men by now," he replied. "The last hill we climbed gave me a good view west ... and it appears we have no pursuers."

Relief gusted through Tara at these words.

Lowering herself onto the mossy ground, she looked on as Maclean finished lighting the fire. Soon, he had it going, pale smoke wreathing up into the still evening air.

"Luckily for us, the weather has turned mild," Maclean said, feeding a large gnarled branch of gorse onto the fire. "It'll be chilly later, but we shouldn't freeze." He then opened the wrapped parcel next to him, revealing a hunk of bread and some boiled eggs, still in their shells. He'd bought the food earlier in the day when they'd passed through the tiny hamlet of Ardalanish.

Tara's belly growled loudly at the sight of the food. Maclean had bought them each a hot grouse pie too from Ardalanish, but that seemed like hours ago now.

Her companion glanced up at the sound, a smile tugging at his mouth. He'd been serious all day; his flash of wry humor now was oddly reassuring. "Hungry, eh?"

Tara sniffed. "Aye."

"Here." He ripped the bread in half and handed her the bigger of the two chunks. He then passed her four of the six boiled eggs. "Eat up."

Tara stilled, her brow furrowing. "Aren't ye hungry?"

His mouth quirked once more before he shrugged.

Hesitating a moment longer, Tara nodded her thanks and deftly peeled an egg. Likewise, Maclean started on his supper. It was a simple one, to be sure, but delicious.

They ate in silence, although, strangely, it was a companionable one, free of the tension that had previously characterized their interactions. They were no longer captor and captive; the dynamic between them had changed. And the knowledge that Logan Black wasn't breathing down their necks also created a more relaxed atmosphere.

Meanwhile, the last of the daylight faded around them.

They'd made camp in a hollow, close to a trickling burn, under the shelter of a sparse hazelwood. It was a bonnie spot, far from the nearest village or stronghold, far from the cares of the world.

Out here, it was easy to believe that they were the only people alive.

Tara had caught glimpses of the sensitive man beneath the callous manner over the past days, and this evening, the 'real' Jack Maclean was more evident than ever. He'd taken care of her during the day, carrying her without a word of protest, even when his feet stumbled in fatigue. And he'd given her the largest share of each meal, even though his appetite would surely be greater than hers.

His unexpected kindnesses unbalanced Tara. However, the man was keeping things back from her—and she was determined to get to the bottom of why he hadn't handed her over to the pirate as planned.

Brushing the crumbs off her skirts, Tara accepted the skin of ale he passed her and took a few grateful gulps. And when she handed it back to him, she purposely met his eye. "Are ye going to tell me the reason for yer change of heart now, Jack?" she said.

Tension flickered over his face, yet she kept her gaze steady. They weren't friends, but she wanted him to be truthful with her.

"It doesn't matter, does it?" he muttered, looking away. "I'm not using ye to seek reckoning any longer. That should be enough." He picked up a stick and poked the embers of the fire between them, sending a spray of sparks up into the darkness.

Tara waited until they'd died down before answering. "No. It's not enough." She stared him down until he met her eye once more. "A man doesn't change heart from one day to the next without good reason." Her gaze narrowed then. "Don't tell me ye suddenly grew a conscience?"

He snorted. "Maybe." Maclean raked a hand through his hair then, a sign her questioning was getting to him. "I always had one, lass ... I just let my need for revenge drown it out."

"But not any longer?"

"No," he murmured, a warning in his voice now. "Not any longer."

Their gazes held. Tara was pushing him, yet something inside her wouldn't let her back down. Maclean's action wouldn't go unpunished. Her father would make sure of that. But, in the meantime, it was important to her that she understood his motives.

"Why?"

Maclean muttered a curse under his breath. "God's bones, woman ... just let this go."

Tara leaned forward. "No. After everything ye've put me through, ye owe me an explanation."

He stared back at her, the fire crackling between them. Maclean clearly didn't want to be honest with her—yet his reluctance just made her even more curious.

"Ye don't want to know the reason," he said finally, looking away from her as he jabbed at the fire once more with his makeshift poker.

"Let me be the judge of that."

His throat bobbed, yet he continued to avoid her eye. Silence stretched between them before he finally spoke once more. "Sometimes, I think fate is playing games with me," he said then, his voice hoarse. "Or maybe this is my punishment for abducting ye ... whatever the reason, I can't escape this ... affliction."

Tara frowned. *Affliction?* Was he unwell? She held her tongue. She'd pushed the man into talking, and she wasn't about to stop him now.

He glanced her way again then, and the raw pain in his eyes made her breathing catch.

Christ's blood. Maclean *was* suffering.

"Somewhere between stealing ye away and the early hours of this morning, something within me seized upon ye," he admitted then, holding her gaze. "And now that it has, it won't let go. Lord knows, I've tried to fight it, but last night, when I couldn't sleep, the truth finally settled into my bones." Reaching up, he dragged a hand over his face, muttering another curse. "I want ye for my own, Tara."

For a heartbeat, Tara just stared at Maclean.

It took a while for his words to sink in, for her mind to make sense of what he'd just admitted. She wasn't sure what she'd expected him to say—but it certainly wasn't this.

And if it wasn't for the agony in his eyes, she'd have laughed in his face.

"Ye *want* me?" she asked finally, enunciating each word carefully, as if they were foreign to her.

Maclean swallowed hard. "*Want* is a mild term for what I feel for ye," he said roughly. "It's a fever in my blood, a cross upon my soul. It steals my peace every waking moment."

His words, and the rawness of them, made her flinch.

Seeing her reaction, Maclean's mouth twisted. "I told ye not to ask … but ye insisted. I never intended ye to know."

Heat flushed over Tara. Aye, she heartedly wished she *hadn't* pushed him.

It made no sense at all. Jack Maclean loathed her and everything she stood for. She was a Mackinnon, after all.

How it must pain him to admit such a thing.

And yet there was a part of her that didn't believe him. "Ye can't be infatuated with me," she pointed out then, her voice sharpening. "We've only known each other three days."

He gave a bitter laugh. "That was long enough, it seems." Maclean shook his head then. "And it's not infatuation I feel for ye, Tara … it's a soul-deep conviction that ye are meant to be mine."

Tara's heart started to pound in her ears. "How can ye know such a thing?"

"I've no idea … I don't go around losing my wits over every woman I meet." Maclean scrubbed at his face with his hand then, as if he could rub the sentiments he'd just expressed away. "I've always been smug about the fact I've kept my heart free of love's snare, lass. But I'm not laughing now."

"But ye *hate* me," Tara replied, her voice dropping as horror stole over her. The knave was speaking not just of want but 'love' now. Panic beat in her chest. She'd been brought up in an environment where emotions were kept tightly leashed; hearing such raw feelings expressed like this made her feel as if her world were spinning out of control.

Maclean shook his head, a faint blush staining his high cheekbones. "I told myself I did … but how could I hate a woman as strong, brilliant, courageous ... and beautiful ... as ye?" He sucked in a deep breath then, his broad shoulders sagging just a little.

Tara had nothing to say to that.

Jack Maclean had just spilled his guts, had just admitted things that had shocked them both.

She was literally lost for words.

Another silence swelled between them, while the fire crackled and popped, oblivious to the admission that had rocked both their worlds.

For her part, Tara was in equal parts mortified and stunned.

But there was also a traitorous part of her that thrilled to hear such words. He thought she was strong, brilliant, courageous, and beautiful? No one had ever said such things to her—not even the man she was to wed. And there was no doubting Maclean either. The ache in his voice told her he meant every word.

Realizing that there was a warm kernel in the center of her chest that was expanding with every heartbeat, Tara curled her hands into fists, digging her fingernails hard into her palms.

She then reminded herself who the man seated across the fire was.

A Maclean who'd abducted her, terrified, bullied, chased, and insulted her over three days of their acquaintance.

Aye, he'd saved her from being raped by Ramsay and his cronies. Aye, he'd changed his mind about giving her to a pirate and taken her swiftly away before Black caught her. He'd also tended to her sore ankle and carried her for miles on his back.

But he was still a villain.

It didn't matter if he thought she was lovelier than Helen of Troy, or that she was the soul he'd waited a hundred lifetimes to find. The fact was that he was the enemy.

The tender flame that flickered in her chest extinguished then, and coldness seeped through her.

Tara didn't speak again that evening. And neither did her companion.

17: YE ONLY HAVE MY WORD

JACK AWOKE TO find a root digging into his side. Wincing, he rolled over onto his back, his eyes flickering open. Above him, the sky was beginning to lighten. He'd slept like a stone.

It was hardly surprising since he hadn't managed to rest at all the previous night.

Even so, his chest tightened.

Curse it, Tara would probably have fled while he slumbered, desperate to escape the foul letch who'd just admitted his feelings for her.

Addlepated shitbag, he berated himself. *Why didn't ye just lie to her?*

His ribs constricted further. He had no answer—only that when Tara had fixed him with her disarming steel-grey stare and demanded honesty from him, he'd been unable to deceive her.

He'd lain there the night before in Fionnphort considering his choices. *Ye are at the gates now, lad,* he'd told himself, his stomach hardening. *Once ye go through them, there'll be no going back.*

He'd been so obsessed about reckoning that it had blinded him to all else. He'd never thought about the consequences. Before he'd embarked on this plan, Jack hadn't spared the matter of how Logan Black might treat Tara any thought. But as he emerged from the fog of hate, he did. He didn't know the mercenary well. Black was tough. An opportunist. Having good relations with the Macleans suited him, and so he left their boats alone.

Even so, Black wasn't someone to cross lightly. His hate for the Mackinnon might have made him cruel. He might have hurt Tara.

Jack had berated himself in the darkness, even as a cold sweat beaded upon his skin. *Clodhead. Ye understood all this when ye took her.* He had, but his perspective had changed. The cloak of anger and bitterness that had enshrouded him since losing his father had fallen away.

He felt naked without it.

He felt sick without it.

His throat had tightened then. God's troth, he was punishing the wrong person. The lass didn't deserve any of this. Tara deserved to be treated like a princess. Instead, he'd stolen her from her clan and hauled her across Mull. Her twisted ankle was his doing too.

He'd earned her hate.

He should suffer for what he'd done.

His behavior would affect more than just Tara and her father though. As clan-chief, Loch would bear the consequences of his cousin's actions. And Jack's brother, Rae, who ruled Dounarwyse, would too. The Mackinnon's wrath would blister them both.

But as many as his regrets were, Jack had now just added another to the list.

The moment he'd told Tara the truth, he'd wished he could call the words back. He hadn't been surprised when she'd retreated into cold silence. He'd expected nothing less.

Steeling himself, Jack rolled right, his gaze shifting to the opposite side of the cold embers of the fire. And to his surprise, Tara Mackinnon lay there.

She was still asleep, lying on her side facing him, with her head cradled in the crook of her arm. The lass slept peacefully, her brow smooth, her breathing easy.

For a few instants, Jack merely drank her in, shocked that she hadn't run away.

Aye, she was the loveliest thing he'd ever seen.

Christ on a cross, listen to yerself. Jack clenched his jaw. *Next, ye'll be writing the lass a sonnet and making her a daisy chain.* If his friend Finn were here right now, he'd heap scorn upon him for becoming exactly the sort of man he'd once derided.

But there was a part of Jack that didn't care, and he continued to gaze at Tara. He shouldn't stare. If she woke up and caught him, she'd be upset.

In truth, he'd expected her to become hysterical at his admission the eve before. However, he should have realized that wasn't Tara's way. Unlike him, she was adept at keeping her emotions leashed. As he'd told her, she *was* strong. It would take more than a love-sick idiot to frighten her.

Jaw set, Jack pushed himself into a sitting position. He then reached for the bladder of ale he'd purchased from Ardalanish the day before and took a gulp. At least his head and neck were feeling better this morning. Sleeping rough usually left his neck and spine in knots, but apart from the pain in his side, from where he'd unwittingly rolled onto a tree root, he was surprisingly rested.

His mouth twisted at the irony of it. Maybe spilling his guts to Tara had lifted a weight from his soul. His admission changed nothing, but at least he was no longer burdened by it.

Rolling to his feet, Jack set about readying himself to depart. They still had another full day's journey ahead of them and should reach Duart the following morning.

His activity roused Tara from her sleep.

Yawning, she sat up and rubbed her eyes. Yet, when her gaze settled upon him, it narrowed.

"We've nothing to break our fasts with," Jack announced, deciding it was wise to keep to practical matters. "However, we aren't far from the village of Carsaig. I've one or two pennies left." He patted the now-light purse at his belt. "It should be enough to get us food for the day."

Tara nodded, although her expression remained wary.

Rising to her feet, she stretched her stiff limbs and glanced around.

It was a cool morning. Unlike the day before, the sky was cloudy, and a sharp breeze had kicked up from the west. They wouldn't be walking with warm sun upon their faces today.

Despite that the fire had died overnight, Jack kicked dirt over it. He then set off east, hoping that Tara would follow.

She did.

Perhaps she was beginning to trust that he wouldn't go back on his word. Tara was no longer his captive. He'd no longer tell her what to do. If she stayed with him, it would be her choice. It wouldn't take them long to reach Carsaig, but if she decided to stay in the village, he wouldn't stop her.

She hurried up the slope behind him. Glancing over his shoulder, Jack noted she wasn't limping as badly as the day before. However, the new crutch she'd found was helping her too.

He wanted to offer to carry her if she tired—but he wouldn't. After what he'd revealed, she'd likely spit at him.

Jack turned his attention forward once more, slowing his gait so that she could keep up. At the brow of the hill, he halted and looked back the way they'd come. Just like the eve before, when he'd gazed west, he saw no sign of pursuers.

Tara crested the brow of the hill, and seeing the direction of Jack's gaze, glanced west as well. "We really are safe then?" she asked, breaking the tense silence between them.

Jack nodded. "It would seem so."

"Won't Black be vexed?"

"Aye ... and he's not likely to forget either. However, it looks as if he's letting us go."

Her silver gaze met his then. "And will I be safe at Duart?"

Jack tensed. "Of course."

Tara's mouth pursed. "It's not a foolish question, Maclean. How do I know yer clan-chief won't decide to hold me captive and wield me as a weapon against my father?"

Their gazes held a long moment before Jack answered, "Ye don't. Ye only have my word."

Tara gave a loud snort, an incongruous sound from such a feminine creature. "Yer *word*?"

Jack favored her with a wry smile, even if wretchedness twisted his guts. "I know it isn't worth much."

"Ye're right, it isn't."

Jack held her gaze, his own level. "All the same, I promise ye no one will hold ye at Duart against yer will, Tara. As soon as we arrive, I will organize an escort to take ye home."

She put her hands on her hips then, her jaw tightening. "But ye aren't the laird. Loch Maclean is."

"Aye, and although I've been blinded by hate all these years, my cousin has a much broader view. He has no wish to incur yer father's wrath ... any more than he already has ... and will want to return ye to yer kin." Jack's mouth twisted then. "Besides, when we get to Duart, he'll be too furious with me to focus on much else."

18: RIDDLES AND OPINIONS

BITING INTO A walnut-and-dried-plum bun, Tara then chewed slowly. It was delicious, but she wanted to make it last.

They'd reached Carsaig after around an hour and a half's walking. The village was tiny, just a scattering of half a dozen bothies. There had been little in the way of provisions, although Maclean had handed over a penny to a shepherd's wife in exchange for a cloth bag of freshly baked buns.

They were now walking east again, and despite the brooding sky above, and the rocky terrain she had to be careful not to turn her sore ankle on, Tara found herself captivated by her surroundings.

Carsaig was one of the prettiest spots she'd ever seen. They walked close to the coast once more, and from here, she had a clear view across the Firth of Lorn to the southeast and a cluster of isles on the horizon. They'd barely left the village behind when they approached dramatic cliffs, with columns of rock beneath them.

The sight was so impressive that Tara stopped a moment, swallowing the last of her bun.

Ahead of her, Maclean halted, glancing back over his shoulder. "It's quite a sight, isn't it?"

Tara nodded. "Where are we?"

"The Carsaig Arches."

"It looks like the ruins of an ancient fortress."

"I don't think men made this place," he replied, his mouth lifting at the edges as he too turned to gaze up at the stacks of stone and lofty arches and pillars, "although I know what ye mean."

Maclean resumed his climb then, up the narrow path that circuited the cliffs. After a moment, Tara followed. The way was perilous, and with loose shale underfoot, she had to be careful not to slip. Her stick helped though, and she was getting adept at using it. As they climbed, she noted how her companion slowed. He also glanced back over his shoulder often to check on her.

There were times when Tara would have been grateful for his hand to pull her up. Yet she didn't ask for it. After the things he'd admitted the night before, she was wary of touching him. Strangely though, she was no longer *scared* of Maclean. Indeed, she'd slept easily overnight, unafraid that he'd try anything.

Daft lass, she chided herself, puffing as she crested the top of the cliffs. *The man's still a rogue. Only a halfwit would trust him.*

Leaving the beauty of Carsaig at their backs, they continued east. The way became slower as the terrain along this part of the coast was mountainous and rocky. And all the while, the sky grew darker and the wind stronger.

Tara's brow furrowed every time she glanced up at the sky. She didn't like its ominous color, especially to the west, the direction the wind was coming from. She could only hope the rain held off.

At noon they stopped for a short while on the edge of deep, shadowy pools, where clear water bubbled over the rocks. There, they finished the last of their buns. Tara didn't speak while she ate, and neither did Maclean. After a while, their silence grew awkward, and Tara was relieved when they were on the move again.

Walking a couple of yards behind Maclean, she noted that he'd stoop to pick up stones now and then, inspecting each one carefully before tucking it away in a pouch at his belt.

His behavior intrigued her, and eventually, curiosity got the better of her. "What are ye doing?"

"Collecting stones for my slingshot." He patted his left hip, where a slender leather coil hung. "I'd rather not go to sleep on an empty belly tonight." He cut her a glance then and a quick smile. "I'll see if I can catch us a grouse."

Tara arched an eyebrow. "With a slingshot?"

His mouth curved into a boyish grin. "Aye … the right hit will knock the bird clean off a branch."

Tara stilled at the sight of his grin. Maclean was handsome when serious, but disarmingly so when he was amused. It brought his face alive, dimpled his cheeks, and made his green eyes sparkle.

He turned away then, leading her over rugged hills that gradually grew more wooded.

They didn't speak for a long while after that, and eventually, the silence started to wear on Tara. The afternoon was dragging on, and despite her stick, the walk was taking its toll on her ankle. Its dull ache gnawed at her; the pain was making her grumpy. The wind now had spots of rain in it, warning that the bad weather was on its way.

Shifting her gaze to Maclean's broad back for what felt like the hundredth time that hour, Tara huffed a frustrated breath. "Ye are keeping yer own counsel today," she observed.

Her companion jerked, for her words had clearly dragged him from his thoughts, and he slowed his stride, waiting for her to catch up. Meeting her eye, he inclined his head. "Bored?"

Tara pulled a face. "Tired."

"We still have a few more hours before the sun sets," he pointed out. "Shall we distract ourselves with a game?"

Tara frowned, making her reluctance clear.

Maclean shrugged. "I was going to suggest a game of riddles … but if ye aren't keen we—"

"Riddles?" Tara's brow smoothed.

"Aye." He paused then, flashing her another disarming smile. "Here's one for ye … *no one can hold me in his palms or sight. I scatter sudden clatter far and wide. I want to hammer oaks with mournful might. Yes, I strike sky and scour countryside."*

Tara considered his words, and a moment later, when a powerful gust caught at her cloak, making it billow around her, she grinned. "The wind."

Maclean shrugged. "Aye, that was an easy enough one. Do ye want to take a turn?"

"I'm not sure I remember any."

"Nonsense. Everyone knows a riddle or two."

Tara pulled a face. In truth, she'd never been that good at riddling, although she enjoyed listening while her father's men tested each other over tankards of ale. Nonetheless, she wasn't about to let Maclean get the best of her, so she dug through her memories. "Very well … here's one," she said after a pause. *"When I am alive I do not speak. Anyone who wants to takes me captive and cuts off my head. They bite my bare body. I do no harm to anyone unless they cut me first. Then I soon make them cry."*

Maclean snorted a laugh. "That's too easy. An onion."

Tara drew herself up, casting him an arch look. "Well, *ye* come up with something cleverer then."

His eyes glinted at her challenge. "Aye, lass … here ye go." He paused then for dramatic effect. *"I am something amazing that hangs by a man's thigh. Under my lord's nap. A hole at my head, I am stiff and hard. I keep my place well. What am I?"*

Tara stared at him a moment before heat bloomed across her cheeks. "Crude churl," she muttered. "I should have expected this."

Maclean's eyebrows raised. "Expected what?"

"That ye'd drag this game to yer own base level."

He snorted. "I'm not … is it my fault if yer mind leads ye there?"

Tara drew herself up, hands fisting at her sides. "What are ye saying?"

"That my riddle is entirely innocent … but yer thoughts *clearly* aren't."

His words caused anger to ignite in her belly. "How dare ye?" With that she hobbled off ahead, both equally flustered and vexed that Maclean was able to provoke such strong emotions in her. Back home, she rarely lost her temper. It wasn't the Mackinnon way.

"Don't ye want to know the answer to the riddle?" he called after her.

"No!"

"I'll give ye a clue … ye tried to steal one of these, poorly I might add, from me the day before yesterday."

Tara's step faltered, and she cast a glare over her shoulder. "What?"

"A key … that's the answer."

Heat flushed over Tara, her cheeks burning now at the mischievous twinkle in Maclean's fern-green eyes. The dog was having far too much fun at her expense. "I suppose ye know many riddles like that, do ye?" she muttered. "Ones that suggest one thing but mean another."

He nodded. "Soldiers will do anything to distract themselves from the cold on freezing winter nights." He paused then before adding. "However, it was my mother who instilled a love of riddles in me. She used to tell me a different one every night when she tucked me into bed."

Despite herself, Tara was intrigued. She waited for Maclean to catch her up before she cut him a curious look. "*Every* night?"

"Aye … she never missed one." He flashed her a rueful smile. "Until I turned twelve and my Da told her I was too old to be put to bed by my Ma."

Envy twinged deep in Tara's chest then as she remembered her own childhood. "Ye are lucky to have had such a kind mother," she murmured. "Mine never tucked me into bed once, that I recall." She certainly hadn't sung to Tara or told her a story or riddle either.

"She must have," Maclean replied, surprise rippling over his face.

Tara shook her head. "That was my handmaid, Orla's, task. Ma never bothered herself with her bairns. I can count the times she ever hugged me on one hand."

His eyes grew wide at this admission. Tara's own candor surprised her too. She wasn't sure why she was confiding in him. "She died recently, didn't she?"

"Around a year and a half ago," Tara answered. "That's why Da is now looking for a new wife."

Maclean remained silent for a short while after these words, and when he did speak, his tone was cautious. "And what did ye think of his choice?"

Tara cast him a sidelong glance as they walked. "Astrid Maclean, ye mean?"

"None other."

"I don't have an opinion on it."

Maclean snorted. "Of course, ye do. Ye are a woman with an opinion on everything, and I'd like to hear it."

Tara frowned. Somehow, he'd just managed to insult and compliment her at the same time. Silence swelled between them before she finally muttered, "She's young."

"Aye ... and?"

"She wasn't right for him," she replied. "Although I think my father was sweet on her."

Maclean raised an eyebrow. "I got the impression it was just a political choice on his part."

"Didn't ye notice the way he looked at her when we visited Duart last autumn?"

Tara had, and it had been discomforting to watch. Her father's gaze had been ... hungry. He'd never looked at her mother like that over the years. She could see why he lusted after Lady Astrid. The lass, who was only three years her elder, had a pale, ethereal beauty, blended with fire.

Perhaps, after a long marriage to a cold woman, her father wanted something different.

Maclean shook his head. "I was too busy imagining what it would feel like to drive a dirk into yer father's heart to pay attention to that." He paused then, his expression turning rueful. "And when I wasn't glaring at the Mackinnon, I was staring at his bonnie daughter."

19: A MAN WHO LOVES FOREVER

"AYE, OF COURSE, ye were," Tara replied, trying to ignore the jolt of her heart. They'd done an admirable job all day of avoiding the subject of the eve before—but now, he'd just brought it up. "Ye were imagining my ruin."

Maclean's handsome face shuttered. "I was," he admitted quietly. "But even then, ye captivated me ... I just didn't want to admit it to myself."

Tara frowned. She didn't care to hear such admissions. They flustered her. "So, to answer yer earlier question clearly," she said pointedly. "I *was* against my father wedding a Maclean. I think it would have likely ended in disaster."

"I agree," Maclean replied, his gaze fixed ahead now. "Although, our opinions matter little in the end. And now that yer father threatens to raze Dounarwyse in retribution, a great battle between our clans is on its way."

A lump of ice settled in Tara's belly at these words. Aye, she'd said some blood-thirsty things to Maclean regarding his clan over the past days—and she'd spat them at him with vengeful spite—but now she considered the reality of what would happen if Mull was thrown into war. The death and suffering that would ensue. "And what will yer clan-chief do if Dounarwyse is besieged?" she asked after a pause.

Maclean's expression hardened. "Loch has seen a lifetime's worth of war over the years, but he won't back down from a fight, and he'll defend Dounarwyse with his life if it comes to it." He paused then, his gaze boring into hers. "As will I."

They stared at each other a moment longer, tension rippling between them. Meanwhile, the chill in Tara's stomach spread up to her chest. A sense of foreboding crept over her then.

Of course, her abduction would only fuel the fire of her father's hatred for the Macleans.

If Dounarwyse fell to him, he'd show its inhabitants no mercy.

Swallowing, she turned away from Maclean, gripping her stick tightly as she went to move forward on the rocky path. However, an instant later, his hand caught her arm, firmly pulling her back. Tara's pulse leaped, and she whipped around to face him once more, her lips parting as she readied herself to tell him off. But her companion had a finger to his lips now, warning her to remain silent.

He then nodded right, to where a hawthorn tree bristled against the sky. And there, perched on a high branch, sat a large fat red grouse.

A grin flowered across Maclean's face, and he slowly released her arm before reaching for the slingshot looped through his belt with one hand, while he retrieved a stone from his pouch with the other. "Looks like I've found us supper," he whispered.

The light was fading as the standing stones came into view, emerging from the gloaming like ancient sentinels.

Stepping out from a stand of twisted oaks and ash, Jack's gaze settled upon the worn, lichen-encrusted stones that formed a rough circle, pushing up from the boggy ground. A faint smile tugged at his mouth then as he remembered years gone by, when he, Loch, and Finn would explore the isle together.

The Lochbuie Stones were one of his favorite haunts. He'd often camped under the boughs of the nearby trees, under the shadow of Ben Buie—the mountain that loomed to the north—and watched as the sun kissed the stones at dusk and dawn.

There was no sun to bathe them this evening though, for the sky was still ominously dark.

Tara limped past him then, leaning heavily on her stick. Although she hadn't once complained about her ankle throughout the day, he marked the pain that now etched her face.

Jack's smile faded, guilt tugging at him. He hated that he was responsible for her injury. It was a reminder of how much he'd let hate cloud his judgment.

Ignoring him now, Tara made her way into the stone circle and stopped, gazing about her.

Jack watched her, taking in her proud carriage and the elegant sweep of her neck. She was tired and sore after their long journey, but she still carried herself like a queen. He could almost imagine her as one of the ancients, standing in the center of this mysterious stone circle with swirls of blue woad painted upon her skin, her fiery hair tumbling down her bare back as she lifted her hands to the gods.

His mother had told him tales of the peoples that had once inhabited this land—those who would have erected these great stones in another age. She'd told him that the ancients dressed lightly in leather and fur, and often went about in nothing but their skin. The men were fierce, yet so were the women.

Another smile tugged at the edges of Jack's mouth then, his mood lightening a little. Aye, he could imagine Tara as a warrior woman of times gone by.

As he looked on, she hobbled over to one of the stones, the largest of them that thrust upward from the boggy ground like a spear. She then placed her hand upon its rough surface.

Meanwhile, Jack glanced around, assuring himself that they were alone here. He'd already decided they'd make camp near this spot but wanted to ensure there wasn't anyone lurking nearby.

"These stones remind me of another cluster … a little smaller than this, just outside Tobermory," Tara spoke then, drawing his attention once more. She'd moved on to another stone and was tracing its surface with her fingertips. "Those also bear these strange markings. I wonder what they mean?"

Jack drew close, his gaze traveling to the long scratches that bisected the stones. "No idea," he murmured. "If only these stones could talk … think of the tales they could tell."

Tara's full mouth curved into a smile in response, her grey eyes glinting at such a suggestion.

However, Jack promptly forgot about his words. All he could focus on was Tara Mackinnon's bonnie smile. Over the past few days, he'd given her little to smile about. Her expression had been serious at best, angry or frightened at worst. But her smile now lit up the dull day as if the sun had just come out.

"Aye," she murmured, her attention shifting to the stone they both touched now. "How I wish I could step back in time and see the people who made this circle."

"I'd like that too," he admitted, even as his chest started to ache with longing. Not to travel to times long past, but to take Tara in his arms and kiss her.

Pulling himself out of his reverie, Jack dropped his hand and moved back from the stone. He then unslung the dead grouse from over his shoulder. "Come on," he said briskly. "This bird won't cook itself. I'd better find us shelter and build a fire."

Tara turned to him once more, her expression sobering. "Aren't we close to Moy Castle here?"

"Aye."

A groove appeared between her eyebrows. "Why aren't ye calling upon them rather than camping outdoors?"

Jack pulled a face. He understood why she'd ask him that. Tara would be missing her home comforts. "Because if I do that, I'll be besieged with questions … and I'm not in the mood to answer any of them." That was the truth, although Jack didn't add that he couldn't guarantee Tara's safety at Moy Castle either. He trusted Loch, yet he wasn't so sure about the chieftain of the Macleans of Lochbuie. He moved away from the stone circle and headed toward the line of trees to the north of it. "Besides, Leod Maclean, the laird of Moy Castle, is a bitter man and poor company."

"Bitter?" Tara asked, following him out of the stone circle.

"Aye, the story goes that he lost his first wife, whom he loved, and took a second one, whom he does not. Elizabeth is much younger than him … and it's said that they quarrel night and day." He cut her a wry look then. "Can ye see why I'd rather sleep outdoors, even with the threat of rain?"

"Perhaps," she huffed with a half-smile.

Seated before the crackling fire, under the shelter of a large twisted oak, Tara watched Maclean pluck and gut the grouse he'd caught.

She'd been skeptical that he'd be able to kill the heavy bird with a slingshot, but, as he'd boasted, one shot knocked it clean out of the tree. The poor thing had been lying on the ground, stunned, when he reached it. He'd then promptly snapped the grouse's neck, tied its feet together with some string, and slung it over his shoulder before they continued east.

Although she wouldn't admit such to him, Tara had been impressed. And she was so again as she watched the deft, sure movements of his hands.

"Ye look like a man used to living off the land," she observed as he skewered the grouse onto a stick and placed it on a makeshift spit he'd erected over the edge of the fire, where the embers glowed hot.

"I've always enjoyed hunting and being out in the wild," Maclean admitted. "And there have been times over the past decade when these skills have saved my hide." His gaze flicked up, meeting hers then. "I know we bested the English in the end, but Edward the Younger's army gave us no end of trouble. There were days ... and weeks ... when I wondered if I'd ever see Mull again. It's just as well my Da taught me how to survive."

Tara took this in, noting how his voice softened when he mentioned his father. Her chest tightened then. Of course, he'd worshipped the man. That was why he'd let hate and the need for vengeance consume him.

"Is yer mother still alive?" she asked then, suddenly curious to know more about Maclean's family and the environment he'd grown up in. As much as she tried to deny it, the man intrigued her.

He shook his head, turning the grouse on the spit. "She fell down the tower house steps a year before Da's death," he replied, his voice subdued. "Broke her neck."

Tara stiffened. Such accidents were common in castles, especially upon slippery steps. She'd taken a few tumbles as a bairn. Nonetheless, she marked the way his gaze shadowed. No, Jack Maclean wasn't a man who let things go. Even many years on, his mother's death still affected him.

"Ye loved her deeply, didn't ye?" she asked softly.

He nodded, even as his lips curved into a sad smile. "As all bairns adore their mothers."

Tara's breathing grew shallow. She'd never met someone who felt things as keenly as he did. She liked how sensitive he was, yet it was both a blessing and a curse.

He's a man who loves forever. A man whose loyalty is bone-deep, a voice whispered. *He's someone I could confide my deepest, darkest thoughts to ... and he'd listen.*

Swallowing, Tara cut her gaze away from his. What idiotic thoughts she was entertaining. This was the knave who'd stolen her away, who'd been prepared to hand her over to someone else with an ax to grind against her father. God knew what Logan Black would have done with her.

Tara shuddered. No, she didn't want to think about it. It didn't matter how comfortable she felt with him, she needed to remind herself that Jack Maclean was her enemy.

He didn't go through with it though. The voice was back, more insistent now.

"Are ye cold?"

She looked up to see her companion was studying her, his brow furrowed.

"A little," she lied. "Although the fire is warming me up."

"I'll put another log on." Reaching over, he retrieved a branch of ash from the pile that Tara had collected while he'd gotten the fire started and placed it onto the hearth. Sparks billowed up, although the edge where Maclean spit-roasted their supper remained a bed of hot embers.

Their gazes met across the fire then and held. And curse her, Tara's pulse quickened. Hades, she wished he wouldn't look at her like that. The softness in his eyes transfixed her. His gaze caused a strange neediness to flower deep in her chest. It made her want to tell him how alone she'd felt as a bairn, how she envied him his warm relationship with his family.

It even made Tara wish to confide in him how when her mother died she hadn't wept.

20: ON THE EDGE

THE GROUSE WAS delicious. Tara devoured the half carcass that Maclean handed her before licking her fingers clean of grease.

"Enjoy that, did ye?" he teased, a half-smile curving his lips as he watched her. He'd already finished his meal and was wiping his hands on some moss.

"Aye," Tara replied with a sigh, not bothering to pretend otherwise. "Ye cooked that grouse to perfection."

His smile flowered into a wide grin, and Tara's heart jolted.

She hadn't meant to be so enthusiastic. However, a strange mood had settled over her this evening. Maybe it was the presence of the nearby standing stones, but she felt at one with the world and everyone in it. At peace. Oddly, she felt happier in this moment than she ever had, listening to the crackle of the fire and surrounded by a bower of oak branches.

"I like this place," she admitted then, lowering her gaze, and focusing on the log that burned in the fire pit between them. "It welcomes ye."

"Aye … I used to camp here often in the past. The Lochbuie Stones have always called to me."

Their gazes met across the fire, and both their smiles faded. Of course, the standing stones weren't the only reason Tara felt at ease this evening. Ironically, Maclean made her feel as if she could be herself. With him, she didn't worry about maintaining a reserve. He welcomed her observations, her responses.

She was about to respond to him when a fat drop of water splashed upon her face. It was swiftly followed by another.

Maclean murmured an oath and shot a glance up at the canopy above them. "There's the rain." Rising to his feet, he skirted the edge of the fire and settled himself against the trunk of the oak behind Tara. "I suggest ye move this way too," he added. "It'll be the driest spot."

The patter turned to a steady tattoo, and soon cold water was dripping down Tara's face. Disappointed to leave the warmth of the fire, Tara edged back from it and took her place next to Maclean. He was right, this was the most sheltered area of the canopy. The fire did its best to fight the rain, yet it soon started to smoke and hiss.

Meanwhile, Tara drew her cloak about her and relaxed against the oak trunk. Her and Maclean's shoulders were lightly touching, and she told herself she should move away from him. But she didn't.

Just as his company relaxed her this evening, there was also something reassuring about the contact. Once again, he made her feel safe, protected.

The irony of it wasn't lost on her—although this time she pushed aside her mind's chatter and just enjoyed the moment.

"Are ye warm enough now?" he asked after a spell. His voice was veiled, polite, as if he was aware that they were sitting too close and didn't want to startle her.

"I think so."

"Ye risk catching a chill overnight in that thin cloak of yers. Here ... mine's thicker. Shall I wrap it around both our shoulders?"

Tara should have told him not to bother, should have told him she didn't want to share his cloak. Instead, she merely nodded, leaning forward so he could sling his fur-lined cloak around them both. And when she leaned backward once more, she found her side pressed entirely against his.

Her heart leaped into a canter, while an odd excitement fluttered low in her belly. *What are ye doing?* A voice squealed in her head, but she ignored it. The heat and strength of Maclean's body against hers was indeed comforting, and he would be her only source of warmth overnight.

She inhaled the masculine scent of him then. Her belly fluttered once more before panic arrowed through her. No, she couldn't let herself respond to him like this.

She had to remind herself who they both were.

Fighting herself, Tara kept her gaze ahead, deliberately not glancing his way. Meanwhile, the night grew darker now that their fire had gone out. The drum of the rain on the canopy overhead had a lulling effect upon her, and after a long day of walking, tiredness dragged Tara down into its embrace.

After a while, she relaxed against the tree trunk. "It's nice under here," she admitted eventually. "Peaceful."

"Aye." Maclean's voice was soft yet held a strained edge. "We're sitting in nature's bower."

"It almost makes ye forget the last few days ever happened," she admitted then, still not looking his way. There wasn't any point anyway, for darkness shrouded them both.

"I wish we could," he replied. "I wish I could retrace my steps and make different choices, Tara."

Her pulse leaped at his use of her given name, as it always did. "Aye?"

"Aye … although there's just one problem."

"And what's that?" She was only too aware of how close they were sitting, of the pressure of his thigh pressing against hers. Why didn't she shift away?

"If I could go back and change things … ye and I would never have had this time together."

Tara's heart kicked hard against her ribs at this admission. He really shouldn't say such things, and yet his words tore at the restraint she'd used as a shield. Jack Maclean made her *feel* things. It was as if she'd been half asleep before meeting him. "Wouldn't that be for the best?" she asked, wishing her voice didn't suddenly sound so husky.

"I'm not sure it would have been."

Silence fell between them, tension shivering in the damp air.

A heartbeat passed and then another, and then his fingers slid along her cheek. His touch was soft yet sure, and Tara's breathing caught.

He was too bold. She should slap his hand away.

Neither of them spoke as his fingertips traced the sweep of her jaw, the arch of her cheekbone, as if committing the contours of her face to memory. Tara's eyes fluttered shut as she allowed the sensation in. Eventually, she whispered, "It would certainly have made both our lives *easier*, Jack."

Jack. She liked his name.

"Aye, lass." His breath feathered across her cheek then. "But 'easier' doesn't mean they would have been better."

He had a point. Indeed, right in that instant, Tara didn't want to go back and change a thing. Her restraint had fled, and all she wanted, desperately, was for Jack to kiss her.

His palm cupped her cheek then, and her breathing caught once more when his lips brushed her brow. His scent, his masculinity, overwhelmed her.

Heat swept over Tara, and with it, a heady excitement. Turning toward him, and reaching up, she explored the strong line of his jaw with her fingertips, enjoying the scrape of stubble, before she traced the sensual swell of his lower lip.

Her heart pounding like a hunting drum, she arched toward him, her chin lifting.

It was a silent invitation and one that he took.

Jack's mouth slanted across hers in a passionate, claiming kiss.

The shock of his embrace made Tara gasp, yet he just took it as an opportunity to part her lips. His tongue speared into her mouth, sliding against her own, encouraging her response.

And she did just that, stroking her tongue along his, tasting him. She lifted a hand then, splaying it across his chest. Her fingertips dug in as Jack deepened the kiss.

Their tongues tangled now, their lips bruising, their teeth nipping.

Dizziness assailed Tara. She'd never imagined a kiss could be like this—although she had nothing to compare this to. This was her first one.

Time drew out. Jack kissed her thoroughly, deeply, his hand still cupping her cheek. He softened his embrace now, taking his time as he explored her mouth with a gentleness that made hunger twist in Tara's belly.

It was sensual torture, but now that she'd tasted it, she wanted more.

All good sense had fled, as had any thoughts of caution. This evening had wrapped them both in an enchantment—one she had no desire to free herself from.

Groaning, Tara slid her hand up Jack's chest, to his shoulder, before tangling it in his thick hair. She pulled him closer, her teeth grazing his lower lip.

A strangled sound escaped him, and then he hauled her onto his lap.

Seated astride Jack, Tara arched her back as he slid his hands under her cloak and down her spine. He then cupped her backside and drew her closer still, so that their groins met.

And even through the layers of clothing that separated them, she felt his arousal—hot and thick—straining against his braies.

Tara couldn't help it, she rolled her hips against his hardness, gasping as wild excitement ignited in her lower belly, followed by a rush of wet heat between her thighs. Lord, how she loved this. How she wanted to discover where it led.

Jack tore his mouth from hers then, burying his face in the hollow where her neck met her shoulder. "We should stop."

"No," Tara gasped, awed by her own lustiness. The word had almost come out as a sob. He'd just given her a taste of pleasure, and she couldn't bear to have it ripped away.

"Vixen," he growled, nipping at the soft skin of her neck with his teeth. "If this continues, I'll soon be buried inside ye."

His words inflamed Tara, as did the feel of his teeth, his lips, and the glide of his tongue on her skin.

"Aye," she gasped, her body trembling now. Suddenly, she wanted nothing more than to be joined with him. She wanted to let sensation rule for once—to discover what truly letting go was like.

"And if that happens, ye could end up with bairn," he reminded her, his voice raspy, as if it was taking all his strength to keep his wits about him. "I've already harmed ye enough ... but if my seed quickened inside ye, it would be yer ruin."

They were sobering words and should have doused her passion as quickly as a pail of icy water over the head. And yet, they didn't. Instead, Tara offered a solution. "I've overheard the lasses in the kitchens discussing their experiences with men," she admitted, trying to concentrate as the tip of his tongue flicked into the hollow of her throat. "They say that if their lover pulls out before he spills his seed, it will prevent a bairn from growing."

Jack made a throaty sound, halfway between a laugh and a groan. "Aye ... if he doesn't forget himself."

21: SIN

"AND WILL YE forget yerself?" she whispered back, thrilling at her own bravery.

Jack did groan then. Murmuring an oath, he pulled her head down to his, kissing her fiercely.

Tara responded with equal enthusiasm, tangling her fingers in his hair as their tongues dueled.

As they kissed, she was vaguely aware that he'd pushed her cloak from her shoulders. She felt a tug and realized he was now unlacing her surcote. Untangling her fingers from his thick mane, she leaned back to give him better access. Moments later, the whisper of cool air against her skin warned her that he'd pushed her surcote, and the kirtle and lèine she wore underneath, off her shoulders.

Jack explored her naked torso with slow sensuality, his fingertips tracing across the plane of her belly, the arch of her ribcage, and up to the swell of her breasts.

And when his fingers grazed her hard nipples, Tara gasped.

Jack murmured an endearment then, cupping her breasts with his hands, and stroking their aching tips with his thumbs.

Pleasure arrowed straight down to Tara's core, and she arched toward him, demanding more. What a revelation this was—suddenly, she was greedy to discover just how good this man could make her feel.

Jack dropped his hands from her breasts then and took hold of her hips, lifting her up so that she was kneeling rather than sitting astride him. This position brought her breasts level with his face.

An instant later, the rasp of his stubbled cheek slid across the sensitive buds of her nipples before he drew one deep into his mouth and began to suckle her.

Tara groaned, loudly, as the flesh between her thighs started to ache. His touch ignited something feral inside her. Her greed spiraled into a ravenous hunger that gnawed at her belly—for something she'd never experienced. She'd listened to the whispers of the cooks and scullery maids at Dùn Ara, but she was innocent in carnal intimacy.

The way Jack suckled her made her wild for him. Her fingers scrabbled at the laces of the gambeson he wore over his lèine. However, she couldn't seem to get any closer to his skin.

"Wait, lass," he mumbled against her breast.

Breathing hard, Jack pulled back, and although she couldn't see anything more than vague shadows and outlines, the sounds that followed let her know that he'd just yanked off his gambeson and lèine.

Tara leaned down, her hands exploring the muscular bulges of his upper arms before sliding to the crisp whorls of hair that covered his strong chest. Like hers, his nipples were peaked. He inhaled sharply when she glided her thumbs over them.

An instant later, his mouth had latched on to her other breast, and he suckled her with such sensual determination that Tara sagged against him, her hands going to his shoulders to brace herself.

Jack didn't stop there. Hitching up her skirts, his hands slid up her legs to her parted thighs. And when he pushed her legs even farther apart, his fingers sliding between them, Tara let out a soft, keening cry.

"Aye?" he crooned before he started to stroke her in gentle sweeps. He then circled the hard bud nestled within the petals of her sex.

Tara shuddered, pleasure coiling in her lower belly. Suddenly, she had no words at all.

This was magical. She wanted him to never stop. Sometimes, late at night while Orla snored upon her cot near the hearth, Tara had explored her own body, and had stroked herself between her thighs. The pleasure she'd discovered had surprised her, yet it paled in comparison to the savage need that coiled inside her now.

Jack's touch made her entire body tremble. And all the while, he still lavished attention upon her breasts, suckling one and then the other, until Tara writhed against him.

The needy ache that had been gathering in her lower belly like a storm crested then, and pleasure pulsed and rippled through her loins.

Tara's ragged cry echoed through their oak bower, joining the drum of the rain. Her knees buckled, and she collapsed on Jack's lap.

He gave her no time to recover though. Instead, his mouth captured hers for a savage kiss. His hands slid from between her thighs and up her back, to tangle in her hair, pulling her head back as his lips left hers and explored the slope of her jaw and the column of her throat.

"God's blood, Tara," he rasped. "Ye are delicious."

She murmured something incomprehensible in answer, grinding her aching core against him. He'd brought her to a climax, yet she wanted more. And judging from the bulge that strained against his braies, so did he.

Reaching between them, she fumbled with the laces of his braies and freed his shaft.

The darkness prevented her from seeing him, so she explored the length of his engorged manhood with her fingertips, marveling at its heat and the silkiness of the skin that covered its hardness.

Jack murmured a curse against her neck, a shiver rippling through his strong body as she caressed him.

Taking hold of her hips once more, he drew Tara closer and positioned the cleft between her thighs over the swollen head of his rod. "This might hurt ye, but we'll go slow," he murmured, his breath whispering in her ear.

Tara nodded, trusting him. The lasses she'd overheard had spoken about their first time 'stinging' a little, although some had scoffed at this, saying it hadn't hurt at all. It seemed the experience was different for every woman, and she would soon discover it for herself.

Jack lowered her onto his shaft, sliding into her carefully.

The first couple of inches were easy, and then she felt herself tighten around him.

Tara halted, letting herself adjust to the invasion. Dragging in a deep breath, she exhaled, gathering her courage. She then sank down on him, impaling herself in one movement.

It did sting, and she gasped at the ache that followed, her hands tightening upon his shoulders.

"Tara?" Concern laced Jack's voice.

"It's all right," she murmured, even though she wasn't quite sure. "It's just ... Hades, ye're *big*."

He chuckled. "Music to a man's ears."

Tara snorted, giving his cheek a playful swipe. The stinging had gone now, and the ache had subsided to a sensation of fullness.

"Roll yer hips, lass," Jack said then, his voice lowering. "Test how it feels."

Tara did as bid, moving her pelvis in a cautious circle.

Hot pleasure arrowed straight up her core into her belly, and she gasped.

Jack's body tensed under hers. "Did that hurt?"

"Lord, no," she whispered. She then repeated the act, whimpering at the overwhelming sensations that followed. "It feels indescribably good." She rotated her hips once more, losing herself in the pleasure that rolled through her, while Jack rocked her back and forth, showing her how to slide up and down his rod.

"Tara," he groaned, an edge of desperation in his voice. "Ye are heavenly."

She huffed a laugh, riding him harder now. "And ye are sin," she panted, throwing her head back as the tension in her womb coiled tighter. And he was—the kind of sin that could ruin a woman. Their behavior tonight was ill-advised and reckless, but Tara now rode Jack's rod as if her life depended on it—as if both their lives did.

No one would take this discovery, this breath-stealing pleasure, away from her.

Her movements became wild and jerky as she clawed her way toward the edge of a cliff.

And then Jack tipped them both sideways onto the mossy ground at the base of the oak. Rolling Tara onto her back, he shoved her skirts about her waist and grabbed hold of her knees, pushing them back against her chest so that her sex thrust up toward him.

Jack's eyes glinted in the darkness. "I'll give ye sin," he growled, rubbing the tip of his rod over her wetness. "I'll make ye want nothing else."

An instant later, he plunged into her.

Tara cried out. This position had almost folded her torso double, allowing him to penetrate even deeper than earlier. And the sensation that had enraptured her when she'd sat astride him was even more intense now. With every thrust, wet heat surged deep in her belly—the Saints preserve her, this was turning her inside out—and then she shattered, a scream ripping from her throat as ecstasy pulsed through her.

Jack plowed Tara through her climax, slamming home again and again while she writhed and shuddered under him.

And then, suddenly, he withdrew from her.

A heartbeat passed before warm wetness spurted across Tara's naked belly.

Through the fog of pleasure, she realized that, whereas she'd lost control, Jack had held on to his wits. Instead of spilling deep inside her, he'd managed to withdraw in time.

A blend of relief and disappointment washed over her. Relief because he'd spared her the consequences of a bairn; and disappointment because not having him lose himself inside her made their coupling feel, somehow, incomplete.

Even so, her body was boneless and molten in the aftermath.

She lay there panting, staring up at the dark shapes of twisted tree branches above her, while the blood roared in her ears. And as she recovered, Tara waited for recrimination to creep in, for hot shame to sweep over her.

But it didn't. She wasn't sorry at all, it seemed, and the realization surprised her.

"I've made a mess of ye, lass," Jack muttered. "Here, I'll find some moss to clean ye up."

Shortly after, the soft glide of moss over her belly roused Tara from her thoughts. "Ye didn't make a mess," she assured him, propping herself up onto her shoulders as he finished cleaning her off. "But thank ye for remembering."

He harrumphed. "I can't believe I did ... there were a few moments when I lost myself ... when I wanted nothing more than to spill deep inside ye."

Heat swept over Tara at this admission, and her breathing grew shallow once more. However, she didn't admit that she'd yearned for the same. Both their emotions were roused in the aftermath of their passion; it would be easy to say something foolish she'd regret later.

She had to remind herself of reality. This encounter had been unplanned and unexpected, but tomorrow they'd arrive at Duart Castle, and she'd be sent back to her family. The Mackinnons and the Macleans would then go to war.

This was a stolen moment in time—one that couldn't be repeated.

"I wish I could see ye," she admitted then. And she did. She wanted to see the expression on his face, to be able to gaze deep into his eyes after what they'd just shared.

He huffed a soft laugh. "Best not," he replied, his voice thick. "Ye don't want to see a grown man cry."

Her chest constricted at these words, and she pushed herself up into a sitting position, reaching for him. And when she touched his cheek, she discovered it was wet.

Recrimination spiked through her. There was she, enjoying this encounter on a physical, carnal, level, while her lover's feelings went far deeper. She hadn't forgotten his admission the eve before—yet despite the passion that had sparked between them, she couldn't return the sentiment.

"Jack," she whispered. "I—"

"It's all right." He caught her hand and turned it over, placing a gentle kiss upon her palm. "Don't mind me," he said huskily. "Fear not, by morning, I'll have my mask firmly back in place."

BOOK TWO: FREED

22: STRIKING A BARGAIN

DUART CASTLE LOOMED to the east, its high curtain walls slicing into the sky.

But the sight of Jack's home brought a flicker of nervousness along with relief.

Aye, he had a few things to be uneasy about.

Loch's reaction to what he'd done for one.

He was ready to weather the consequences—and wasn't expecting his cousin to go easy on him—but his arrival at Duart also reminded him that soon the closeness that had formed between him and his enemy's daughter would end. They'd no longer be alone together, and they'd resume the roles expected of them.

Jack cut a glance over at Tara then. They'd spoken little that morning, and the silence between them had been tense.

Of course, it would be.

Memories of the night before intruded then. The sweetness of Tara's mouth. The softness of her skin. The feel of her round breasts filling his palms. The wet, tight heat of her quim. Tara riding him. Her under him as he rutted her like an animal. His tears afterward. Enfolding Tara in his arms and sleeping with their limbs entwined.

Jack's throat thickened. They were memories that would stay with him. Memories he hoped he could hold on to in the years to come.

If he lived that long.

Feeling his gaze upon her, Tara met his eye. She then favored him with a half-smile. "Ready?"

No. I'll never be ready to be parted from ye.

Swallowing the impulse to tell her what lay in his heart, Jack nodded.

Their gazes held for a moment before Tara cleared her throat. A faint blush tinged her cheekbones as she glanced away. "I'm not sorry about last night," she murmured.

Jack's heart kicked hard against his breastbone at this admission. "I'm relieved to hear it," he replied, trying to sound cavalier and failing.

Tara's attention flicked back to him. "I mean it."

"So do I," he said, swallowing. "I was worried ye would wake up this morning and blacken my eye."

Tara laughed, pushing a bright-red curl off her forehead. "If I thought punching ye in the face would help, I'd have done so days ago."

"Aye, well ... I wouldn't be surprised if Loch knocks my teeth down my throat shortly," he replied. "If ye want retribution, ye'll get it."

Jack wasn't exaggerating. In truth, he hadn't spared Loch more than a glancing thought when he embarked on his revenge. But now that everything had changed, his cousin crept increasingly into his thoughts. Loch would be incensed—and rightly so. Now that Jack was no longer blinded by his need for vengeance, he could view his behavior objectively.

Base. Twisted. Cruel.

"I don't want retribution against ye, Jack," Tara said softly. "I just want to go home."

Her words knifed him in the guts. Of course, she wanted to return to Dùn Ara. Last night had been a truce between them, something foolish and reckless that only made him sicken for this woman even more.

But Tara didn't feel the same way about him. Why would she? There was no denying though the fire that had ignited between them—an animal hunger she'd given into.

They were climbing the incline now, having just passed through Duart village. The women hanging out washing had gawked at them as they walked in, as had the men shepherding sheep on the hillsides beyond.

Tension knotted in Jack's gut.

This was but a taste of the awkwardness that was to come. He needed to steel himself for it.

"Have ye gone daft, man?" Loch shattered the ominous silence that had filled the solar while Jack recounted his tale. "Why the devil would ye bring Mackinnon's daughter here?"

Jack's pulse jolted at these words. Understandably, his cousin was vexed by what he'd just heard. However, Jack hadn't expected the clan-chief to give such a brutal reply.

"Lady Tara needs to get home," he replied, even as his face warmed. "I thought ye could help her."

Loch's mouth pursed, his peat-dark eyes narrowing. "Did ye?"

Jack drew in a deep breath, curling his hands into fists at his sides as he waited for the storm to hit.

Of course, they weren't alone in the solar. The laird's wife, Mairi, sat by the fire, as did Loch's sister, Astrid. Loch's wolfhound, Luag, sat between the two women, his keen gaze observing the newcomers. Meanwhile, Jack's brother, Rae, stood at the window.

Rae's presence was a surprise, an unwelcome one. However, it seemed that when Jack didn't return to Duart from Dounarwye Castle, Loch had sent word. Rae had then ridden south to inform him that Jack departed days earlier, and that he had no idea of his whereabouts.

Meanwhile, Jack and Loch stood in the center of the large chamber, with Tara looking on quietly from the side.

As he'd told his tale, he'd felt her gaze upon him.

Jack had recounted the story honestly, from start to finish—although he left out the detail about the kitchen lass at Dùn Ara helping him for coin. Tara would be returning to that fortress, and Aynsley would meet a terrible end if the Mackinnon discovered what she'd done. Jack also didn't reveal the real reason for his change of heart or that he and Tara had lain together; some things should remain private.

But the rest was all true, and as he'd recounted the details, his gut had cramped. Satan's cods, he was a shitweasel. Had he really hatched such a devious plan? Had he really thought he'd get away with it? The truth was, he'd been so focused on getting his long-awaited revenge that nothing else mattered.

A ponderous silence settled in the solar after Loch's challenging response. The arched window on the south side of the chamber was open, allowing the morning sun to filter in and pool across the wooden floor. The bleating of sheep on the hills beyond the castle intruded, followed by the faint wail of a bairn somewhere in the nearby village.

Eventually, as he waited for Loch to say something else, Jack's attention flicked around the room, taking in Tara's veiled expression, Mairi's horrified one, and Astrid's scowl. His brother's face had gone as hard as flint.

"Ye have taken a stick to a hornet's nest … ye do realize that?" Loch continued finally, each word enunciated with care—a sure sign he was struggling to keep his temper on a leash. "The situation is bad enough without ye stirring things up."

Jack nodded, although he refrained from reminding Loch that *he* was actually to blame for the recent tension between the Macleans and MacKinnons. Such an observation wouldn't sweeten the laird's mood.

"Ye should know that Mackinnon himself sailed by here just yesterday morning," his cousin added then. "He moored his birlinn offshore and sent one of his men up here with the news his daughter was missing." A nerve ticked in Loch's cheek. "I told him we'd not seen or heard anything … but then, when Rae arrived later that afternoon, I guessed ye had something to do with her disappearance."

Jack tensed at these words. He should have anticipated this; his cousin was shrewd, and he knew Jack better than anyone besides Finn.

"Where's my father now?" Tara asked, speaking for the first time since they'd walked into the clan-chief's solar.

Loch gave Jack a hard look that warned he'd deal with him later before his dark gaze shifted to Tara. "He sailed north … likely returning home." He cut Jack a scowl then. "The only silver lining in this mess is that ye didn't hand Lady Tara over to a mercenary." Loch took a menacing step toward him. "But once Kendric Mackinnon hears what ye've done, he'll be savage in his retribution … and I can't say I blame him."

"He'll focus on Dounarwyse," Rae spoke up then, his voice gruff. "He's already let us know he'll begin his attack there."

"Aye," Loch growled, casting Tara a narrow-eyed look. "Although we'll discuss that later, Rae."

Heeding the warning edge to the clan-chief's voice, the laird of Dounarwyse fell silent, while Jack frowned. Of course, Loch didn't want to speak of such things in front of Tara—for she could take back anything she heard here to her father.

"Sooner or later, we'll weather an attack from our neighbors," Astrid said then, breaking the tense silence that followed. "But Mackinnon doesn't have to learn that Jack is responsible for his daughter's disappearance."

Loch cast his sister a surprised look before shifting his attention back to Tara. Jack marked how her chin lifted and the steeliness in her silver eyes as she stared back at the laird.

"I could hold ye captive here … to use against the enemy," Loch said, frowning. "But I won't." He paused here, giving Tara a moment to take in his words, before continuing, "I can understand why ye'd tell yer father everything on yer return home … but he's already irate after I broke faith with him. Do ye want a blood feud to erupt between our clans … one that could potentially last generations?"

Tara's throat bobbed, even as her gaze remained level.

Jack's chest tightened. God's blood, she was brave. Regal. Magnificent.

"So, this becomes my responsibility, does it?" she asked finally, her voice husky.

Loch's gaze shadowed. "Aye, lass," he murmured. "It doesn't seem right, does it?"

"No."

A sickly sensation washed over Jack at this exchange, the sting of humiliation swiftly following. But he deserved this—and more. Meanwhile, Loch and Tara continued to stare at each other as a battle of wills ensued.

Eventually, Tara spoke. "Organize for a boat to sail me back to Dùn Ara tomorrow, and Jack's name won't be mentioned."

Rae snorted, while both Astrid and Mairi stiffened in their seats. Astrid's dark-brown eyes had narrowed. Next to her, Loch's wife viewed the exchange with an incredulous expression upon her lovely face now—as if she couldn't believe Tara Mackinnon had spoken thus to her husband.

Jack could.

Tara was a Mackinnon, but she wasn't like her father—or Jack for that matter. Hate and bloodlust didn't blind her. She was a lady, yet she understood the true cost of war—for both their clans.

Loch cocked an eyebrow. "Aye?"

Tara nodded. "I shall tell my father that I was struck by pre-wedding nerves upon my trip to Tobermory ... that I ran off in a panic. I eventually strayed into Maclean territory before being captured and brought to ye."

"And he'll believe such a tale?"

Tara favored Loch with a thin smile. "If I tell it well enough, aye."

"That's ... decent of ye, Lady Tara," Astrid spoke up once more, her expression sharp now. She'd suggested the subterfuge yet appeared wary. "But can we trust ye to keep yer word?"

Tara glanced over at Astrid, and the two women's gazes fused. "Ye don't have any choice in the matter," she replied, her tone cooling once more, before she added, "I'm not doing this for the Macleans, but the Mackinnons … a blood feud will destroy this isle."

Astrid inclined her head. Her lips parted then as she readied herself to answer. But before she could, the solar door crashed open, and a lean, leather-clad figure stalked in. "Sorry I'm late," Finn MacDonald greeted them, his sharp hazel gaze sweeping the room before it rested upon Jack. "I was delayed."

Across the chamber, Astrid's mouth clamped shut, her eyes hardening.

Meanwhile, Loch muttered an oath under his breath. "Aye, well … we aren't repeating it all for yer benefit."

"Ye might want to know *why* I was delayed," Finn drawled, folding his arms across his chest.

Loch scowled. "I'm not in the mood for riddles today, Finn," he replied, his voice hardening. "Spit it out."

Unconcerned, the Captain of the Duart Guard merely shrugged. "All right then. Logan Black has moored the *Revenge Tide* offshore and paid ye a visit." Finn's sharp gaze flicked to Tara then, no doubt marking the way her eyes snapped wide at this news. "It seems Jack made him a promise … and he wants him to keep it."

23: I SHALL HAVE MY RECKONING

THE MACLEAN CLAN-CHIEF snarled a filthy curse, one that made Tara flinch, before he rounded on Jack. "I'm far from being done with ye, cousin," he bit out. "Once we've dealt with Black, ye and I are going to have a private word."

To his credit, Jack didn't wither under Loch's glare. Even so, his handsome face was pinched, his eyes shadowed. He favored the laird with a nod, acknowledging the threat.

"What about Black then?" Lady Astrid asked, rising to her feet.

Loch turned to the man who'd just entered, a sharp-featured individual he'd called Finn. Clad in leathers, with a fur-lined cloak swinging from his shoulders, the man had mussed light-brown hair and a hungry look about him. "Bring him up here."

Alarm arrowed through Tara at this news. She didn't want to meet the pirate Jack had promised her to.

Likewise, Jack's features drew taut. "Can't we meet him down in the outer courtyard?"

"No," Loch snapped. "Logan Black was part of yer witless plan ... and I shall hear his side of it."

Meanwhile, Finn had turned on his heel and left with the same suddenness that he'd appeared.

"Ye aren't going to give me to him, are ye?" Tara demanded. She tried to keep the panic out of her voice yet failed. Suddenly, she felt as if she'd entered a den of wolves. Jack had told her she could trust Loch, but the faces surrounding her weren't friendly, and she didn't like the glint in their eyes when they glanced her way.

She was a Mackinnon amongst Macleans. Unwelcome.

"No, Lady Tara," Loch replied, an edge to his voice now. His expression was grim and his jaw flexed. "But if Jack made him promises, I will have to find a way to make things right ... Logan Black is an ally of the Macleans, and I have no wish to turn him into an enemy."

Tara stared back at him, her panic still simmering. What a fool she was, for taking this man at his word.

An awkward silence followed, and then the laird's wife smoothly rose to her feet. "I think we could all do with some wine to settle our nerves," she said, moving to an oaken sideboard, where a jug of wine and a stack of wooden cups waited.

"Aye, thank ye, Mairi," Loch replied, his tone softening.

In response, his wife glanced over her shoulder, favoring her husband with a smile.

The look that passed between them made Tara catch her breath.

Jack had told her he'd seen love matches, but she hadn't. Her parents' marriage had been distant, and none of her aunts and uncles seemed happily wed. As such, it was a shock to see such warmth pass between husband and wife.

Loch Maclean's face literally transformed when Mairi smiled.

Envy tugged at Tara's belly then. She couldn't imagine Callum MacDonald ever looking at her like that.

Mairi deftly poured the wine and loaded the cups onto a platter. Tara watched her nimble movements. Of course, the woman had run *The Craignure Inn* before wedding Loch. She'd once spent her days serving others.

Taking the cup Mairi passed her, Tara managed a tight smile. "Thank ye."

The laird's wife nodded, her tawny eyes crinkling at the corners as her mouth curved. "Don't worry," she murmured. "Ye'll be safe here, Lady Tara." Mairi then moved on before Tara could reply.

Only slightly more reassured than earlier, Tara glanced over at Jack then. Tension still rippled off him, and his expression was now stern, making him look like the man standing by the window.

They'd been briefly introduced upon entering the solar—Rae Maclean was Jack's elder brother, and the family resemblance was remarkable. The chieftain of Dounarwyse perched on the window ledge, his face stern. His dark-auburn hair was cropped short against his scalp, adding to his severe look. And at present, Rae didn't look any happier than Jack. He took a cup of wine from Mairi with a nod, his gaze never leaving his brother's broad back.

They'd all taken a sip or two of their wines when a heavy tread on the stairs outside, and then on the landing, made Tara's pulse spike.

A few moments later, a big man with a wild mane of dark-brown hair strode into the solar. Finn followed behind him, closing the door.

"Black ... it's been a long while." Loch stepped close, and the two men clasped arms, a greeting typical between warriors.

"Aye, Maclean," the mercenary replied with a careless smile. "Last time we saw each other, we were both no older than eighteen and well into our cups."

"I won that drinking game if I recall." Loch flashed Black a grin.

The mercenary snorted. "Barely." He took the cup Mairi passed him then, favoring her with an appreciative smile, before his gaze shifted from the laird and his wife, traveling to Jack, and then Tara. His dark-blue eyes narrowed.

Tensing under his scrutiny, Tara stared back.

She'd imagined Logan Black to be frightening to look upon, but he wasn't. He possessed rough, virile good looks, although she sensed the banked violence and aggression in him. No, this wasn't someone to be messed with.

Her stomach dropped then.

Jack had known that, yet he'd turned his back on the arrangement they'd made all the same.

Fighting the urge to glance Jack's way once more, Tara continued to hold the mercenary's eye. She wouldn't let him intimidate her.

After a few moments, Black's mouth quirked, and he shifted his gaze back to Jack. "Wanted her for yerself, did ye?"

Jack's brows crashed together, a muscle in his jaw bunching. "Watch it, Black."

The mercenary's smile flowered into a toothy grin. "Cunning dog."

"Jack made a mistake promising ye Tara Mackinnon," Loch cut in, his brow furrowing, "but luckily came to his senses."

Black's grin faded, a dangerous expression stealing over his features. "Aye, but he made me a promise."

"The deal's off," Jack replied curtly.

"No, it isn't."

"Logan." The warning in Loch's voice made Tara clench her fingers around the cup. "Don't insult me by insisting on this."

The wolfhound that had been sitting placidly by the fire started to growl low in its throat then, although Loch settled the dog with a gesture.

The mercenary shot the clan-chief a glare. "Ye should ensure Jack keeps his end of the bargain."

"Ye aren't getting even with Kendric Mackinnon by taking his daughter," Loch growled. "That's low ... even for ye."

The two men's gazes fused, an aggressive silence swelling between them before Black shattered it. "Over a decade has gone by since we last saw each other, Maclean," he growled. "Ye will have surely changed, as have I. A Mackinnon raiding party slaughtered my parents and younger sister five years ago." He cut Tara a look that made her tremble. "And I shall have my reckoning."

A sickly sensation swept over Tara then. She wanted to call him a liar, yet if Black's family had been murdered by Mackinnons, he had every right to hate her clan. She couldn't imagine how she'd feel if their positions were reversed, how it would have twisted her up inside.

As it had Jack.

"Revenge isn't as sweet as ye might think," Jack spoke up, bitterness lacing his voice now. "Trust me, I should know."

Black snorted, although his gaze never left Loch's. "I repeat. I shall have my reckoning."

"Ye should listen to my cousin," Loch answered, not budging an inch. Watching the Maclean clan-chief, a grudging respect tugged at Tara. On her previous visit to Duart Castle, she'd found him insufferably arrogant—but she saw a different, more thoughtful, side to him now. "Vengeance takes on a life of its own," he continued. "And it will end up yer executioner."

Black's lip curled, and he took a step forward, eyeballing Loch. "Aye, but ye know what the bible says … eye for eye, tooth for tooth … life for *life*."

Tara shuddered at the menace in these words. God's troth, what had Black been planning to do with her?

"An eye for an eye just starts a cycle that can never be broken," Loch replied, his voice low and hard. "Ye think revenge will take away the hate that gnaws at yer gut … but it won't. It's a disease. And in the end, it'll consume ye." Tara marked the pained expression on Jack's face at these words, yet the laird remained focused on the mercenary. "It's also a waste of a good man."

Black gave a dismissive snort.

"What if I made ye an offer ye couldn't refuse?" Loch asked then.

The mercenary's midnight-blue gaze narrowed. "It would depend on the offer."

"Land and a holding of yer own?"

Black jerked as if the laird had just slapped him. "What?"

"Give up a mercenary's life and yer quest for vengeance, and swear yer loyalty to me," Loch continued.

"Become one of my chieftains, and I'll give ye the ruined tower and lands around Croggan." Black's gaze widened at this, but the laird hadn't yet finished. "I want the southeastern coast of Mull and Loch Spelve watched over. Ye are the man for the job."

A hush fell over the solar, all gazes settling upon Logan Black.

Everyone looked just as stunned by Loch's offer as the mercenary himself did. Jack's lips had parted, Rae was gripping his cup so tightly his knuckles had gone white, Finn's hazel eyes were startled, while Mairi and Astrid shared shocked looks.

Tara too couldn't believe the laird had offered this man, this *pirate*, such a boon.

Recovering from his surprise, Black frowned. "What if I don't wish to give up a seafarer's life?" He cast Tara a hot look that made her heart falter. "Or my prize?"

"Tara Mackinnon *isn't* yers," Jack cut in, his voice lowering dangerously. "Just let it go … as I have."

The mercenary cocked an eyebrow, issuing a silent challenge.

Loch made an impatient noise in the back of his throat. "I know ye are a sea dog, Black … but ye can't own the waters ye sail. I'm offering ye *land* and a tower ye can rebuild, stone by stone, and make yers." He paused then, his brow furrowing. "I'm offering ye a *legacy*."

The mercenary and the laird locked gazes, and long moments slid by. Loch's frown eventually deepened. "This offer won't be made twice. Think hard before ye refuse me, Black … for if ye do, the *Revenge Tide* will no longer be welcome to dock at Maclean ports upon this isle. If ye won't become my ally, ye shall be punished for yer part in Jack's ill-considered plan. Do ye want to end up reviled?"

The pirate's lips thinned at this threat.

Tara held her breath, awaiting his answer. It was a generous offer indeed, yet it was clear that Logan Black was a proud man—one who wasn't used to answering to anyone or being forced into anything. Meanwhile, outdoors, a dog started barking. The wolfhound by the hearth pricked its ears up.

Logan Black stepped back from Loch then, glancing Tara's way for the first time since locking horns with the laird. "Ye're a fine lass indeed," he murmured, casting an appreciative eye over her. "And contrary to what ye might think, I didn't intend to slit yer throat." He paused then, his lips tilting at the corners.

Tara didn't answer him. Black might not have intended to harm her, but the thought of belonging to him made her blood run cold all the same.

Winking at her, the mercenary turned away, flashing Jack a sly smile, before he focused on Loch once more. His expression hardened, and his dark-blue eyes glinted. "No need to be so heavy-handed, Maclean."

Loch merely stared back at him, not giving an inch.

Their gazes locked before a faint smile eventually tugged at the corners of Black's lips. "Very well then ... I accept yer offer."

24: WILLING TO PAY THE PRICE

"THESE WILL BE yer lodgings for the night." Mairi led the way into a spacious chamber dominated by a huge canopied bed. The laird's wife then turned to Tara, her brow creasing. "I hope ye find the room to yer liking."

"Aye, thank ye," Tara assured her, casting a gaze around the room. Indeed, it would do very well. Sheepskins covered the floor, tapestries depicting hunting scenes hung from the stone walls, and a fire crackled in the hearth. "Are all yer guest chambers this big?"

"This was built to be the Lady of Duart's bedchamber," Astrid announced, following the other two women into the room. "However, my parents always shared the laird's chamber" —she cut Mairi an insinuating lòok then— "as do Loch and his wife."

Mairi's mouth merely curved at this comment.

"Well, it is fine indeed," Tara replied, awkwardness stealing over her.

Mairi and Astrid were both polite, yet there was a reserve in them that reminded her she wasn't truly welcome here. Highland hospitality dictated they treat her with respect, and the laird's wife and sister were doing their duty.

Even so, Jack had spoken true—Loch Maclean wouldn't keep Tara here against her will. Indeed, he was more than keen to see her on her way. Before she departed the clan-chief's solar with Mairi and Astrid, leaving the men to continue their discussion in private,

the clan-chief had assured her that Finn MacDonald—
the Captain of the Duart Guard—and his men would
escort her home by the laird's private birlinn the
following morning.

"I'd wager ye aren't comfortable staying here …
amongst Macleans," Astrid said then, no doubt reading
her expression.

Tara turned to Loch's sister, meeting her eye. The
woman was slender and pale, yet there was a directness
to her gaze, a firmness in her jaw, that revealed the iron
beneath the fragile façade.

"Not really," Tara admitted.

"Aye, well, lucky for ye, Jack came to his senses."

"Indeed."

The two women's gazes locked for a few moments
before Mairi cleared her throat. "There will be an oath-
swearing ceremony later, followed by a special supper,"
she informed Tara, casting Astrid a wary glance. "Would
ye care to join us?"

Tara's attention shifted to the laird's wife. "Am I
welcome?"

Astrid harrumphed. "Of course." There was a
challenge in her voice, as if she dared Tara to hide away
in her chamber until the following morning.

Tara lifted her chin, meeting Astrid's eye once more.
She wouldn't be cowed by the laird's forthright sister.
"Then, aye, I will join ye."

"Good." Mairi sounded vaguely relieved while Astrid
watched their guest with a sharp look that made it
difficult not to squirm. "Astrid and I will find ye some
clean clothes." Mairi gestured to the soiled, dusty, and
travel-worn garments that Tara wore. "And I'll have
those laundered, ready for yer departure tomorrow."

Tara nodded, gratitude washing over her. "Thank ye."

"I imagine ye'll want a hot bath too," Astrid added,
favoring Tara with an arch look. "After days of being
hauled across the wild by my cousin."

A sigh escaped Tara at these words. "I'd *kill* for a
bath," she admitted.

Jack watched Loch pour himself another cup of wine and waited for the storm to break.

After the women left, and Logan Black had been shown to his chamber—for he'd been invited to stay overnight so that he could swear his oath to the laird publicly that evening—only Loch, Jack, Rae, and Finn remained in the solar.

And none of them spoke.

Jack still nursed his first cup of wine. He wasn't in the mood for drinking.

Setting the jug down and picking up his refilled cup, Loch turned, fixing Jack in a level stare. "Ye are lucky indeed that things have worked out as they have," Loch rumbled. "Or ye'd have two black eyes and a broken jaw by now."

Jack pulled a face. He didn't doubt it.

All the same, Jack still couldn't believe everything had been sorted out so swiftly. Tara had agreed not to tell her father she'd been abducted, and Logan Black had been pacified.

But that didn't erase what he'd done, or the ramifications for him that were sure to come.

"I'm not going to ask what possessed ye to do such an idiotic thing," Loch went on, "for I know how yer need for vengeance against the Mackinnon became a sickness of sorts." He paused then, his eyebrows knitting together. "But I must assure myself of something. Are ye done with it now?"

"Aye," Jack replied without hesitation. "It was like being lost in the fog, Loch ... and I'm glad to be free of it ... to be able to see clearly for the first time in a long while."

"So, ye no longer want to drive a dirk into Kendric Mackinnon's throat?" Finn asked.

Jack glanced his friend's way. Finn was leaning against the wall, arms folded across his chest, regarding him with incredulity.

"I wouldn't go that far," he replied. "I'd still love to end that bastard's life."

Across the chamber, still seated by the window, Rae snorted. "Aye, well, ye'll have to wait in line for that."

Jack flashed Rae a rueful smile. The Mackinnon had plenty of enemies, his brother among them.

"I'm relieved to hear ye've come to yer senses," Loch cut in, his tone impatient now, "although that doesn't change what ye did."

Jack focused on his cousin once more. "I know," he murmured. "And I'm willing to pay the price."

Loch scowled. "I should make an example of ye," he growled before taking a gulp of wine. "I should have ye flogged and left in the stocks for a week."

Jack's gut clenched. Loch was ruthless. It was what had made him a formidable military leader and now a clan-chief to be reckoned with. Jack's actions could have caused a lot of damage; he shouldn't go unpunished. He had no wish to be publicly flogged and humiliated, yet he steeled himself for what was to come. "Aye, Loch," he said roughly. "It's yer choice."

"It is," his cousin replied, stalking across to him. Loch halted just a couple of feet away, his peat-brown eyes boring into his. "And fortunately for ye, I'm in a merciful mood." He paused then, his gaze narrowing. "I'll spare ye the flogging and public disgrace … but, as of this moment, ye are no longer my marshal. Ye are stripped of rank and will now serve under Finn in the Guard."

Jack jolted—not because he was shocked that Loch had stripped him of the role he'd given him when he'd stepped into the role of laird at Duart—but because his cousin was allowing him to stay on here at all.

Loch was being lenient indeed, but even so, it was a blow to have his role stripped from him.

In many ways, he'd taken his position within the castle for granted, yet he didn't any longer. He'd enjoyed the responsibility of being Duart's marshal, where he'd been in charge of the military presence within the stronghold. He'd also overseen the smithy, grooms, and stable lads working inside the keep, and the transporting of goods to and from Duart. His role ensured he'd worked closely with both the laird and the Captain of the Guard—but now he'd have nothing to do with the running of the castle and would be taking orders from Finn and the senior guards.

It would be quite a step-down, yet one he deserved.

"Move yer things out of the marshal's tower before noon," Loch went on. "Ye will be sleeping in the barracks from now on."

Jack nodded slowly as if in a trance. "Is that all?"

Loch scowled, a muscle flexing in his jaw. "Do ye wish for a more severe punishment, cousin?"

"No."

"Good." Loch drained the dregs in his cup and turned away from him. "Then get out of my sight."

Tara sank into the steaming rose-scented water with a deep sigh.

"Is the bath to yer liking, Lady Tara?" Cait, a buxom woman of around thirty with a mass of thick auburn curls piled atop her head, glanced up from where she was laying a stack of drying cloths on the stool next to the cast iron tub that now sat before the hearth. There was a wary edge to her maid's voice, with an underlying resentment that Tara had expected.

Cait Maclean wasn't overjoyed to be waiting on a Mackinnon.

"Aye," Tara replied, her eyes fluttering shut as the heat soaked into her limbs. "It's perfect."

"I've brought up some rose soap," Cait added, her tone clipped now. "Would ye like me to wash yer hair?"

"Aye."

Tara pushed herself up so she was sitting properly, before inclining her head back, aiding the maid as she scooped up water in a cup and poured it over her hair, wetting it. Cait then began to massage soap through her tresses and into her scalp.

"Christ's bones, ye have hair even brighter than mine," Cait said under her breath then, forgetting her reserve. "As red as fire."

Tara gave a soft snort. "Aye … but if I'm honest, it's always been my bane."

"Really?" The woman sounded intrigued despite herself. "Why?"

"It makes me stand out … ye can't hide in a crowd with hair the color of mine."

Cait harrumphed at that.

"Excuse me?" Tara opened her eyes and glanced up at her maid, giving her an arch look.

Chastised by Tara's response, Cait's cheeks flushed. "Ye wouldn't blend into a crowd anyway, Lady Tara," she muttered. "Not as bonnie as ye are."

Tara gave her maid a long look before pointing out, "Neither would ye," It was true: Cait was striking with her lush curves, hazel-green eyes, and a riot of auburn curls. Tara wouldn't be surprised if half the men who worked in this keep lusted after her, for she had an unconscious sensuality about her—one that Tara envied a little.

Cait shrugged. "Aye, well, that's only because the lads can't keep their eyes off my paps."

Tara huffed a laugh and turned away, allowing the maid to resume washing her hair. The scent of rose that already drifted from the bath water grew more intense. Tara closed her eyes, enjoying the sensation of the woman's hands massaging her scalp. Aye, Cait wasn't a friend, but the attention she was receiving reminded her of how Orla had looked after her back at Dùn Ara.

Poor Orla, she'd be ailing with worry by now. It would be a relief to arrive home and reassure her that all was well.

Anxiety fluttered up then, causing her pulse to quicken, and shattering the pleasure of having her hair washed. Soon, she'd be back amongst her kin, readying herself to sail to the Isle of Skye and begin her new life as Callum MacDonald's wife.

Soon, the Macleans would be her enemies again.

Cait didn't speak while she finished washing her hair, and Tara found herself enjoying the silence. In contrast, Orla chattered non-stop while she helped her bathe. But Cait was far younger than her spinster maid—and the two of them were newly acquainted.

However, as Cait rinsed off the last of the soap suds, before wringing the water out of her long hair, curiosity wreathed up inside Tara.

"Are ye wed, Cait?"

"I was," the maid replied, her tone wary again. "I'm widowed now."

"Oh, I'm sorry."

"Thank ye." Cait's voice warmed a little. "I lost Neil a few years ago now, but I still miss him."

Tara took the soap the maid passed her and started to wash under her arms. "Ye don't wish to marry again then?"

Cait moved around to sit on a stool facing her. Their gazes met, and then the woman shrugged. "Och, I was lucky with Neil, and I doubt I would be so again. Most men aren't worth the trouble." Her expression turned wistful then. "When ye find enduring love once ... nothing less will do."

Tara's breathing hitched at this answer. *Enduring love*. How fortunate Cait had been. "I will wed soon," she admitted softly.

"And does the sight of yer husband-to-be make yer pulse race?" Cait teased.

Tara thought of solid, serious Callum MacDonald. He was only five and twenty, yet the clan-chief of the MacDonalds of Sleat's firstborn son acted like someone twice his age. And when he'd kissed her hand upon taking his leave after the betrothal had been arranged, she felt nothing. "No," she murmured. "He doesn't."

25: IS THIS HOW IT ENDS?

SMOOTHING THE EMERALD skirt of the surcote she'd just donned, Tara viewed herself in the long looking glass. After her bath, and clad in clean clothes, she looked and felt like a new woman. How odd it was to be standing here, a Mackinnon in a Maclean keep, wearing the Lady of Duart's clothing.

"Lady Mairi chose well," Cait admitted from behind her. "Green goes well with red hair."

"Aye," Tara murmured, adjusting her neckline a little. "My hair clashes with a lot of colors." The surcote and kirtle she wore under it were both slightly loose. They belonged to Mairi, who had more voluptuous curves than she did.

Underneath, she wore a blood-red kirtle that also set off the green nicely.

Tara stilled then. *Blood.* Suddenly, she was transported back to Tobermory just five days earlier. She recalled her shock at the man's voice behind her, and then the stomach-churning fear when she'd spied the dirk he'd been holding.

How could one week alter so many things?

The biggest change was that she no longer feared and despised Jack Maclean. Indeed, she'd willingly lain with him. Delicious memories of what they'd shared fluttered up then, and warmth stole over Tara.

The events of the past days had caused a shift within her. She felt full of contradictions—less sure of her opinions and at the same time more certain of her own mind. The time she'd spent with Jack made her question everything.

The warmth that flooded over Tara intensified. God's blood, all these new sensations confused her.

But if she no longer saw Jack as the enemy, how *did* she feel about him?

"That's better," another female voice intruded, and Tara glanced over her shoulder to see Lady Astrid standing in the doorway. Her mouth quirked then. "But the surcote needs this." She held up a lovely gilded girdle.

Crossing the chamber to Tara's side, Astrid deftly slid the girdle around her waist and buckled it. She then pushed it down a little, so that it emphasized the swell of Tara's hips and the nip of her waist. "There ye go."

"A fine choice, Lady Astrid," Cait said with a wry smile.

Tara turned from the looking glass, her gaze flicking between Lady Astrid and Cait. "Thank ye," she murmured, taken aback by Astrid's gesture. Earlier, the laird's sister had been wary of her indeed, but it now seemed she was trying to make an effort to be welcoming. "I'm not sure a Maclean would get the same treatment at Dùn Ara."

Astrid pulled a face. "I'm *sure* we wouldn't." She shrugged then. "But Mackinnon or not, ye are still our guest."

Tara nodded warily. Sensing her discomfort, Astrid's expression softened. "Ye look much more rested than when ye arrived."

"I am," Tara assured her. After she'd bathed, she'd slept for a few hours, waking mid-afternoon to a light meal of bread and cheese. Outside her small window, the light had now faded. Supper was approaching.

"Everyone will be amassing in the great hall," Astrid added. "Logan Black must swear his fealty to Loch in front of his clansmen before we sit down to eat." Then, to Tara's surprise, the laird's sister moved around to her side and linked her arm through hers. "Shall we go down together?"

Logan Black sank to one knee before the clan-chief, holding the dirk upright by the blade. Loch stood there, his expression grave, while the entire great hall—Tara included—looked on.

An expectant hush settled then before the deep bass of Black's voice shattered it. "I swear by the cross of our Lord Jesus Christ, and by the holy iron that I hold, to give ye fealty and pledge ye my loyalty to the name of the clan Maclean. If ever my hand shall be raised against ye in rebellion, I ask that this holy iron shall pierce my heart."

The mercenary's voice was low yet earnest, something which surprised Tara.

Giving up an exciting existence upon the high seas to become a laird of his own land would be quite a change for the mercenary, and he'd been loath to relinquish his old life. Nonetheless, she was relieved he'd abandoned his claim on her.

Black lowered the dirk and kissed it where the haft met the tang. He then sheathed the dagger and, still kneeling, clasped his hands together before raising them to his laird. Loch's dark eyes gleamed as he stepped forward, grasped Black's hands, and lifted them to his lips in acceptance. An instant later, he raised him to his feet.

Lady Astrid, who stood solemnly at her brother's side, handed the clan-chief a gem-encrusted silver goblet. Loch took a sip and then handed it to the oath taker.

Black drank from the cup as well before handing it back to his laird.

Loch's mouth tugged into a smile. "And I, Loch Maclean, clan-chief of the Macleans of Mull, accept yer oath."

Black's rugged face split into a grin before he bowed and stepped to one side, allowing the laird to move forward to address the crowd. "My loyal clansmen," Loch called to them. "I give ye Logan Black, the chieftain of Croggan."

A thunderous applause exploded inside the great hall. The noise rattled the tables and echoed high into the rafters.

Tara observed their enthusiasm yet didn't join in.

Instead, she fought a restlessness that had been growing all afternoon.

She was an outsider and by rights shouldn't even be sitting here, rubbing shoulders with Macleans. Soon the warriors surrounding her would be going to war against her people. Aye, she'd marked the looks she'd received upon entering the hall on Astrid's arm—and noted how some of the women whispered and a few of the men scowled. Despite that they'd have learned her presence at Duart wasn't of her choosing, Kendric Mackinnon's whelp wasn't a welcome sight.

They'd be as relieved as Tara that she was leaving at first light the following day.

Now that the oath-swearing ceremony was over, the inhabitants of the hall took their seats.

Tara joined those at the clan-chief's table, finding herself seated between Lady Astrid and Captain MacDonald. The chieftain of Dounarwyse had also joined them, and sat at the end of the table, next to MacDonald. Meanwhile, as a special guest, Black had been given a place next to the laird and his wife.

However, Tara noticed that Jack wasn't invited to sit with them. He was present, yet he took a seat at one of the long trestle tables a few yards away.

Like her, he'd bathed, and his dark-auburn hair curled in damp waves around his collar. He wore a snowy-white lèine tucked into clean braies, and his jaw was freshly shaven. Tara's heart gave a sharp kick at the sight of him. Curse it, the man looked far too good.

Their gazes met across the hall briefly, but Tara deliberately didn't let their look draw out. Earlier, Jack had wisely left out the real reason for his change of heart when he'd explained himself to the laird. No one had any idea of what had transpired between them, and since it would never be repeated, it was best it stayed that way.

Lifting the goblet to her lips, Tara took a sip and reminded herself that she'd be wise not to steal too many glances in Jack's direction.

With the stares she was attracting this evening, it would be a relief when supper was over and she could retire to her bedchamber.

"We've readied the laird's birlinn, Lady Tara," Captain MacDonald spoke then, drawing her attention. "We shall leave at first light tomorrow, if that suits ye?"

Tara nodded. "Aye, thank ye." Impatience surged up then, churning inside her. As much as MacDonald's words reassured her, she suddenly wished that they could depart *now* rather than in the morning. She cast Jack another quick, darting look then. He was speaking to the man next to him, his brow furrowed.

Will ye leave without saying goodbye?

Tara's mouth thinned. The man had abducted her; she owed him nothing. And yet, after what they'd shared the night before, it felt wrong, somehow, to slip away without speaking to him.

"How many men are ye taking with ye?" Loch asked, catching his captain's words from a few feet away.

MacDonald cast him a sidelong glance. "Four … along with eight local lads to help row."

"That's not enough," Astrid cut in. "Ye'll be sailing into the wolves' den … ye should take at least double that number of men-at-arms."

The captain's lean face tightened. He clearly didn't like Astrid challenging him on this. "Last I looked, I took orders from the laird of Duart, not his sister," he replied coldly.

"Ye take orders from *both* of us," she countered.

"My sister has a point, Finn," Loch said, cocking an eyebrow. "Despite that ye travel in goodwill, Macleans aren't welcome at Dùn Ara. Take thirteen of yer best men … they're all capable of wielding an oar, trimming the sail, or steering the galley." The laird paused there, casting Tara a rueful look, before continuing. "It would also be prudent not to wear any clan sashes for the journey or carry anything that marks ye as Macleans."

"I'd already thought of that," MacDonald replied, his expression still pinched. "And I planned to take just four warriors so that we didn't attract too much attention to ourselves … but if ye wish otherwise, so be it."

"I do," Loch replied firmly. He then turned back to where Mairi was conversing with their new chieftain. From the snatches of words Tara caught, Black was regaling her with tales of his adventures.

Meanwhile, an awkward silence settled at Tara's end of the table.

God's teeth, it was uncomfortable enough sitting here surrounded by Macleans without dealing with the tension between her supper companions. She'd have been blind not to notice how Astrid and Captain MacDonald glowered at each other. It was made worse too by the fact that Jack's elder brother, Rae—a quiet man it seemed—had nothing to say.

Reaching for her goblet of wine, Tara took a sip, grateful that supper was being served. The sooner she ate, the sooner she could leave.

Cait, the red-haired maid, appeared then. The woman met Tara's eye briefly as she set a tureen down at their end of the table and gave a slight nod.

Tara favored her with a brittle smile in response.

The tension between Astrid and the captain made her feel as if she were caught in a vise. Glancing at MacDonald's profile, she cleared her throat. "Captain," she ventured, eager to ease the awkwardness. "Have ye lived at Duart a long while?"

His sharp hazel gaze flicked back to her. "I came to foster here when I was a lad … but was away at war for many years … so I suppose, the answer is 'aye'."

"And which branch of the MacDonalds do ye hail from?"

"Of Dunnyveg, upon the Isle of Islay." MacDonald's mouth quirked. "I'm not kin to the family ye are about to marry into, if that's what ye are wondering."

"I was, actually," she admitted, relieved that the tension at the table seemed to have eased a little.

More food arrived. Oath-taking was an important business, and so the cooks had dug deep into the last of the winter stores. Cait had returned and now set a large wheel of aged cheese down before the laird. As she did so, she caught Logan Black's eye.

The new laird of Croggan gave the woman a long, appreciative look and then flashed her a roguish grin. Many lasses would have blushed, yet Cait held his gaze boldly, her full lips lifting at the corners.

Tara swallowed a wry smile at the maid's response. Cait might not have wished to wed again, but she could enjoy a man's attention, it seemed.

Without being able to stop herself, Tara's gaze traveled across the hall then, to Jack—again. He ate silently, not joining in the conversation and merriment around him as the other men-at-arms helped themselves to food.

Is this how it ends?

Tara's breathing grew shallow then. If she let things be, this eve would be the last time she'd ever set eyes on Jack Maclean.

Surely, ye aren't lamenting such a thing?

No, of course, she wasn't. Yet despite that she'd been chafing at the bit all day to make for home, Tara now hesitated.

There were loose ends that had to be tied up.

She couldn't depart from Duart Castle without bidding Jack farewell.

26: MY PUNISHMENT

TARA RETURNED TO her bedchamber after supper. However, she didn't remain there. Instead, she retrieved her cloak from its peg next to the door, wrapped it around her, and descended the stairs to the lowest level of the keep. Cait would be up later, once the last of those still celebrating vacated the great hall. The maid would then help Tara undress and ready herself for bed.

But in the meantime, Tara had a small measure of freedom, and she intended to use it.

Tomorrow at dawn, she'd be on her way home—but before she left, she needed to look her former captor in the eye once more, so she could close the door on this short but tumultuous chapter of her life.

Venturing out of the keep, and minding her tender ankle on the steps, Tara found herself in the inner courtyard, where she paused a moment to survey her surroundings. Ringed by arched windows, its walls covered in ivy and climbing roses that were yet to bloom, the cobbled space was empty at this hour. Cool air feathered across her face as she glanced up at the sky. The last of a fiery dusk was starting to fade.

This was a peaceful spot in a busy keep; Tara wouldn't have minded seating herself by the well to enjoy the sunset. However, she didn't linger. Instead, she made for the archway that led through to the outer courtyard, where the guard barracks were housed. Perhaps she'd find Jack there. He'd left the great hall shortly after supper, not staying on to drink and dice as some of the other men had.

She couldn't blame him. As Jack would have anticipated, his return had brought him shame and punishment. But it could have been much worse for him—and it was a storm he'd have to ride out.

Tara had just entered the outer courtyard when she spied Captain MacDonald, who'd just stalked out of the keep through the main doors and was now descending the stone steps two at a time.

"Lady Tara," he greeted her, his gaze skimming over her cloaked form. "Are ye going somewhere?"

She shook her head. "Not until tomorrow."

"It's almost dark ... best head indoors."

"I will," she assured him, lifting her chin at his authoritative tone, "However, I wish to find Jack first. Can ye tell me where he is?"

The captain's eyebrows raised. Clearly, he found it odd that having just escaped her captor, she'd want to see him. Indeed, it was, but Tara let her words lie. She didn't have to explain herself to this man.

A pause followed before MacDonald shrugged. "Ye'll find him up on the eastern walls," he replied, his hazel eyes narrowing. "Mind yer step up there though ... the stone is mossy."

Reaching the top of the wall, Tara stopped for a moment to take in the expansive view. Her home, Dùn Ara, had a high vantage point, but it was nothing like this. From Duart, she could see nearly all the way to Oban. No wonder Loch Maclean's forebears had built a fortress here—no one could sail the Sound of Mull unobserved.

The evening was a lovely one, without a breath of wind. The last of the sunset glowed upon the ridges of the mountains to the west. To the east, she spied a cog moored just offshore, near the cove beneath the headland.

The *Revenge Tide* floated on the calm water, its single mast piercing the gloaming. At the sight of Logan Black's ship, Tara's pulse quickened. The cog reminded her how differently things could have gone—if Jack hadn't lost his wits over the woman he'd stolen away.

Heat blossomed in Tara's belly as she recalled the things he'd told her, the way he'd touched her. They were memories—both delicious and forbidden—that she would keep close for the rest of her days.

Shaking her head to clear it, for such thoughts would muddle her mind this evening, she started walking down the wall then. Ahead, she spied a tall figure holding a pike, standing at the northeastern edge of the ramparts. Tara's traitorous pulse quickened. Even clad in boiled leather with an iron helmet upon his head, she recognized Jack instantly.

Doubt wreathed up then.

Maybe Captain MacDonald was right to look askance at her. Coming up here wasn't appropriate. She should let things lie between her and Jack. Bidding him farewell wasn't necessary. Deciding that, indeed, she'd retrace her steps, Tara inched backward.

However, the scuff of her boot on stone caught Jack's attention, and he turned swiftly, his eyes snapping wide at the sight of her. "Tara," he greeted her brusquely. "Ye shouldn't be up here."

Tara's chin kicked up, and inwardly berating herself, she resumed walking toward him once more. "I know … but I wanted to say goodbye."

Tension rippled over his face. "That isn't wise, lass."

"No." Tara halted once more before pulling a face. "I realize that now … but since I'm here …" Her voice trailed off, and she suddenly felt foolish. An awkward silence fell then, and she cleared her throat. "Farewell, Maclean."

His mouth quirked, even as his gaze shadowed. "Goodbye, Vixen."

Tara snorted. "I can't believe I'm admitting this … but I think I might miss being called that."

His smile widened. "Aye?"

"Aye … but don't let it go to yer head, ye arrogant cur."

Jack's expression sobered, and he put his pike aside and moved nearer then, stopping when there was barely a foot between them. "Don't worry, I won't."

His nearness made Tara's pulse skitter.

Goose, she chided herself. *Going in search of him was one of yer daftest ideas ever.*

"I won't forget ye, Tara Mackinnon," Jack admitted then, his voice roughening.

Tara sucked in a sharp breath. "Don't say that," she whispered, even as heat flushed over her. She needed to step back, to create some distance between them, but her feet wouldn't move.

"I can't help myself." He lifted a hand, stroking her cheek.

Tara stopped breathing entirely then, and she froze to the spot. It took everything she had not to lean into his touch.

Heartbeats passed before Jack stepped forward, bridging the remaining gap between them. His head then lowered, and his mouth captured hers.

The kiss was achingly gentle, and he didn't hurry it. His tongue slowly mated with hers, exploring her mouth with a sensuality that made Tara's toes curl inside her boots. He didn't seem to care that they stood on the walls, for all the world to see.

And for a few moments, she didn't either.

The Saints forgive her, he tasted good. She wanted to drown in him, to feel his strong, tender hands claim her body again. But that wasn't to be. The night they'd shared under that sheltering oak by the ancient stones while the rain pattered down around them shouldn't have happened. They both knew it. And so shouldn't this kiss. They were pushing the boundaries here, yet they did it anyway.

Tara lifted her hand, her fingers sliding against the hard surface of the boiled-leather breastplate he wore, traveling up to the naked skin of his throat.

Her touch roused him, and Jack lifted his mouth from hers.

He didn't draw away from Tara, not yet. Instead, he cupped her cheeks with his hands, his gaze roaming over her face as if committing every detail to memory. She did the same, taking in the curve of his lips, the slant of his aquiline nose, and the sweep of his strong jaw. Lastly, she gazed into his eyes. Fern-green and glistening with emotion.

"I have to go," she whispered. Her feet unstuck themselves then, and she moved back.

Jack let his hands fall from her face. Lips parting, he took a step forward, as if intending to follow her, but then pulled himself up short. "Then go," he said hoarsely.

Their gazes locked one last time before Tara turned on her heel and hurried away.

Jack watched Tara depart.

Even so, every fiber of his being howled for him to follow the lass, to haul her into his arms, to kiss her again until they were both gasping for breath.

But what would happen then?

Wanting Tara Mackinnon was impossible. And if he didn't find a way to rein in his need for her, he'd destroy himself.

This is my punishment ... for stealing her away. Jack's gut clenched. Aye, and it was a cruel one indeed, but fitting considering what he'd done. He was in agony. No punishment Loch could have ever dished up would hurt more than this.

Growling a curse, Jack turned around and stalked back to his post. He then picked up the pike he'd put aside when Tara approached him and faced the sea once more. However, this time, he couldn't focus on anything but the painful thud of his heart.

"Jack." A man's gruff voice intruded then.

Clenching his jaw, Jack turned to face the intruder. Satan's cods, couldn't he have a few moments to pull himself together?

Apparently not, because his brother stood before him.

Arms folded over his broad chest, Rae observed him keenly.

"What do ye want?" Jack croaked.

"That's a warm greeting."

"Aye ... well, I'm not in the mood for company."

Rae inclined his head. "I just saw Tara Mackinnon fleeing indoors, her face stricken ... would that have anything to do with it?"

Jack's gut twisted, even as he turned away, his gaze fixing on the horizon once more. "Did ye want something, Rae?"

"Aye," his brother replied. "I've come up here to ask if ye wish to come home."

Jack jerked before he whipped around to face his brother once more. "What?"

Rae continued to observe him, his mouth lifting at the corners in a rare smile. "Loch did what he had to ... removing yer rank and privileges ... but ye don't have to remain at Duart if ye don't want to. Dounarwyse has always been yer *true* home."

Jack stared at him, struck dumb for a few moments, before his throat tightened. "Ye'd suffer me under the same roof?"

Rae snorted. "Aye, we're kin, after all."

Silence fell atop the wall then as the brothers continued to eye each other.

They'd fallen out years earlier when Jack took issue with Rae's handling of affairs after their father's death. He'd scorned his serious elder brother—the one who chose stability over revenge. Every rare meeting since had been strained. However, Rae's offer made guilt stab Jack through the chest.

Bitterness and hate had truly skewed how he'd seen the world. But now, Jack saw the truth.

Rae was a stalwart chieftain who'd doggedly held Dounarwyse for the past fifteen years, even while Kendric Mackinnon bayed at his borders. He'd been little more than a lad when he'd stepped into the role and had done the best he could.

Even so, Jack found it hard to believe his brother actually wanted him back. "Are ye *sure* ye'd suffer me underfoot?" he asked warily.

Rae's half-smile widened. "Ye wouldn't be … I need someone with battle experience to captain my guard. Loch's given me a host of warriors, but they're unruly, and my current captain can't manage them."

Jack considered Rae's words, even as a kernel of warmth unfurled deep in his chest. He was still tied in knots over Tara, but his brother's offer touched him. He was close to Loch and hoped his disgrace wouldn't create a permanent gulf between them. For years, the three men—Loch, Jack, and Finn—had been as close as brothers, fighting for Scotland. But the war was over, and their focus and priorities were shifting like sand.

None of them could hold on to the way things had been, and now that Jack had shed his blinding need for vengeance, his own perspective on his relationship with his cousin had changed. Loch had made a fresh start at Duart with Mairi. Maybe Jack needed a new beginning as well. It was tempting, and yet he hesitated.

As such, he held his brother's gaze for a moment longer before replying, "Thank ye, Rae. I shall think on it."

27: WITH THE DAWN

"READY YERSELF TO depart at dawn."

Jack had finished his shift on the watch, and was crossing the outer courtyard toward the barracks, when a familiar voice hailed him from the shadows.

It was late, and he hadn't expected to see anyone about. Halting, he glanced right, to where Finn stepped out. His friend wore a smug smile as if he was pleased with himself about something.

However, Jack wasn't in the mood, and he frowned. "Depart for where?"

"Ye are one of the thirteen men who're coming with me to Dùn Ara."

Jack stiffened. "Loch won't allow that."

"Loch doesn't know."

Jack approached his friend, his frown sliding into a scowl. "What are ye up to?"

"Nothing," Finn replied with the air of someone who was most definitely brewing up trouble. "But Loch asked me to pick my best warriors … and ye're one."

Jack's pulse quickened. He'd just said farewell to Tara, and had spent the rest of his shift, after Rae departed, mulling over his life choices.

But now, Finn had teased him with the possibility of prolonging his contact with the woman he ached for.

There was a sane voice in the back of Jack's head that told him he should refuse, should tell Finn to choose someone else. Yet, another voice, louder and stronger, overrode it. He was only putting off the inevitable, but if he got to spend one more day in Tara's company, it would give him a day's worth of memories he'd treasure.

Nonetheless, he checked himself. "Loch won't like it."

"Loch put ye under my charge," his friend countered smoothly. "He'll understand when I explain it to him." Finn paused then, pulling a face. "He's too busy at present ... readying us to face the Mackinnons, to give ye too much thought."

Jack frowned. That seemed true enough. Upon his arrival at Duart that morning, he'd noted the castle was busier than when he'd left. The Duart Guard had swelled to nearly fifty men-at-arms. The keep's weaponsmith toiled long hours, readying pikes, dirks, and swords, the clang of steel echoing through the outer courtyard, while the local blacksmith had delivered a haul of arrowheads that very afternoon.

More men and weapons weren't enough though. What the Macleans really needed were allies.

During supper, Jack had seen the intense look on Loch's face as he'd spoken with Logan Black. His cousin was canny indeed, for he'd just gotten himself a new chieftain. Black had a good-sized crew, many of whom would follow their captain, and once he arrived upon his new lands, he'd quickly attract men keen to serve him— men he'd train to fight.

Aye, Loch had a lot on his mind at the moment. Even so, Jack still hesitated. "And ye trust me ... after what I just did?" he challenged. "Ye don't think I'll try to run off with Lady Tara again."

Finn smirked. "And will ye?"

Jack's mouth thinned. They both knew he wouldn't. He studied Finn's face then, trying to glean what was going on beyond the mask. It was impossible to know though, and he was too tired to argue. Huffing a sigh, he nodded. "Very well ... have it yer way. I'll be there."

Tara spent her night at Duart Castle tossing and turning.

Lying upon her comfortable bed, covered in crisp sheets and a luxuriously heavy quilt, she should have slept easily—especially after everything she'd been through—but her mind was too active.

Cait had retired upon the narrow cot in the corner of the bedchamber. Her maid also slept restlessly, and Tara had slipped into a fitful doze when the sound of the door clicking shut roused her.

Propping herself up on her elbows, Tara's gaze traveled to where Cait had been sleeping, only to find her cot empty. The fire had died down to embers but cast enough light for her to see that the woman had slipped away.

There was a chamber pot behind a screen in the opposite corner of the room, yet maybe Cait had decided to use a privy elsewhere. Or perhaps she was hungry and had gone down to the kitchen to fetch herself something to eat.

Tara thought about putting on some clothes and doing the same—only she wasn't hungry. Instead, she lay there waiting for Cait to return to the bedchamber, her mind churning.

It had been a mistake to go up to the walls to bid Jack farewell, for the attraction between them still smoldered, and it had taken very little for it to reignite.

His sensual kiss had made her yearn for more.

Muttering a curse, Tara rolled over onto her side and buried her face in the pillow. *Enough of this*, she railed at herself. *Go to sleep!*

Eventually, lying like that made it hard to breathe, so she rolled over onto her back and stared up at the shadowed rafters, willing sleep to come. But it wasn't to be. Time crept by, and although Tara dozed fitfully, sleep eluded her. Cait didn't return to the chamber either, and by the time the first rays of dawn light edged around the corners of the sacking covering the windows, Tara was gritty-eyed and grumpy.

Rolling out of bed, she splashed cold water on her face before going through her morning ablutions. She then pulled on her laundered clothes that Cait had brought up the eve before.

She could have done with the maid's help to tie the laces, but since the woman seemed to have disappeared, Tara managed herself. All the same, it took her longer than usual to dress.

Irritated that Cait had abandoned her, Tara gulped down some boiled, cooled, water from an earthen cup next to her bed before slinging on her cloak.

She then tested out her ankle. It felt better this morning, if a little stiff. A day's rest had helped it heal a little.

The time had come to go—even though she'd only been at Duart Castle a day, it was long enough.

Leaving the bedchamber, Tara descended the winding stairwell, her way illuminated by flickering cressets. Arriving downstairs, she found her escort ready and waiting in the outer bailey. The laird wasn't with them, and neither was Mairi or Astrid. Tara wasn't surprised. It was still early; the sun hadn't yet cleared the eastern walls.

Nonetheless, what did surprise her was that Jack was among the group of men waiting for her.

After her restless night, Tara's step faltered at the sight of him standing behind Captain MacDonald, and she came to an abrupt halt. Their gazes fused for an instant before she glanced over at MacDonald.

The captain was scowling, his mouth compressed with irritation.

"Sorry I'm late, Captain," she greeted him. "My maid disappeared ... so I didn't have any help with dressing."

"We need to go," MacDonald muttered, "or we'll miss the tide."

Tara nodded, flicking a questioning glance in Jack's direction once more. "I'm ready."

The mood was tense as the group filed out of the keep, passing under the guard tower and down the incline beyond.

Tara's escort all had grim expressions upon their faces. She couldn't blame them really, for they were Macleans about to venture into Mackinnon territory. She also couldn't help but notice that they were all well-armed, with dirks and polearms. However, the warriors wore no clan plaid or anything that would mark them as Macleans.

The group made its way over the headland, taking the steep, winding track that led down to the crescent-shaped white-sand beach beneath. Duart Bay was a sheltered spot, and below, Tara could make out the outline of a small birlinn. There was no dock here, so they'd pulled the single-masted galley high onto the sand.

"Did ye sleep well?" Jack asked Tara as he waited for her to pick her way down a particularly rough section of track.

Tara glanced up to meet his eye and then pulled a face. "Not a wink."

He harrumphed. "Me neither."

Her boot slipped on a loose stone, and Jack's hand shot out to help her. Without hesitation, she took it, steadying herself. Her fingers curled around his, and relief flooded through her.

"I didn't think I'd see ye again," she murmured as they continued down the perilous track that hugged the rugged cliff-face. "Neither did I," Jack admitted, his tone rueful. "Until Finn informed me of it, late yestereve." He paused then. "I don't think Loch knows … but I didn't argue. It was a chance to see ye again, and I selfishly took it."

Despite herself, Tara's heart fluttered at these words.

As they neared the beach below, and the way grew easier, Jack could have let go of her hand, yet he didn't—and Tara didn't release her grip either. Once they stepped onto the beach, there would be no excuse to touch, but for now, she continued to pretend she was unsteady on her feet.

Meanwhile, she caught sight of a wooden rowboat below, with what looked like four occupants, on the water beyond Duart Bay. They were rowing out toward where the *Revenge Tide* had anchored. Tara couldn't see most of those onboard clearly, although she caught sight of a big man with brown hair at the stern.

It seemed that Logan Black was also keen to make an early start, to journey to his new holding at Croggan.

Spying her, Black raised a hand and gave a lazy wave.

Jack snorted softly. "Black's looking pleased with himself this morn."

"Aye … ye would too," she replied archly. "Loch was generous indeed."

"He was, but his act wasn't selfless. He's gathering allies … and he'll likely need them."

Tara's belly tensed. "I shall keep my word," she said, meeting his eye once more. "My father will never know what really happened."

She'd hoped her words would reassure him, yet Jack's brow furrowed and his green eyes shadowed. "I don't like ye taking responsibility for my behavior," he growled. "Or having ye lie for me."

Tara's mouth curved. "No, but ye'll just have to suffer it, Maclean. This isn't about ye anyway … but about lessening the bloodshed … on both sides." Her expression sobered then, worry tightening her belly. "I likely can't stop my father from attacking Dounarwyse, but *maybe* I can prevent him from swearing to kill every person living there."

Jack's features tightened at these words, yet after a brief pause, he nodded.

They reached the beach then, their boots sinking into the powdery sand, and Jack slid his hand from hers.

Waiting a few yards back, Tara watched as the men heaved and pushed the flat-bottomed birlinn off the dry sand and down to the tideline. It was a sleek craft with an eagle's head carved into the prow. When the first waves lapped against the hull, Captain MacDonald turned and motioned to Tara, beckoning her down. "The *Sea Eagle* awaits ye, Lady Tara," he called.

Tara walked toward him. Jack kept pace with her, and when she reached the birlinn, he offered her his hand once more, helping her into the boat. However, as soon as she was safely onboard, he released her.

The men pushed the *Sea Eagle* into the water, their grunts and shouts mingling with the cry of the gulls that swooped overhead. The tide had recently reached its highest point and was now starting to ebb. Once they were in the shallows, the last of her escort scrambled onboard and took up their long oars, propelling the galley out of the bay. This birlinn was one of the smallest and lightest Tara had seen, with room for just twelve oarsmen. However, anything bigger couldn't be dragged easily onto the sand at Duart Bay.

Once they were in open water, they unfurled the single sail.

There was a brisk wind out here that made Tara's skin tingle. She was grateful she'd braided her hair before leaving her bedchamber, although the salty wind still managed to pull tendrils free and whip them in her eyes.

Seated near the stern, out of the way, while the men worked, Tara looked back at Duart Castle. It loomed overhead, its sturdy walls illuminated by the morning sun.

The nervousness that had tightened her stomach earlier, when she'd spoken to Jack about the lie that she was about to tell her father, increased, tying her belly in knots now.

She didn't like the idea of deceiving him, yet she knew how vengeful her father could be. If he ever discovered a Maclean had stolen her away from Tobermory, he'd never let it go.

He'd make it his life's purpose to destroy them.

Tearing her gaze from Duart, even as foreboding prickled her skin, Tara glanced Jack's way. He had his back to her as he trimmed the sail. Meanwhile, MacDonald bellowed orders as the *Sea Eagle* rode the swells and tacked her way north.

Even though she knew she shouldn't, her attention lingered upon Jack, noting the way the sun caught the red strands in his dark-auburn hair and the flex of his powerful shoulder muscles under his billowing lèine as he worked.

Tara's pulse quickened then, and as when they'd held hands earlier, her heart gave a flutter. *Daft woman*, she chided herself as she cut her gaze away. *Put yer eyes back in their sockets.*

Jack Maclean had stolen enough of her attention of late—she now needed to focus on what lay ahead.

28: SET IN STONE

THEY TRAVELED SWIFTLY up the coast, with the wind behind them. Presently, the birlinn passed a broch, perched upon a green headland, overlooking the Sound.

"That's Dounarwyse, isn't it?" Tara called out to Jack, who'd moved up to the stern and was now coiling some rope. Glancing up from his task, he followed her gaze.

A smile flowered across his face, one that dimpled his cheeks and made the corners of his eyes crease. "Aye," he replied, raising his voice to be heard over the slap of the water hitting the hull and the screech of gulls that followed the birlinn. "Bonnie, isn't it?"

"Aye," she agreed with an answering smile. Indeed, the castle's grey-stone walls had a grace to them, and the steep drop to the water below was covered in a wash of bluebells this time of year. It was much smaller than Duart, but a sturdy fortress nonetheless, with thick encircling walls to hold off attacks.

Tara's pulse started to pound as she recalled her father boasting many a time over the years that one day Dounarwyse would be his. She'd once smiled at his words, but she didn't now.

After spending time with the Macleans, her view on things was far more muddied—and if she were honest, she thought her clan should leave the Macleans of Dounarwyse be.

Finishing his task, Jack moved up and took the place of the warrior at the steering oar, attached to the rudder, at the stern. He then lowered himself onto the seat next to Tara. They were so close, she could feel the heat of his thigh.

"My brother surprised me yestereve," Jack said, his voice lower now that they were seated next to each other. "He's offered me the position of Captain of the Guard at Dounarwyse."

Tara inclined her head. "Really? Will ye accept?"

"I haven't decided."

"Why the hesitation?"

Jack pulled a face. "I'm not sure … maybe loyalty to Loch. We've been through a lot over the years together."

Tara nodded. She could understand his reluctance. However, she instinctively knew that Jack needed a change. "Ye'd still be loyal to Loch," she pointed out, "but yer brother likely needs ye too. Maybe ye should say 'aye'."

Their gazes held before Jack's expression softened, his lips tilting up at the corners. "Perhaps I should."

Silence fell between them, as they watched Dounarwyse slide by, and Jack concentrated on steering the birlinn. Tara glanced over her shoulder then to see what the other occupants of the galley were up to.

Captain MacDonald was still shouting instructions to his crew. Despite that the wind had caught the sail, six oarsmen worked to propel the birlinn through the water. It was no wonder they were traveling so fast.

Tara's gaze rested upon MacDonald, her brow furrowing. She found the man an enigma. There was something both sharp and aloof about him, and he was almost impossible to read.

Turning back to the stern, she leaned a little closer to Jack, catching his eye. "I was seated between Captain MacDonald and Lady Astrid at supper yestereve," she said, giving him a meaningful look.

Jack gave a soft snort. "Aye … I didn't envy ye that. If looks could kill, those two would have been gasping their last."

"So, they detest each other?"

"Aye."

"Why?"

Jack sighed. "It's a longstanding hate, lass ... one that took seed over a decade ago." He glanced MacDonald's way as if checking to see if he was listening. However, the captain's attention was still focused elsewhere. "Around a year before Finn, Loch, and I answered the Bruce's call, Finn was sweet on a local lass. Margaret Garvie was her name, although we all knew her as Maggie. She was a flighty wee thing and best friends with Astrid." Jack paused here as if telling the tale pained him slightly. A moment later, his jaw tightened, and he pushed on. "I'm not sure how all the events unfolded, for Finn never fully confided in me ... but as I understand it, Finn stole a rowboat from a fisherman at Craignure one summer's eve and took Maggie out onto the Sound to impress her. Somehow, they got into trouble. Maggie fell into the water and drowned."

Tara frowned, darting another glance in MacDonald's direction. She couldn't imagine the man 'sweet' on anyone. He was too calculating, too cynical. Yet perhaps the tragedy had made him that way.

"How awful," she murmured.

"That was only the start of it," Jack replied. "The locals blamed Finn for Maggie's death. Fisherfolk are a superstitious lot and have great respect for the sea. To lose one of their own to it was a terrible thing. Some wondered if he'd been daft enough to whistle out on the water ... and call up the wind ... while others even said he'd drowned her deliberately when she rebuffed his advances." Jack halted, his mouth thinning. "Astrid was among those who believed he'd played her foul. She and Maggie were as close as sisters ... and she was heartbroken by her death."

"So, what happened?" Tara asked, her breathing growing shallow. Although she barely knew Astrid and MacDonald, there was something about their tale that drew her in.

"A group of grief-stricken and enraged locals tried to lynch Finn," Jack said, his voice lowering. "They'd have hanged him from the crossroads north of Craignure too if the laird hadn't got wind of it. He saved Finn's life ...

and upon hearing his side of the tale, Iain Maclean absolved him of any blame."

"So, Finn didn't kill her?"

"He insisted that it was an accident. Maggie went swimming and got into difficulty. He tried to save her yet failed." Jack's features tightened slightly. "The laird and Finn met in private, so no one else knows what exactly was said ... and Finn has never spoken of it." He paused then, his expression turning rueful as he added. "Of course, it never helped that Finn hadn't made himself popular over the years ... the three of us—Loch, Finn, and I—were known as troublemakers locally."

Tara arched an eyebrow. "Why doesn't that surprise me?" she murmured, casting one more look MacDonald's way.

The captain had finished barking orders at his men and turned toward the stern now. His gaze narrowed as it settled upon her and Jack.

Once they sailed by Tobermory, Tara's belly started pitching nervously. Dùn Ara was just a short distance away.

Likewise, the mood onboard the birlinn grew subdued. The men ceased conversing amongst themselves, their faces tensing as they continued west.

Mull's northernmost tip was lovely indeed, with a mountainous, rocky coastline and dense green foliage spilling down to the water in places.

It was a coast that Tara knew well, a landscape she loved.

But she couldn't enjoy it today. All she could think about was that she would soon stand before her father—and spin him lies.

Few folk were brave enough to attempt to hoodwink Kendric Mackinnon. Tara broke into a cold sweat just at the thought of his cool silver gaze pinning her to the spot. However, she'd promised Loch she'd do this, and she knew in her gut this was the right choice.

Aye, as much as she loved her father, she wasn't blind to his viciousness. He'd think nothing of leaving Mull awash with blood if he discovered what Jack had done.

And if she were honest, she was disappointed that he hadn't come after her on horseback, tracking her abductor across Mull as she'd hoped. She'd been relieved to hear that he'd taken his birlinn south, stopping at Duart to find out if anyone there had seen her, yet his behavior wasn't what she'd expected.

She'd thought her father would tear the isle apart with his bare hands to find her.

Finally, they rounded the last cove, and there, sitting high upon its perch of stone, was her home. Dùn Ara's thick curtain walls of stone and lime gleamed in the bright spring sun. Just like the other fortresses that studded Mull's craggy coast, the Mackinnon stronghold held a commanding view over the sea and the land around it.

If anyone tried to attack—and a few had attempted to lay siege to Dùn Ara over the years—they'd see them coming.

One of the men nearest her muttered an oath under his breath. Tara tensed, yet she refrained from cutting the warrior a look of censure. She understood why being this close to the fortress unnerved him.

She didn't speak to Jack as he angled the *Sea Eagle* toward the thin stacked-stone jetty that protruded like a spear from the rocky headland. Her father's birlinn, a much larger galley that held forty oarsmen, was moored there, and there was another, large, birlinn tied up next to it—a craft Tara didn't recognize.

Her brow furrowed. It looked as if her father had guests.

Beyond the jetty was a stony inlet with noosts, where a row of colorful fishing boats had been pulled up into the hollows above the tide mark.

Jack maneuvered the *Sea Eagle* alongside the jetty, while two other warriors threw ropes up to tie up the boat.

"Ye'll understand if we don't disembark with ye, Lady Tara?" Captain MacDonald said, approaching the stern.

"Aye ... yer arrival will have been noted," she replied, rising from the plank she'd been sitting on. "I shall not linger over my farewell."

"That's wise." MacDonald stepped close then, his hazel eyes narrowed. "Not all decisions are set in stone, Lady Tara," he said then, his voice lowering. Tara frowned, not grasping his meaning, yet he continued. "Should ye decide yer upcoming marriage isn't what ye want, ye can walk away from it."

Behind her, Jack murmured an oath, but the captain ignored him. "We shall moor at Tobermory overnight and depart as soon as the sun rises," MacDonald went on. "And if ye wish to, ye can join us."

Tara stared at MacDonald. Had she misheard him? "Surely, the Maclean clan-chief would have something to say about this?" she said, recovering from her shock. Indeed, his offer went against the promise she'd made to Loch Maclean, and it would ensure she broke forever with her kin.

MacDonald's eyes glinted. "Aye, but there would be a silver lining too ... one Loch would appreciate."

His words were cryptic, yet Tara was no fool. "My father would lose the support of the MacDonalds of Sleat, ye mean?"

The captain smiled, although his gaze remained sharp. "Aye."

Tara frowned. The man was sly, although he'd misjudged the depth of her loyalty to her kin. She'd not let her father down. She'd promised to wed Callum MacDonald, and she would go through with it.

"Enough of this nonsense, Finn," Jack muttered, rising to his feet. "Ye are wasting time."

MacDonald didn't answer; he merely inclined his head and stepped back.

Heart pounding in her ears, Tara turned away from the captain. Did he really think her capable of running away from her clan? To what end, exactly? A hot, prickly wave of mortification swept over her then. Had MacDonald seen her and Jack upon the wall together?

Wordlessly, Jack vaulted up onto the stone jetty and then reached down and grasped her hand, pulling her from the birlinn.

And as Tara got her footing, their bodies brushed for an instant.

Righting herself, she stepped back, drawing her cloak about her. She glanced up at the castle then, her gaze alighting on the company of warriors that was now descending the winding path, chain mail and steel glinting in the sun. "Ye need to go," she said, anxiety coiling in her breast.

Jack nodded. However, his gaze held hers for a heartbeat longer.

"Farewell, Jack," she whispered.

A nerve flickered in his cheek. With MacDonald and the other men looking on, and all within earshot, he could say nothing without incriminating himself. So, Jack stepped away from her, dropping to a crouch before he jumped back into the birlinn.

He resumed his position at the steering oar, although his gaze never left Tara's face.

Unmoving, she watched MacDonald's men unmoor the birlinn, and then twelve of them took their places at their oars, propelling the streamlined craft away from the stone jetty.

And still, Tara remained there, watching.

Jack raised a hand, as did she. Then, drawing in a deep, steadying breath, she dragged her gaze from his face and turned.

The company of men had reached the foot of the rocky outcrop now and were marching toward the jetty. However, they were too late to greet the *Sea Eagle*, for she was already ten yards away, and gathering speed fast.

Tara released a deep sigh. *I'm home.* Aye, she could now leave her ordeal behind her and look to the future once more.

A tense reunion with her father.

A marriage to Callum MacDonald.

Squaring her shoulders, and steeling herself for what was to come, Tara stepped forward to meet the Dùn Ara Guard.

29: BETRAYAL

"SO, YE RAN away, did ye?" Kendric Mackinnon's powerful voice vibrated through the clan-chief's solar. "Ye merely picked up yer skirts and fled out the back of the ribbon merchant's shop?"

Tara nodded, even as her pulse hammered. She'd kept her story simple, telling her father that she'd stolen a horse in Tobermory and ridden south, taking refuge with kind-hearted farmers along the way, before a patrol of Maclean warriors caught her and took her to Duart Castle. There, Loch Maclean had decided to send his rival's errant daughter home.

Her father didn't reply immediately, something that made Tara even more nervous. She'd told her tale convincingly, but now she doubted her skill as a liar.

Resisting the urge to fidget where she stood, Tara cast a glance around the solar. It was an intimidating chamber that represented her father—from the array of axes, shields, and claidheamh-mòrs upon the walls, to the row of three glowering boar heads above the huge hearth, all beasts that the Mackinnon had slain himself.

But she and the clan-chief weren't alone this afternoon. Her brother and her betrothed were both present, watching the exchange between father and daughter silently.

Tara had expected Bran to join them, although she was surprised that Callum was here. It was his galley she'd seen moored next to her father's earlier.

Her brother looked on, his silvery gaze slightly narrowed, while her betrothed's face was set in grim lines that made him look older than his five and twenty years.

"I'm sorry," she said finally, casting an apologetic look at her husband-to-be when it was clear her father was going to let the silence draw out even longer. "I panicked."

Callum's eyebrows crashed together. "Ye *panicked*?"

"I went in to buy some ribbon, and while I was in the shop, everything suddenly became … too much." Tara deliberately lowered her voice then, injecting a pleading note into it. "I didn't think … I just ran."

"Well, ye—"

"Don't indulge her, MacDonald." The clan-chief, who'd been standing with his back to her, at the open window, swiveled on his heel, his steel-colored gaze fixing upon Tara. "We all know she's lying."

Tara's heart leaped into her throat. She cast a glance at her brother, yet Bran's face gave nothing away. Looking at her father once more, she took a step toward him. "Da, I—"

"Don't bother," he growled. "I've heard enough."

"But I—"

"Ramsay!" the Mackinnon shouted then. "Get yer arse in here."

Tara stilled. *Ramsay?*

A moment later, the door to the solar opened, and a big dark-haired man sauntered inside.

Tara's heart dropped to her boots.

"Did ye hear my daughter's tale?" Kendric demanded.

Ramsay smirked. "Aye, and an artful one it was too."

"Ye'll note it's vastly different to the story ye told me."

"Aye, well … mine is truth, and hers is fiction."

Heat ignited in the pit of Tara's belly then as she recovered from the shock of seeing the outlaw standing in the clan-chief's solar as if he belonged there. She then rounded on her father. "What is this villain doing here?"

Kendric cocked an eyebrow. "Excuse me?"

"He tried to *rape* me!"

A beat of silence followed before Bran uncoiled his lanky form and rose to his feet. "What?"

Callum shot the younger man a look of caution and placed a hand on his arm.

Meanwhile, Kendric's face turned to stone as he focused on Ramsay once more. "Ye omitted to tell me that."

The outlaw was no longer smirking, although he held the clan-chief's eye boldly. "Another lie," he replied, folding meaty arms over his barrel chest. "As I said … we ran into yer daughter and Jack Maclean, southwest of Ben More. She was hysterical and told us Maclean had stolen her away. We tried to rescue her, but Maclean fought my men off … and I barely escaped with my life."

"How many of ye were there?" Bran demanded.

Ramsay cast the younger man an irritated look. "Five."

Bran snorted. "Five against one … that's some odds."

Ramsay's heavy brow furrowed.

"My son has a point," Kendric murmured. "How is it, he bested ye?"

"Jack Maclean's a wicked fighter … a seasoned warrior," Ramsay grumbled.

"Maclean had some help from me," Tara announced then. It was clear her lie had been uncovered. However, she wasn't going to let her father believe this bastard's poison. "I smacked Ramsay in the head with a stone and sent him running."

Bran smirked at this, while Ramsay's face went dark red.

"Did ye, lass?" Her father turned to look at her once more, and it took every bit of courage not to wilt under the force of his glare. "So, ye admit ye spoke falsely to me then?"

Tara drew in a slow, steadying breath. Hurt arrowed through her, constricting her chest. Why hadn't he drawn his dirk and slit Ramsay's throat upon hearing that he'd tried to rape her? Her brother appeared more upset by it than her father. "Aye," she replied huskily. "But I have good reason."

Her father's gaze hardened. "Let's hear it then."

Tara swallowed, squaring her shoulders as she faced him down. "I don't want our clans to go to war, Da ... that's why I didn't tell ye the truth."

Her father's silver eyes narrowed into glittering slits, and she felt his gathering anger. "Ye would defend a *Maclean*?"

She shook her head. "No ... but ye must wonder why the enemy delivered me safely home?"

A muscle flexed in her father's jaw. "Aye," he admitted grudgingly.

Tara drew in another deep breath, relieved that he was at least willing to listen to her. "After Jack Maclean had dealt with Ramsay and his rabble, he took me southwest to Fionnphort. But when we reached the coast, Maclean's mood altered. He became withdrawn and moody. I imagined we were going to board a boat on the coast, but instead, he led me east to Duart Castle, where he confessed all to the laird."

She halted then, searching the clan-chief's face for any sign that he believed her. However, he now wore an incredulous expression.

"Are ye telling me that Loch Maclean wasn't behind this abduction?" he growled.

"He wasn't," she assured him. "He'd been looking for his cousin and was furious when he discovered what he'd done. He then organized for his men to bring me here." Her father's mouth twisted, yet Tara pushed on. "Aye, Jack Maclean did a terrible thing, but the clan-chief had no part in it. And he has tried to remedy things."

A beat of silence followed before her father responded. "Loch Maclean has already insulted me. And now he lets his cousin steal away my daughter. There will be no end to the ways that I will make the whoreson pay." Anger vibrated off the clan-chief's strong body. Kendric Mackinnon was a striking man with long thick red hair that was shot through with silver these days. When Tara had been a bairn, she thought her father the most handsome man in the world, but for the first time, she marked a harshness to his features, a cruel set to his mouth.

Panic surged through Tara at these words then. God's blood, this was exactly what she'd been trying to avoid. "But he ensured I was returned to ye safely, Da," she gasped, taking a step forward. "Surely, that's what matters?"

To her shock, her father growled a curse. "What matters, girl, is that my enemies are about to be *crushed*." His eyes glinted then. "This will make my revenge upon Loch Maclean all the sweeter. I should *thank* ye."

Tara gaped at him, hardly able to believe that he'd admit such a thing.

An unexpected blade of anger jabbed her through the belly then. Suddenly, it was as if the scales had fallen from her eyes. For the first time, she saw the truth.

She'd always believed she was her father's princess, but she wasn't. All that mattered to him was power—and his comely, fire-haired daughter had been a means to gain it. Was that why he'd indulged her all these years?

Heart pounding, she glanced over at where Ramsay MacDonald stood, legs apart, arms still folded across his chest. The outlaw wore a smug expression now, his eyes gleaming with victory.

"Da," she said finally, as she struggled to leash her temper. "That outlaw tried to rape me. Aren't ye going to—"

"Leash yer tongue," the clan-chief snapped. "Another word from yer deceitful mouth and I shall knock ye across the room."

Tara stifled a gasp. Her father had never raised a hand to her, although she knew by his tone that he didn't speak idly. Ramsay and his companions had intended to brutalize her, and her father had merely brushed it aside.

Oblivious to his daughter's upset and outrage, Kendric shifted his attention to Callum MacDonald. "I take it our agreement still stands?"

The younger man stiffened, his oak-brown eyes widening at the Mackinnon's brusque question. There was a challenge in the clan-chief's voice, as if he was daring MacDonald to try and back out of his betrothal to Tara.

Callum's throat bobbed, and he gave a wary nod.

His response clearly wasn't enthusiastic enough for Tara's father, for he scowled. "Do ye think Jack Maclean's had his way with her, is that it?"

Tara's blood started to roar in her ears. God's troth, this scene had spiraled into a nightmare.

"Well ... did he?" Callum asked, his tone hardening as a blush rose upon his cheeks.

Kendric pinned Tara with another of his gimlet stares. "Did that bastard rape ye?" he demanded.

Tara's hands curled into fists at her sides, rage pulsing through her in time with each beat of her heart.

"Did he?" her father boomed, taking a threatening step toward her.

"No," Tara rasped. And it was the truth. She'd given herself willingly to Jack. There had been no coercion of any kind.

Kendric arched an eyebrow at Callum. "Does that appease ye?"

Her betrothed hesitated, and another wave of heat doused Tara from head to toe. It seemed he didn't find her as appealing as before her abduction. However, after a few moments, Callum replied. "Aye."

"Good," the Mackinnon replied briskly. "Ye and Tara will set sail for Skye in the morning. As we originally planned, ye will wed her at Dunscaith Castle."

Callum nodded at this, although his face remained taut. Wisely, he feared Kendric Mackinnon's wrath and would do his bidding.

"But as soon as the ceremony is done with, we must bring our plans forward," the clan-chief added. "I will need the six forty-oar birlinns and the host of warriors ye promised ... *immediately*."

"Aye, Mackinnon," Callum replied, his tone clipped. "I will not break a promise."

Nausea bit at Tara's throat at this assurance, dread slicing through her anger and grief. The very thing she'd tried to avoid was about to come to pass; her father was now bent on reckoning and would attack early.

"Good." The clan-chief huffed a deep, satisfied sigh then, crossing to the sideboard, where he picked up a jug and poured himself a large cup of wine. "Now, let's toast to our alliance."

30: I HAVE TO TRY

"WHAT'S YER GAME?"

Finn glanced up from where he was tying the birlinn to the mooring. "What do ye mean?"

"Don't act all innocent." Jack crossed his arms and looked down his nose at his friend. "What was that 'Not all decisions are set in stone, Lady Tara' blather?"

"Oh, that." Finn flashed him a sly smile. "Ye were never going to say it, so I thought I would."

"Say *what* exactly?" Jack demanded, his jaw clenching. He wasn't in the mood for one of Finn's games.

Sailing away from Tara had ripped his guts out. And now, as Finn had promised Tara, instead of sailing back to Duart as planned, they'd moored at Tobermory.

Finn didn't answer Jack, turning instead to the rest of his crew, who'd disembarked onto the dock. "Remember, lads ... ye are MacDonalds of Dunnyveg, merchants on our way home from Skye. Keep yer heads down while we're here ... and try to avoid getting into any fights." Finn paused then, casting a narrowed gaze over them. "We leave at the crack of dawn. Anyone who's late will be left behind."

This comment drew wry looks and pulled faces from some of the men. However, they all nodded and mumbled their agreement.

Finn watched them move off down the dock, joining the throng heading toward the jumble of shops that lined the waterfront. He then turned back to Jack. "Do ye remember what happened on the last day at Bannockburn?" he asked, his expression sobering.

Jack frowned, confused as to why Finn wasn't answering his question. "Aye," he replied warily.

"I was distracted and didn't see the knight swing down from his destrier behind me." Finn's features tightened as he recalled the incident. "He'd have cut me in half with his broadsword if ye hadn't jumped in."

Jack nodded. "Ye cheated death that day, lad ... but why bring it up now?"

"I owe ye a blood debt, Jack."

Their gazes fused for a moment, and Jack was tempted to deny such a thing, yet the gleam in Finn's eyes warned him against making light of his words. Finn wasn't someone who spoke of personal matters easily.

Sighing heavily, Jack raked a hand through his hair. "I don't understand."

Finn's mouth tugged at the corners. "I saw ye and Lady Tara on the wall yestereve. Ye've lost yer wits over the lass, haven't ye?"

Jack's heart thumped guiltily against his ribs, yet he didn't answer. He didn't need to; his feelings were likely written all over his face.

"I thought so." Finn's voice held a rueful edge now. "Ye've dug a dirty great hole for yerself."

"Aye," Jack muttered. "Ye think I don't know that?"

A pause followed before Finn huffed a sigh. "I've been looking for the chance to repay ye for a while now. It's why I spoke to Lady Tara as I did ... and why we're mooring here overnight. Let the lass have at least one opportunity to change her mind. Why not give the pair of ye a chance at happiness?"

Jack's throat constricted. He was touched by his friend's gesture, while at the same time exasperated. "Ye've wasted yer time. Tara isn't in love with me," he replied hoarsely. "And she won't abandon her kin ... or her responsibilities."

Finn shrugged. "Maybe not ... but I'm giving her the chance to alter course, should she so choose."

Jack shook his head, even as his chest constricted. He shouldn't have been surprised by Finn's act. On casual acquaintance, one would be fooled into thinking that he didn't care deeply for anyone. Finn had severed all ties with his family on Islay, and ever since Maggie's death, he hadn't shown softness toward any woman. However, he was doggedly loyal to Loch and Jack. "Don't think I don't appreciate the gesture," he murmured. "But ye must realize that if Tara did run away, Loch would skin ye alive?"

Finn flashed him a grin. "No, he wouldn't … not once I pointed out that, thanks to me, the MacDonalds of Sleat won't be allying themselves with the Mackinnons of Mull."

Jack snorted a laugh. "Ye really thought this through, didn't ye?"

"Aye … always." Finn shifted to Jack's side then and slung an arm over his shoulders, steering him down the docks toward the waterfront. "Come on … it's time we found ourselves an alehouse and got a hot meal and some ale. A few games of knucklebones should distract ye." Finn cast him another careless grin before adding, "I might even let ye win."

"It's been so dreary here since ye disappeared, Lady Tara," Orla said as she bustled around the bedchamber, packing feverishly in preparation for their departure the following morning. "I've missed ye terribly."

"And I have missed ye," Tara replied with a wan smile. It wasn't a lie—she *had* missed her maid. However, ever since Tara had joined her upstairs, and once she'd managed to disentangle herself from Orla's smothering embrace, the woman hadn't stopped babbling.

Tara had bathed and changed into clean clothes, yet all the while, Orla had talked without barely taking a breath. Tara found herself missing Cait's company back at Duart Castle. The woman might have been wary of her, but she didn't feel the need to fill every silence with words.

"Dùn Ara is grim without yer lively presence," Orla went on as she placed another neatly folded lèine into the large wooden trunk they were bringing to Skye. "I'm relieved that I'm going with ye to Dunscaith Castle."

"Dùn Ara isn't so bad," Tara replied distractedly. She was going through the jewelry she'd bring with her. There was a lot of it—brooches, rings, and necklaces studded with amber and garnets. Most of the items had been her mother's. "Ye always love a good gossip with the cooks and scullery maids."

"Aye, but ever since one of the lasses ran off a few days ago, the cook's been in a foul mood."

Tara glanced up, surprised. "Which lass?"

"Aynsley."

Tara's gaze widened as she recalled the sunny lass with golden hair and an impish smile. "Really? I hope she hasn't gotten herself into trouble."

Orla shrugged. "She was the laziest of the scullery maids," she sniffed. "Always skiving when she should have been working." Her maid then launched into her opinions of all those who worked in the castle's kitchens.

It wasn't long before Tara's mind wandered.

In truth, she had little patience for Orla's prattle this evening.

She was too upset. Too disappointed. Too angry. Her chest ached, and it was difficult to breathe.

She'd always thought her father adored her. Aye, her family wasn't a demonstrative one, yet in many ways, he'd always favored her over Bran. He was hard on his son, readying him for the day he'd step into the role of clan-chief. Her father might not have used endearments often with her, but he'd indulged his only daughter over the years, buying Tara the finest surcotes, and ordering expensive perfumes, oils, and soaps for her from France.

But he hadn't been worried about Tara's wellbeing or overjoyed to see her safely returned to him, and he'd taken Ramsay MacDonald's word over hers.

The only thing he could focus on was beating his enemies, no matter the cost. He was hungry for conflict, and his vision for an Isle of Mull under Mackinnon control was within his grasp. Aye, she'd glimpsed the victory in his eyes when Callum had reassured him that he'd still take Tara as his wife.

Seated upon her bed, while Orla still rambled on about the kitchen servants, Tara's vision blurred.

Never had she felt so alone, so betrayed. And right now, the last thing she wanted was to become Callum MacDonald's wife.

Tara's throat constricted, and she knuckled away the tears that trickled down her cheeks.

"Oh, lass. Don't mind me blethering on like an old fool. Ye must be exhausted after yer ordeal." Orla rushed to her, stroking Tara's back as she had when Tara had been upset as a bairn.

But she wasn't a bairn anymore, and she wasn't weeping over some trifling thing. Swallowing a sob, Tara buried her head in her hands.

"There, there … shall I get ye a nice hot cup of caudle? That'll make ye feel better."

Tara didn't reply; she was too busy trying to stem the grief that clawed its way up her throat. *Oh Lord, I shouldn't have come back here.*

This afternoon, in her father's solar, the truth had hit her like a mallet to the chest.

Her father was incapable of love. His domineering, calculating character had likely doomed his marriage from the start. No wonder her mother had been so cold; being wed to such a man would cause a woman's soul to wither.

The clan-chief saw both his son and daughter as pawns, to move around to suit his purposes. To use no matter the cost.

It was also clear that her betrothed didn't really want her—not any longer. His father craved an alliance with the Mackinnons of Mull, although she sensed if Callum could have withdrawn from the agreement, he would have.

Tara didn't want Callum either. She never had, not really. She'd been blinded by her need to please her father and her blinkered loyalty to her clan.

But spending time with Jack had lifted the veil from her eyes, and there was no putting it back. It was a cruel irony that the man who'd abducted her had also been her liberator. Those few days with him showed her another world, one where she was truly seen and valued for herself.

But that world was drawing out of reach. And if she didn't do something—tonight—she'd be trapped in this life forever.

"Aye, Orla," she gasped, wiping away her tears. "Don't mind me … I'm just overwrought after everything that's happened." She managed a watery smile then. "But I *would* like a hot cup of caudle."

Orla flashed her a relieved smile in response, happy to have come up with the solution. "Aye, lass … I'll be right back."

Watching her maid bustle from the chamber, Tara weathered a pang of guilt. As overbearing as she could be, Orla was a kind soul. She deserved better than to be manipulated and lied to.

However, Tara had to act quickly, decisively, if she was to ever save herself.

Not all decisions are set in stone, Lady Tara … should ye decide yer upcoming marriage isn't what ye truly wish for, ye can walk away from it.

MacDonald's words whispered to her then, and her skin prickled.

The captain had shocked her—and she'd suspected that his motivations were self-serving—but his offer had taunted her ever since.

The Macleans weren't sailing back to Duart Castle straight away. They were spending the night in Tobermory. Captain MacDonald was taking quite a risk. If she'd been truly loyal to her father, she'd have told him that the Maclean birlinn was mooring on Mackinnon soil overnight. Her father wouldn't have wasted time tracking them down and killing them.

But, somehow, MacDonald had known she wouldn't betray Jack, despite everything she'd endured of late.

And he was right. She'd cut off her own hand before she'd reveal such a thing to her father.

Kendric Mackinnon was no longer worthy of her loyalty.

I must reach Tobermory by daybreak.

Hands trembling, as excitement and fear pulsed through her, Tara leaped off the bed and dug around for a small cloth bag among her things. Retrieving one, she returned to the bed, opened the jewelry box she'd just closed, and poured her jewels into it.

She thought about retrieving a leather satchel from the wall and stuffing a few items into it but dismissed the idea. No, it was too risky. The only items she'd bring would be the clothes on her back and her bag of jewelry, for the way she'd take out of the castle was perilous.

She'd only be able to make her escape once it was dark, once most of the inhabitants of Dùn Ara slumbered.

Slipping the bag into her cloak, which hung behind the door, Tara started to pace the chamber.

What are ye doing? Panic curled up then, threatening to consume her.

Tara fought it. "Fleeing for my life," she whispered.

Ye'll never make it.

"Maybe not," she spoke aloud once more, "but I have to try."

31: THE DEVIL TO PAY

"IT GROWS LATE, Lady Tara. Do ye wish to retire?"

"Not yet, Orla. I shall take a stroll through my mother's rose garden first."

The older woman raised her eyebrows. "At this hour? Ye won't *see* anything."

"The torches on the walls throw plenty of light over the garden." Tara paused then, guilt tugging at her once more. "We will be leaving early tomorrow, and the garden is a special place for me." She glanced away so her maid wouldn't see the lie in her eyes. "I wish to bid Ma farewell."

A pause followed before Orla made a sound in the back of her throat. "Of course, lass. Let me fetch my cloak, and I shall join ye."

"I'd prefer to take a stroll alone," Tara said firmly. "I won't be long ... but I need solitude in order to say goodbye properly to my mother."

Orla stiffened, likely surprised by this sudden show of affection for a woman who'd only ever treated her daughter with aloofness. Instead, Orla was the one who'd shown her warmth and kindness. And in return, Tara was deceiving her.

But as sorry as she was to treat her maid like this, she couldn't confide in her. Orla was stoutly loyal to the clan-chief and would betray Tara to him in a heartbeat.

"My ordeal has made me more emotional than usual," Tara added with an apologetic shrug. "Please, indulge me."

"Ye won't be long?" Orla looked unconvinced, no doubt remembering what had happened the last time she'd left her charge to her own devices.

"No. I'll be down and back before ye know it."

Orla sighed, although she still looked unhappy. "Aye, well, make sure ye take yer mantle, for it's chilly outdoors this eve."

"I will." Tara rose from where she'd been resting on the bed and pulled on her boots before crossing to the door, taking down her cloak. She then flashed Orla a smile. "See ye shortly."

Slipping from the bedchamber, Tara tried to ignore the tightness in her chest. It was difficult though, for as she descended to the lowest level of her father's keep, anxiety fluttered up.

Sweat dampened her palms. She couldn't believe she was doing this.

Tara's heart kicked hard against her ribs then. There would be the devil to pay if she was ever caught.

Dùn Ara Castle was built on two levels upon the summit of a rocky promontory bounded by precipitous cliffs on one side and thick vegetation on the other. One wouldn't have expected to find a garden here, yet Tara's mother had insisted her husband have one carved out of the rock to accommodate her.

The private space was accessed through the southern curtain wall, and Tara wasn't surprised to find it empty this evening. Few, besides her and her mother, had ever spent time here. Nonetheless, as always, guards had placed burning torches on brackets at opposite ends of the garden just in case the laird or his family decided to take a stroll within it.

Climbing roses covered the encircling walls, while knots of lavender and more roses radiated symmetrically from the heart of the square space. The garden had a barren appearance this time of year, for the roses were just starting to bud and wouldn't bloom for another turn of the moon.

Heart skittering nervously, Tara walked through the garden, her boots crunching on the fine gravel underfoot.

Of course, she wasn't here to take a few turns of the path that circuited the walls and say farewell to Dùn Ara. Instead, cutting furtive glances around her to ensure no one was watching, she made her way over to the southwest corner, where the garden wall and the curtain wall met.

Careful not to jab her fingers on rose thorns, she tentatively felt the garden wall, relief fluttering through her when she found the deep grooves she hadn't touched in years. As a bairn, she'd scaled this wall, and used it as her secret escape route from the castle.

Tara's breathing quickened then. It had been years since she'd exited this way—and she was no longer a lithe lass of thirteen.

What if she couldn't scale the wall?

Tara set her jaw and pushed aside her anxiety. There was only one way to find out.

Without further hesitation, she started to climb, setting her fingertips and toes in the grooves that she'd discovered one summer while trimming roses with her mother.

She'd never told anyone about it, not even Bran. It was her way in and out—and the knowledge that it was hers alone gave her a forbidden thrill.

Nonetheless, she'd sometimes wondered who'd carved these grooves into the wall, and if anyone else ever used this escape route.

Tara had barely climbed three feet when she discovered her worries weren't unfounded. She wasn't as light or nimble as in the past. Scaling this wall was hard, and the muscles in her arms trembled and burned, yet she refused to give up.

By the time she reached the top, her arms were exhausted, her fingers bled from the clawing thorns that had impeded her progress, and sweat poured off her.

Panting, she rested at the top, welcoming the crisp evening air on her glowing face. She'd done it. From memory, getting down from here, although longer, was an easier climb, for someone had set iron handholds into the stone.

Just as well too, for the drop from here was terrifying.

Tara was grateful that the darkness hid the sharp rocks and spiky foliage beneath her.

Climbing down was still difficult though. Her arms burned once more from the strain as she slowly descended the wall to the rocky incline below. Breathing hard, she rested a few moments at the bottom before sliding on her backside down the rock. It was so steep here, there was no other way to do it.

Halfway, Tara heard a ripping sound and realized she'd caught her cloak on something. Yanking it free, she continued on her way, slithering on her back now, gathering speed until her feet hit the bottom.

Relief buckled her knees, and she crumpled there, her heart pounding in her ears.

Hades, if she'd known how difficult that was going to be, she wouldn't have embarked on this plan with such confidence. Her body ached, and her fingers were raw from their encounters with rose thorns and sharp rocks.

However, Tara allowed herself only a short rest. She had to keep moving, for she wasn't safe yet. Orla hadn't been happy to let her go off unescorted; she might come looking for her early.

Rising to her feet, Tara glanced around. Her chest tightened then, for away from the glow of torchlight, darkness swallowed the world. Only thanks to the silvery light of the waxing gibbous moon, which bathed Dùn Ara, was it possible for Tara to make out her surroundings.

"Courage, lass," she murmured, in an attempt to slow her racing heart. "There's no one out here."

Picking her way gingerly through a carpet of brambles and ferns to the narrow track beyond, Tara took care with her sprained ankle. It had healed well over the past couple of days, especially since she'd rested it, yet it still felt a little wobbly, and she risked turning it once more on the uneven ground.

Shoulders rounded as she peered ahead, she made her way around the base of the fortress and headed toward the boat noosts.

Earlier, she'd thought hard on the best way to escape Dùn Ara and had come up with a plan. But for it to work, she had to rely on a friend.

Her pulse spiked once more. She hated putting Aonghus in this position, yet she had no one else to turn to.

Pulling her hood up, lest she pass anyone on the way, Tara walked the rough path to the noosts, the rocky area above the water where a row of fishing boats sat, waiting for the dawn.

As she'd expected, there wasn't anyone about at this hour.

The fishermen were all at home with their wives, in the ramshackle bothies that nestled at the tree line behind the noosts.

All except one.

Ahead, she made out Aonghus Mackinnon's hunched form as she approached the last of the boats and smelled the odor of ale.

A moment later, a dog's high-pitched bark split the night.

Tara skidded to a halt. Curse it, Dora had a bark to wake the dead.

"Who goes there?" A gravelly voice demanded. The distinctive silhouette turned, and eyes gleamed in the moonlight.

"Good eve, Aonghus," Tara greeted him softly, trying to ignore the pounding of her heart. "It's me … Tara."

A pause followed before he answered, his gruff voice a little gentler now. "Och, lass … I didn't think I'd see ye before yer departure tomorrow."

Tara pulled a face, although she knew it was too dark for Aonghus to see it. News traveled swiftly it seemed. Everyone, even those residing outside the castle walls, knew she was leaving with Callum MacDonald at dawn.

"I'm relieved to see ye arrived home safely," he added then. "Everyone here feared the worst."

"I'm well," Tara assured him, moving closer, and then something small and firm barreled into her ankles.

Leaning down, she stroked Dora's wiry coat. The terrier gave her fingers a welcome nip. "But I need yer help."

"Oh, aye?" The fisherman sat with a skin of ale on his knee. Fortunately, it wasn't late, and so his voice wasn't yet slurred.

Tara halted before Aonghus, her gaze roaming his weathered face. Most folk here said Aonghus Mackinnon was a bitter old curmudgeon, but she'd seen the kindness in him the first day their paths had crossed. "I need passage away from Dùn Ara," she admitted then, deciding it was best to get straight to the point. "Tonight."

His eyes widened, although when he replied, his tone was wary. "Why?"

"I don't want to wed Callum MacDonald." It was the truth, although a simplistic one. "If I don't leave now, I'll be forced to."

"So, the rumors are true then, lass." Aonghus's tone turned rueful. "Ye *did* run away?"

"Aye." She wanted to tell him the truth, but the real story was far too long and complicated.

Silence followed this admission, while panic fluttered up under Tara's ribs. It wouldn't be long before Orla grew impatient. Her maid would soon put on her cloak and venture down to the garden to retrieve her—and once she discovered it empty, she'd waste no time in raising the alarm.

"I shall tell ye all once we're underway," she promised, her tone urgent now. "But I've got someone waiting for me at Tobermory ... and I need passage there."

Aonghus took her words in silently, his heavy brow furrowing. Tara's pulse kicked into a gallop once more as she watched him consider her request. Of course, it was risky admitting all this to him. Despite that she trusted the fisherman, she wasn't certain any longer if he'd help her.

Theirs was an unlikely friendship. Most folk avoided the old drunk who kept to himself a lot of the time, but for the past decade, Tara had often visited Aonghus on her strolls around the base of the castle. To Orla's consternation, she always insisted on going alone. After all, she was within a stone's throw of the castle, and over the years, she'd enjoyed sitting beside Aonghus and listening to his tales.

"I don't want to involve ye, Aonghus," she said, stepping closer still. She then withdrew the bag of jewelry from her cloak and jingled it. "But I also know just how unhappy ye are here. If ye take me away, right this moment, this pouch of jewels is yers. Ye can set yerself up elsewhere and finally buy yerself all the comforts life has denied ye."

She halted then, wondering if she'd gone too far.

Aye, Aonghus wasn't content at Dùn Ara. He'd had a hard life, full of disappointments he'd never rallied from. He'd been wedded once, with a son, but the bairn died and his wife had run off with another man. And in the years that followed, he'd become increasingly reclusive, shunning most folk—except the clan-chief's daughter. Even his scrappy terrier liked her. But he was also proud. He might think she was trying to buy his loyalty.

Suddenly, Tara started doubting her plan.

The silence between them drew out, while the gentle lap of water against rock intruded, followed by a burst of male laughter from somewhere up on the walls.

Tara's palms grew damp, nervousness taking hold now. Without Aonghus's help, she wouldn't go anywhere.

"Very well," he said eventually. "I'll not deny *either* of us our freedom."

Tara's belly swooped at the resolve in his voice and the gleam in his eye. Her instinct had been right. Aonghus was a kind-hearted man who cared what became of her, but he also longed to move away from a community where he'd never fitted in and start afresh.

"Come, lass." Aonghus flashed her a toothy grin and stoppered his bladder of ale before clambering out of his boat. He then moved to the stern and pushed it across the rocks toward the water. Dora gave an excited yip and jumped in. "Let's go."

32: WAITING FOR SUNRISE

TOSSING THE KNUCKLEBONE into the air, Jack scooped up the four scattered across the table in front of him. However, when he tried to catch the jack that he'd thrown up as well—it clattered onto the tabletop. He hadn't been fast enough.

Jack cursed, while opposite him, Finn snorted a laugh.

"Distracted tonight, aren't we?"

Jack scowled. They both knew he was. Picking up his tankard, he took a deep draft of ale, watching as Finn scattered the knucklebones and completed the move Jack had just attempted, swiping up all four and catching the jack with practiced ease.

"I don't know why I ever bother playing knucklebones with ye," Jack said sourly. "Since ye always win."

"It's likely the vain hope that one day ye will manage to best me." Finn flashed him a grin. "A man can dream."

Jack muttered an oath under his breath and leaned back in his chair. He shifted his gaze from his friend then, surveying the cramped common room of *The Bonnie Badger*, the tiny inn where they'd taken lodgings for the night. After a meal of gristly mutton and stale bread, they'd played a few games of knucklebones to pass the time.

But Jack was distracted. His thoughts strayed constantly to Tara.

In truth, he worried about her. Kendric Mackinnon was said to adore his daughter, but he was also ruthless. If he sniffed out her lie, he'd turn on her.

Tara was brave to defy him like this.

Jack's gut clenched every time he thought about her. He ached to protect her, to steal her away again, but this time for love, not revenge. He wanted to make her his wife, to show her in a thousand different ways that they belonged together.

Instead, he was sitting here losing at knucklebones and drinking sour ale in an inn that smelled like burned cabbage.

The only time he'd been at a lower ebb was after his father's murder.

"So ... are ye going to tell me what *actually* happened while ye and Lady Tara were trekking across the isle?"

Jack jerked his attention back to Finn, to find his friend watching him with a veiled expression. "I hadn't planned on it," he replied.

Finn shrugged before lifting his tankard to his lips and taking a gulp. "I don't want to hear about all the sighs and longing looks ... but I *am* interested to know what led to yer change of heart."

Jack sighed, dragging a hand through his hair. He could see Finn wasn't going to let this go. "When I stole her away from Tobermory, I was so pleased with myself," he admitted. "But things started to go wrong, right from the start ... and it wasn't long before I was far less smug. Doubt set in soon after ... and as my meeting with Black loomed, I realized I could no longer see my plans through. That's all there is to it, really." He paused then, his mouth slowly pursing. "There's something I didn't mention when I told Loch all this yesterday."

Finn inclined his head, encouraging him to continue.

"At dawn, on the morning before Ramsay smacked me around the back of the head, I saw The Headless Horseman."

Across the table, his friend stilled, a groove etching between his eyebrows. "Are ye certain?"

Jack nodded. "Tara saw the specter too … and blood-chilling it was." Indeed, it was hard not to shudder at the memory. "A headless rider upon a black horse galloped across our path as we walked out from under the shadow of Ben More." Jack paused then before grimacing. "Ye know what that means?"

"Aye," Finn murmured. "It's an ill-omen … foretelling that one of yer branch of the Macleans is about to die." His frown deepened then. "Why didn't ye tell Loch?"

"I was focused on other things when we met … and there wasn't time afterward." Jack pulled a face then. "Besides, he doesn't want to see me at present."

"Best ye let him know about this when we get back to Duart," Finn replied, his brow still furrowed.

"I must tell my brother as well," Jack said then, his mood darkening further. "He too is at risk."

Finn nodded. "Ye can't bargain with fate, but it's best all of ye know what's coming."

Silence fell between the two friends then, and Jack leaned back in his chair, surveying the smoky room once more. It wasn't that busy this eve—with only a handful of fishermen clustered around a table near the fire, dicing. Nonetheless, Jack and Finn had done their best to remain inconspicuous, taking a seat in the darkest corner of the common room.

Taking a gulp of ale, Jack scowled.

"What is it?" Finn asked. "Still worrying about the Horseman?"

Jack shook his head. "I hated leaving Tara behind at Dùn Ara," he muttered. "I know it's her home … but she's in a vulnerable position now. She's putting the blame on herself rather than me. Mackinnon might punish her for it."

"He might," Finn agreed. "Let's hope the lass has the wits to flee tonight."

Jack met his friend's eye. "She won't."

Finn shrugged. "Don't give up just yet." He paused then, his mouth curving. "The dawn will reveal all."

Moonlight gleamed on the water and frosted the tree-clad headland as Aonghus rowed east. The night was quiet save for the whisper of a light breeze and the rhythmic splash of the oars.

Seated at the bow, Tara had kept her gaze trained back the way they'd come for most of the journey. She was terrified that her father would come after her.

But first, he'd have to discover that she'd departed Dùn Ara by rowboat.

Orla would have raised the alarm by now; they'd be scouring the castle for her before widening their search.

Aye, they'd look for her eventually in Tobermory—but she just prayed that would not be until the morning.

Dora nudged against Tara's leg then, drawing her attention. Reaching down, she stroked the terrier's ears before her gaze shifted to Aonghus.

He'd said little since they'd rowed away from her father's stronghold. Instead, he'd let Tara whisper her tale to him—the real story, without embellishment. After she'd finished, Tara had expected him to warn her not to trust the Macleans—Aonghus was a Mackinnon too, after all—but to her surprise, he hadn't.

"So, ye have lost yer heart to this Jack Maclean then?" Aonghus asked eventually, shattering the silence.

Tara tensed, her breath catching at the direct question. "I ..." she began hesitantly. "I'm not sure ... I ..."

Aonghus's gaze glinted in the hoary light of the moon. "Och, stop with the excuses," he huffed. "A lass doesn't defy her father like this unless love is involved."

Tara's breathing grew shallow, even as warmth washed over her.

Watching her expression, Aonghus's mouth quirked into a knowing grin. "Not much longer ... I'll have ye in Tobermory shortly."

Still flushed and confused by his comments, Tara nodded before glancing over her shoulder. Sure enough, they'd just rounded the headland, and there, its home fires glowing softly, was the port village.

Relief gusted out of her in a deep sigh, excitement swiftly following.

Jack.

Christ's blood, was Aonghus right? Her feelings for Jack were far more complex than she'd realized. The past days had been intense and life-changing—and somewhere along the way, she'd fallen for her abductor. Her heart didn't care that he was a Maclean. It knew what it wanted.

Trying to tame her spiraling thoughts, she met her friend's eye once more. "Thank ye for doing this, Aonghus," she murmured. "I shall never forget it."

The fisherman held her gaze for a moment before favoring her with a smile. "Aye, well, ye've done me a favor too, lass."

"I hope so." Anxiety wreathed up then, tightening Tara's throat. "Make sure ye get as far from here as ye can. I don't want my father catching up with ye." She paused then. "And don't spend all yer coin on ale."

"Och, don't fash yerself about me, lass," Aonghus reassured her. "I intend to turn over a new leaf ... as soon as I drop ye off, I shall disappear like a wraith."

Relief suffused Tara at these words. Aonghus had risked everything to help her, and they both knew what would happen if her father ever found him. Even so, she wasn't innocent enough to believe that he'd never touch another drop of ale again—she just hoped Aonghus wouldn't drink the riches she'd given him away.

They both fell silent then as Tobermory slowly inched closer. Soon, the outlines of the fishing boats and birlinns moored on the dock became visible, and Tara's pulse quickened.

One of them would hopefully be the *Sea Eagle.*

"I'll drop ye off and be on my way swiftly," Aonghus murmured, careful to keep his voice low now, for noise traveled over water. "Best we keep our farewell short."

The fisherman rowed his boat up to the far end of the wooden jetty that protruded from the main dock, bringing the small craft in close so that Tara could disembark and climb the ladder up to the jetty itself.

Tara alighted onto the wooden planks that lined the narrow quay before she dropped to a crouch, turned, and peered down at the fisherman and his terrier.

"Goodbye, Lady Tara," Aonghus said, his voice a low rumble. "Live long and well, lass."

She swallowed, her throat thickening. "Aye," she whispered. "And ye too."

Using an oar, Aonghus pushed his boat away from the mooring and expertly turned it east. Then, as she looked on, he started to row in long, easy strokes, propelling his craft away from the jetty.

Tara rose to her feet and drew her cloak tightly around her before surveying the line of vessels moored here. Halfway down the line, she spied a birlinn, and when she walked down to inspect it, she saw that it was a twelve-man craft with an eagle carved onto the prow. A smile curved her lips. She'd found the *Sea Eagle*.

Disappointment settled over her then, for there wasn't any sign of Finn MacDonald or his men. She'd half expected the captain to leave one of his warriors to watch over the birlinn overnight, yet he hadn't.

Standing on the jetty, she cast an eye over the waterfront. There were three rowdy inns in Tobermory, and Jack could be staying at any of them.

Impatience, mingled with anxiety, thrummed through her. How she yearned to see Jack again. However, it was too risky to go looking for him, for someone would likely recognize her. A young unescorted woman with flame-red hair wouldn't go unnoticed. Most folk here knew what the clan-chief's only daughter looked like.

No, she'd not tempt fate by trying to find Jack. Instead, she'd use her wits, stay here, and wait for dawn to find them both.

Tara climbed down from the jetty into the birlinn. Gripping the rigging for balance, she moved amidship, where there was a gap between the planks that formed seats large enough for her to lie down. Doing just that, she drew her knees up to her chest and pulled her cloak close once more. She wouldn't be able to sleep like this surely, although it would be easier to keep warm, and it was more comfortable than sitting.

Rolling onto her back, Tara gazed up at the swathe of stars that glittered overhead and the friendly face of the moon.

Now, all she had to do was wait for sunrise.

Bleary-eyed and ill-tempered, Jack made his way down the waterfront toward the dock. He'd slept poorly overnight—something which had turned into a habit these days—and had lain awake for hours, his mind churning.

And it hadn't taken long for him to start berating himself.

Ye should have fought for her, ye dolt. Anger had chased this thought away though. He'd already caused Tara enough pain and turmoil. No, he had to let her go. Frankly, after what he'd done, he didn't deserve a woman so fine.

Aye, his thoughts had tied him up in knots, and it had been a relief to finally haul his carcass out of bed, don his clothes, and head back to the *Sea Eagle*.

Even so, he'd risen early. It was barely light; the first glimmers of sun were only beginning to lighten the eastern sky beyond the headland, and the last of the stars still twinkled above. And as Jack walked up the jetty to the birlinn, the wooden planks creaking with each step, he noted that there was no one else about. He was the first of Finn's men to reach the boat.

Slowing his gait, he glanced back at the waterfront, spying Finn emerge from *The Bonnie Badger* inn. Jack then focused once more on the *Sea Eagle*—Loch's recent purchase from a shipwright in Oban. It was a light, sleek craft, and the eagle carving upon the prow gave it a predatory edge. He'd noted the day before how fast the birlinn was. The galley was certainly capable of outdistancing other, heavier, boats should the need arise.

However, one birlinn wasn't enough, not when Kendric Mackinnon was forming alliances with the likes of the MacDonalds of Sleat, and so Loch had commissioned a few more galleys, just like this one—small enough to be hauled up onto the sand at Duart Bay.

Reaching the birlinn, Jack abruptly halted.

His gaze slid over the ship's curve, where a flash of fiery red caught his eye.

His breathing hitched.

Tara Mackinnnon was curled up like a wolf pup, wrapped in a pine-green cloak, fast asleep at the foot of the galley's mast.

For a few moments, Jack just stared, certain that his eyes were playing tricks on him. His lack of sleep must be causing him to see things.

But as time drew out and a briny wind tickled his face, he realized he was indeed lucid. And aye, the woman he loved was sleeping just yards away.

Joy unfurled like a fern in his chest, a smile stretching his mouth, before he eventually spoke her name. "Tara."

33: EVER AGAIN

TARA SCRAMBLED UP onto the jetty, grinning so widely that her face ached, and threw herself into Jack's arms.

He wore a stunned expression, yet he caught her easily, crushing her to his chest as he spun her around. And then he set her down and kissed her wildly, his fingers tangling in her hair, his tongue claiming her mouth.

Tara sank into him, returning Jack's embrace with the same passion. Her hands slid up his chest, and then she entwined her arms around his neck, pressing herself against him.

She'd never thought to fall asleep in the boat, yet she had. And she'd awoken from a deep, dreamless slumber to the sound of someone calling her name.

"Ye changed yer mind, did ye, Lady Tara?" An amused voice intruded upon their kiss, drawing Tara back to the present.

She pulled away from Jack, although her arms slid down to link possessively around his waist as she turned to face the lean leather-clad figure who stood a few yards way. "Aye," she told Finn MacDonald breathlessly. "Yer offer was too tempting to refuse."

The captain wore a smirk that she might have found annoying if exhilaration hadn't been thrumming through her. She and Jack had only been apart a few hours, but she'd been certain on parting they'd never set eyes on each other again. How fickle the hand of fate could be. She desperately wanted to tell him what lay in her heart, although with Captain MacDonald looking on, shyness crept in, and she hesitated.

Jack cupped her cheek then, drawing her attention to him once more. "What happened?" he asked softly, his gaze shadowed with concern now.

Tara held his eye. "My father discovered I was lying," she replied. "Ramsay MacDonald got there before me and told him ye'd abducted me."

Jack made a hissing noise between his teeth. "That shitweasel."

Tara swallowed hard. "Aye … and my father believed him over me."

A heavy silence followed this news, although the looks on both Jack and MacDonald's faces told her they weren't surprised.

"And how did he take the truth?" Jack asked eventually.

"As badly as ye might expect," she replied, her gaze meeting his once more. "Callum MacDonald is at Dùn Ara. I'm supposed to leave this morning with him for the Isle of Skye … and then as soon as we are wed, Callum is to immediately send a host of birlinns and warriors to Dùn Ara so that my father can launch an imminent attack on Dounawyse."

"Not any longer," The captain cut in, a hard smile curving his lips.

Tara's gaze flicked to him. Aye, she understood the consequences of her actions. Her father wasn't just losing his daughter, but—more importantly to him—a valuable ally.

"The Mackinnon is going to be mightily vexed," Jack murmured.

"Aye, he'll be bealin," MacDonald replied with a snort. "Which means we should get ourselves out of his territory without delay."

He swiveled to look behind him. Tara's gaze followed to where the rest of the crew approached. Tussle-haired and bleary-eyed, some of them appeared half asleep. Yet, when they spied her standing in the circle of Jack's arms, their eyes snapped wide, and their sleepiness vanished.

"What's this, captain?" One of the men asked as he approached. "I thought we already dropped Lady Tara off?"

"We did," MacDonald replied brusquely, "but now she's joined us again. Time moves against us, lads. We need to get the *Sea Eagle* off its perch. Fast."

Perched at the stern, a foot away from Jack, Tara watched tensely as the twelve men seated on both sides of the galley heaved back on their oars, propelling the birlinn away from Tobermory and toward the open water.

The sun was rising now, a rosy blush staining the eastern sky and turning the sea pink.

However, Tara couldn't focus on the dawn. They were still far too close to Dùn Ara, still within her father's reach. They were right to depart quickly.

But it wasn't quick enough, for when she glanced over her shoulder, looking west, she caught sight of a galley.

Her belly swooped as she recognized its red-and-white checkered sail.

"My father's coming!" she called out, pointing to the headland where the birlinn had just appeared.

Jack cursed before turning to her. "Take the oar," he ordered.

Tara did as bid, although she had no idea how to steer a ship.

"I've got her on course," Jack added then. "All ye have to do is hold the steering oar steady."

Tara nodded, gamely gripping the oar against the stern post while Jack left her side and clambered between the rows of oarsmen to where MacDonald was untying the sail.

Heart hammering against her ribs, Tara looked west once more. Her father's birlinn, which was at full sail, was gaining on them. His oarsmen were working hard too, water foaming up around the galley as it plowed through the sea.

He'd seen the *Sea Eagle* sail out of the harbor, and although her father wouldn't know she was onboard this boat for certain, he knew that a birlinn fitting this description had dropped her off the day before.

He was giving chase.

"Hurry!" she shouted to MacDonald and Jack as they worked to free the sail. "They're gaining on us!"

The oarsmen gave a collective shout and increased their tempo, working as one.

The *Sea Eagle* was flying through the surf now, yet it wasn't enough. They needed more speed.

The tough, thick-threaded wool sail snapped as they released it, before it caught the stiff breeze.

The rigging creaked as the birlinn lurched forward with such force that it nearly dislodged Tara from her perch. Gripping onto the steering oar for dear life, she squeezed her eyes shut as cold, salty water sprayed in her face.

Blinking to clear her vision, she raised her head once more. If she'd thought their birlinn was moving fast before, it was *racing* now. Of course, its smaller size made it fleet indeed. When she looked back at her father's galley, she saw that the distance between them had already grown. And as she continued to stare west, the Mackinnon birlinn grew gradually smaller and smaller.

A slow smile stretched her face.

They were outrunning them.

Glancing back at the oarsmen, she grinned at them. "Keep at it, lads," she called out. "We're drawing ahead!"

The men grinned back, their cheeks red with exertion, sweat and seawater running down their faces.

"Ye heard the lady!" MacDonald shouted over the roar of the waves. Both he and Jack were grinning now as they trimmed the sail to catch the wind properly. "Put yer backs into it!"

Tara's gaze met Jack's then—and as their stare drew out, both their smiles faded. Suddenly, everything around Tara disappeared. Her belly pitched with an excitement that had nothing to do with the movement of the boat, and pressure built under her breastbone.

The feelings that had surged up within her wouldn't be repressed. Her shyness dissolved. She had to tell him what lay in her heart.

"I love ye, Jack Maclean," she shouted over the roar of the sea and the wind.

His lips parted at this admission, his eyes springing wide. His shock was a picture indeed, yet it only lasted a moment.

Jack leaped forward then, leaving Captain MacDonald to look after the sail. Clambering down the galley between the oarsmen, he reached the stern and hauled Tara into his arms.

A heartbeat later, his mouth crashed down on hers for a passionate kiss. Keeping hold of the steering oar with one hand, Tara wrapped her free arm around his neck and returned his embrace with equal enthusiasm.

Tara's joy spilled over then, as did her tears, but Jack kissed them away.

And around them, the men cheered.

It was an exhilarating ride around the topmost point of Mull and then down the east coast. They left Mackinnon territory behind, yet Tara knew that wouldn't stop her father.

He'd still be after them—they couldn't slacken their pace.

By midmorning, the outline of Dounarwyse appeared to their right, its grey walls brooding against a cloudy sky. The wind, which had already been brisk at dawn, had picked up further. It now had spots of rain in it too, warning that the weather was set to worsen.

Jack had taken the steering oar again, although now he beckoned MacDonald over to him. "Can ye risk stopping at Dounarwyse?" he asked.

Tara tensed at these words, even though she wasn't entirely surprised to hear them, while the captain's gaze narrowed. "Aye," he replied cautiously. "But may I ask why?"

"Rae has offered me the position of Captain of the Dounarwyse Guard," Jack said, his gaze holding his. "And I choose to accept."

MacDonald's eyes narrowed further. "Why haven't ye told me this before?"

"Rae made the offer the night before we left Duart … and I wasn't sure how to answer." Jack's mouth curved into a humorless smile then. "We both know that Mackinnon's wrath will be terrible … and that Dounarwyse will bear the brunt of it. Rae needs my help."

"Well, if ye are disembarking here, so am I," Tara informed him, anxiety fluttering up. "Ye aren't sending me on to Duart without ye, Maclean."

Jack shifted his gaze to her. His expression softened then, and his eyes gleamed with love. "I have no intention of leaving ye," he assured her, his voice lowering intimately. "Ever again."

They stared at each other, the moment drawing out, before MacDonald cleared his throat. "Very well … if it's what ye wish, we can spare a brief stop," he replied. "Be ready to disembark fast though … as the lads and I won't be lingering."

Jack leaped onto the rickety wooden pier, putting his arms out to steady himself as his boots slipped on wet wood. He then turned and reached down, grasping Tara's hand, and pulling her from the birlinn.

Meanwhile, one of Finn's men was already unwinding the heavy rope made of moss-fir, readying to depart.

Once Tara was standing beside him, Jack wrapped a protective arm around her shoulders, steadying her against the wind and rain that now lashed in from the northeast.

The weather was progressively deteriorating, but, fortunately, the *Sea Eagle* wouldn't have long to travel before it reached Duart.

"Give Loch my apologies," Jack called to Finn. "Tell him why I made this choice."

"I will," Finn assured him. "Although ye might want to give him some time to let his anger cool before ye darken his door again." He grimaced then. "He may not be happy with me either … although if he gets testy, I'll remind him that it was *him* who baited Mackinnon in the first place."

Jack nodded, even as his chest tightened. "Be sure to point out that Tara's act will likely help us," he replied after a pause. "I doubt the MacDonalds of Sleat will give him the birlinns and warriors he wants now."

"Don't worry." Finn flashed him a rueful smile. "I will."

There was no more time for conversation though, for the birlinn was moving away from the dock, sliding through the heavy surf, the oars churning, while Finn moved to unfurl the sail once more.

Jack cast a sidelong glance at Tara. She was watching him, her face solemn. Her fiery hair was plastered in tangled curls against her head and neck, yet she'd never looked more beautiful.

Exhilaration and joy flowed over him, dousing his worry over how his cousin would react to the news that Tara had rejoined them and gone to Dounarwyse with Jack.

She loves me.

Even now, he could hardly believe it. And in the moments following her declaration—shouted into the wind without a care for who was listening—he wouldn't have minded if a whole fleet of Mackinnon birlinns had been on their tail.

Tara Mackinnon, the woman he longed for yet had
thought he'd never have, loved him. He was the luckiest
man alive.

"I never checked to ensure ye were happy with my
decision to alight at Dounarwyse," he said softly. "I
suppose it's too late to ask ye now?"

Her full lips lifted at the edges. "Aye ... but ye needn't
worry. When ye told me of yer brother's offer yesterday, I
knew it was the right choice for ye." Her arm wrapped
around his waist and squeezed tight. "As long as I'm *with*
ye, of course."

Jack smiled back, even as his pulse went wild. "Of
course." He nodded toward the broch that loomed above
them. "Now, shall we go up and see what my brother has
to say about all of this?" He paused, brushing a damp
curl off her cheek, his voice lowering as he added, "And if
ye wish it, I will ask him to marry us this very day."

34: OUR NEW HOME

RAE'S STUNNED EXPRESSION would have been comical if Jack hadn't been worried about his reaction.

Not to Jack's acceptance of the role he'd offered him—but to his brother turning up, drenched in seawater and rain, with an equally sodden Tara Mackinnon on his arm.

They stood in the hall of Dounarwyse, on the bottom level of the broch's tower house, by a roaring hearth where a pair of hairy highland collies gnawed at bones. Rae hadn't met them on his own. His wife, Donalda, held the youngest of their two sons, Lyle, swaddled against her breast. While Ailean, a wee lad of around three, clung to his mother's skirts, looking upon his uncle and the flame-haired woman at his side with wide eyes.

Donalda was a slender woman with walnut-brown hair twisted into a severe braid at the crown of her head. The woman was pretty with large doe-like eyes and a small pouty mouth that thinned as Jack now recounted what had happened.

Rae's face was harder to read than his wife's, but, nonetheless, Jack finished his tale with his heart in his throat. His brother likely thought him a reckless idiot, and he wouldn't be surprised if he turfed Jack and Tara out into the rain, telling them to walk to Duart and throw themselves at Loch's mercy.

A tense silence drew out, while the hearth crackled, and rain lashed against the walls of the tower house.

Eventually, Jack cleared his throat. "I realize this isn't what ye bargained on, brother," he said, meeting Rae's eye. "And I'm sorry." He paused then, swallowing. "But I swear I will captain the Dounarwyse Guard with pride. I only ask that ye join Tara and me as husband and wife and allow her to reside at Dounarwsye as well."

"So, her father doesn't know she's here?" Rae asked finally.

Jack shook his head.

"It's only a matter of time before he discovers where she is," Donalda said, her tone brittle. "And then he'll bring his wrath down on us."

"He already intends to do that," Tara said, speaking up for the first time since they'd entered the hall. "Although, my disappearance will have driven a spike into his plans ... for the moment, as he's likely to lose allies he'd counted on."

Donalda's mouth pursed at these words, although Rae nodded. "Aye, that's some good news, at least," he admitted. The laird rubbed a hand over his close-cropped hair, his gaze flicking from Jack to Tara. His mouth then quirked into a half-smile. "I can't say this comes as a huge surprise," he murmured. "When I saw ye on the walls after Lady Tara had departed, I suspected something was brewing between ye." Rae halted then, his smile turning wry. "Very well, my offer still stands Jack ... and aye, I will marry ye and Lady Tara."

Relief barreled through Jack at this declaration, while next to him, Tara squeezed his hand.

However, Donalda huffed a long-suffering sigh. "We have no time to prepare for a wedding, Rae," she pointed out.

"There's no planning needed," the laird replied, his gaze never leaving Jack's. "I will perform the ceremony now."

"Is this to be our new home?"

"It is." Jack stepped up behind Tara and wrapped his arms around her torso, placing a light kiss on her neck that made desire shiver through her. "Do ye like it?"

"Aye." And she did. The large chamber, atop the guardhouse, had two small windows. One gave them a view over the barmkin—the courtyard that wrapped around the keep—and the much taller tower house, and the other looked west over the hills that rolled inland.

Upon climbing the stairs to their quarters, the first thing Tara had done was open the heavy shutters to both windows, braving the wind and rain to peer out. The fire that burned in the hearth was guttering now, and the air inside the chamber cooling, so she promptly closed the shutters.

She then turned, still in the circle of her husband's arms, raising her chin to meet his eye.

Jack stared down at her, his expression soft with love.

Tara's pulse quickened. She would never tire of him looking at her like that. "The space is ample and will do us nicely," she assured him.

Indeed, the sleeping quarters had a heavy curtain that divided them from the living space. Two high-backed wooden chairs with cushions flanked the hearth, and a scrubbed wooden table—where a platter of bread, cheese, and cured sausages awaited, along with a ewer of wine—had pride of place in the center of the room.

The rest of the chamber was sparsely furnished, clearly the lodgings of an unwed man before now. Tara would quickly change that, adding feminine touches that would make these quarters home.

"I'm glad ye like it," Jack murmured, reaching up to stroke her cheek. "I was worried ye'd find it … plain … compared to what ye're used to."

Tara arched an eyebrow. "Of late, I've gotten used to sleeping rough and steering birlinns through wild seas." She lifted a hand, placing it over Jack's. "I don't care where I live, Jack … as long as it's with ye."

"I'll never tire of hearing ye say that," he replied huskily. "I still can't believe it."

"Well, ye should," Tara replied as she gazed up at him. "Because it's the truth." She halted then, marshaling her thoughts before continuing. "I think I lost my heart to ye the night we lay together … but it was only when I arrived back at Dùn Ara that I allowed my feelings to surface." She gave a rueful shake of her head. "I didn't admit it to myself though. It took a plain-speaking fisherman to make me see the truth."

Aye, she had much to thank Aonghus for—and she hoped he was far from Mull by now.

Jack's mouth curved. "I'm relieved ye did." He leaned in for a kiss then, although a knock at the door interrupted him.

"Water's here for yer bath," a woman's voice sang out.

"Bring it in then," Jack called back, stepping away from Tara.

An instant later, the door opened and three rosy-cheeked lasses, hauling large pails of steaming water, entered, followed by two big lads with a heavy cast iron bathtub.

Tara gasped with pleasure. Her skin was itchy from sweat and seawater. She'd longed to soak in a bath yet hadn't asked. Baths were a luxury for the likes of the laird and lady of a keep, or their bairns. Not the Captain of the Guard and his wife.

Seeing her reaction, Jack winked. "A wedding gift from my brother."

Tara beamed, watching as the lads set the tub down before the fire and the lasses filled it with hot water. Then, leaving a pile of drying cloths and a cake of soap on a chair, the servants departed, the door thudding shut behind them.

Jack moved over to the table and poured them each a cup of wine before favoring Tara with a smile. "Go on … ye bathe first."

Tara's breathing grew shallow at both the challenge and the promise in his voice.

Things had moved swiftly between them. A week earlier, they'd been enemies. Now they were wed, and she was about to disrobe before him for the first time.

Aye, they'd already lain together—but it had been in the dark.

She suddenly felt shy about removing her clothing and letting him see her in nothing but her skin.

Sensing her nervousness, Jack nodded toward the tub. "Go on, I'll turn my back while ye disrobe."

"Thank ye," she said, her voice suddenly husky, "but could ye unlace my surcote before ye do?"

"Of course."

He approached her then, handing her a cup of wine before moving around to unlace her surcote at the back. Moths danced in Tara's belly as he worked, and she lifted the cup to her lips and took a large gulp. Black plum, her favorite.

"There," Jack said after a pause. "Do ye need any other assistance?"

Tara wet her lips. "No ... I should be able to manage from here."

Jack moved around, taking the cup from her, and walking across to the table, where he pulled out a chair and sat down, his back to the tub.

Tara watched his broad shoulders for a few moments before she heeled off her boots. Shrugging out of her surcote, kirtle, and lèine, she let them pool around her ankles. Then, she tip-toed across the cold floorboards to the tub and stepped into it.

A sigh of pleasure escaped her as she sank into the water. "Dear Lord, this is bliss."

Jack chuckled. "I'm glad it pleases ye."

Tara smiled before reaching forward and picking up the cake of soap. Sniffing it, she let out a squeal of pleasure. "Damascus Rose!"

"Aye, it seems that Donalda has expensive tastes ... it took all my charm to persuade her to part with a cake of her precious soap."

Tara laughed. "Rogue."

Still grinning, she lathered up the soap and began to wash. The delicious scent of sweet, musky rose wafted up, wreathing around her, and she sighed once more. After the day's adventures, this was a gift indeed.

"I'm relieved yer brother has welcomed us," she murmured as she soaped her hair. "Even if his wife isn't quite sure about the arrangement."

"Donalda will thaw," he replied. "Eventually."

"I've noted a few folk looking at me askance since our arrival," she admitted then. "How will they feel about their enemy's daughter residing here?"

"The folk of Dounarwyse are hardy souls," he replied. "They've had to be … sitting so close to the border between Maclean and Mackinnon lands. However, the news that, since ye've married me, yer father won't likely get the assistance he was counting on from the MacDonalds of Sleat … will be circulating the broch. It'll come as a relief."

"But that doesn't mean they're safe." Her fingers clenched around the slippery bar of soap. "He's going to attack Dounarwyse, Jack … it's not a matter of *if*, but *when*."

"I know, lass," he murmured. "And we'll be ready."

They both fell silent then while Tara finished washing. The bath was heavenly, and she could have soaked in it for a long while. However, she was sharing the water with her husband and didn't want him to have to bathe in a cold tub.

Rinsing off, Tara rose to her feet and took a drying cloth, wrapping it around herself. She then took a second cloth and twisted it around her wet hair before stepping out of the tub onto the sheepskin before the hearth. "It's yer turn now," she announced.

Jack turned, his fern-green eyes swiveling straight to her. His gaze raked down her, and even though Tara's modesty was protected by the drying cloth, she might as well have been naked.

His gaze burned into her.

Swallowing, she edged back from the bathtub, scooping up her clothing and moving toward the hanging that separated the living and sleeping areas. "Go on … before the water cools."

Jack gave her a slow smile and pulled his lèine over his head, revealing rippling muscle underneath. He then started to unlace his braies.

Suddenly, breathless, Tara dove for the curtain. And as she ducked behind it and hurried over to the canopied bed against the far wall, she could have sworn she heard her husband chuckle.

Tara's cheeks flamed. *Knave. Two can play this game.*

35: I'LL LOOK AFTER YE, LASS

THE BATH WAS delicious, the warm rose-scented water silky against his skin.

Nonetheless, Jack couldn't relax in it.

How could he when his beautiful wife was sitting half-naked next door? He imagined she was combing out her long red hair right now, untangling it after the storm it had weathered.

She was likely dressed in her lèine, her peaked nipples visible through the thin fabric.

Jack's rod stiffened painfully at the thought.

It had already stood to attention earlier, at the sight of her all pink and glowing from her bath.

Lord, it had taken every bit of his self-control not to unwrap her like a gift before taking her against the wall.

Instead, Jack had reined the lusty impulse in and disrobed before climbing into the tub. He washed quickly, deftly, not luxuriating in the water as Tara had. And when he rose to his feet, his erection reared up like a schiltron pike, demanding attention.

Doing his best to ignore it, Jack dried himself off and pulled on his braies, lacing them loosely.

Despite that he and Tara had already been intimate, she was a little shy and skittish this evening. He couldn't blame her—things had moved so swiftly between them. He too was still reeling from it.

He had to bridge the gap between them, to win her trust.

Padding barefoot over to the curtain, he hesitated. "Tara," he called out. The lass hadn't said a word since he'd stepped into the bath, and he was beginning to wonder if she'd fallen asleep. "Can I come in?"

"Aye," her soft, slightly-throaty reply filtered through the curtain.

Pushing aside the barrier between them, Jack stepped into the sleeping area. The sight that greeted him made his breathing catch in his chest.

His beautiful wife was lying upon the bed as naked as the day she was born.

Her pale skin glowed in the light of the lamp that flickered on the nearby table, and her damp hair was spread out on the pillow in a dark-red halo.

And as his gaze traveled over her, Tara smiled. Her hand slid across her belly, teasing him. Her chest rose and fell swiftly, betraying her arousal. Her small rose-tipped breasts begged to be suckled.

Jack's knees nearly buckled at the sight of her.

As long as he lived, he would never forget how glorious she looked right now.

Tara's hand strayed lower then, traveling down her belly to the nest of damp curls between her legs. And then, slowly, deliberately, her gaze never leaving his, she parted her legs to show him the flower between them.

Jack stopped breathing then, hunger igniting in his gut.

It was too much. Even *he* had limits.

Shaking from the need that now pummeled him like fists, he undid his braies and let them fall to the floor.

Tara's lips parted as her gaze slid down his torso to his groin.

And then, she gave a soft, breathy moan.

That was all it took. In an instant, Jack was on her, lunging upon the bed, his hands cupping her face as his mouth claimed hers for a wild kiss.

Lust ignited like smoldering tinder between them. Tara's tongue speared into his mouth, her teeth grazing his lower lip, her nails raking at his back as their limbs tangled.

Jack's head swam. The devil take him, this woman set him alight. He couldn't believe she was his, and that they were here together. Naked with no interruptions. Aye, her old man would rage when he discovered whom his daughter had wed, but Jack didn't care.

Let the bastard fume. The only way he'd take Tara from him would be from his cold dead hands.

Tara writhed under Jack, her hands sliding down to his groin. There, she cupped his bollocks with one hand while she wrapped her fingers around his rod with the other. And then, she slowly, firmly, stroked him.

Jack's eyes fluttered closed. The woman had a touch that enchanted him, and if she continued to stroke him with such determined, sensual purpose, he'd spill all over her belly again.

He didn't want that. This time, he wanted to plow her thoroughly. He didn't intend to withdraw before his climax either. Instead, he wanted to lose himself deep inside her.

Pushing himself up, he took hold of Tara's wrists and lifted them above her head, pinning them against the pillows. It was a dominant move that thrust her delicious tits in his face.

Groaning her name, Jack bowed his head and began to suckle each one. He started slowly, taking his time, but her groans and gasps quickly unraveled his self-control, and his sucking became feverish.

He let go of her wrists then, and licked and kissed his way down her body.

And then, moving lower still, he hooked his hands under her knees and lifted them over his shoulders so that her lower legs hung down his back. This position exposed her to him, and he gazed greedily upon the cleft between her thighs.

Their previous coupling, as wild and exciting as it was, had been in the dark. How he'd missed being able to see her—all of her.

Lowering his head, he tasted her, his tongue sliding over her sex, teasing and probing.

Tara let out a guttural cry, thrusting up against him, and Jack's self-control snapped. He devoured her, his tongue, teeth, and lips working wildly until her thighs started to quiver, until she shattered against his mouth.

Gasping, Tara fell back against the pillows. Her silver eyes were glazed, her lips parted, as he rose up between her legs.

Taking hold of her thighs—as he had when they'd coupled under that oak tree in the rain—Jack pushed them back, raising her quim up to him once more. And then, staring down at the pink wetness, he thrust his aching rod deep into it.

Tara shouted his name, bucking hard against him, driving him even further inside her.

"Tara," he gasped, thrusting into her again. His body was alight now, lust a fever in his blood. The need to join with this woman, to possess her, consumed him. "I love ye," he growled as he drove deep once more and then rolled his hips.

She whimpered in response, her body shuddering. She was so wet and hot, he felt as if it would drive him mad. "I love ye, Jack," she cried out, her voice cracking. "Ye are all I need ... I ... oh, God!"

A rush of heat enveloped his shaft, the muscles of her core fluttering and squeezing his length as she climaxed, writhing against him with a wild abandon that severed the last of his self-control.

Jack plowed her savagely now, until heat gathered at the base of his spine, his belly clenched, and his vision darkened. And then, with a roar of victorious pleasure, he emptied himself inside her.

Gasping for breath, Tara threw a hand over her eyes. "The good Lord help me," she panted. "If it feels that good next time, my heart may stop."

"Aye ... mine might too."

She huffed a laugh, wiping the sweat from her face with her forearm before raising her gaze to meet Jack's.

He'd propped himself up on his elbows and was staring down at her with such tenderness and love that her breathing hitched. His eyes glistened, and as he watched her, a tear escaped, glittering on his lashes.

Tara's throat tightened, and she lifted her hand, brushing the tear away with her fingertips.

His throat bobbed. "I'll look after ye, lass," he vowed. "And I'll shield ye with my life if it comes to it."

She stroked his cheek. "I know ye will … but let us hope that it never comes to that." She paused then. "I understood the risks I was taking when I fled Dùn Ara."

His mouth curved in response. "Finn is a sly devil … but I'm glad that he made ye that offer." He paused then. "It wasn't all about ruining yer father's plans either. Last year, on the final day of battle at Bannockburn, I saved his life. In truth, I'd do so again without a moment's hesitation, yet Finn wanted to repay me. And when he saw us on the wall together at Duart, he seized his opportunity."

"I'm glad he did," she replied. "It was awful at Dùn Ara, Jack." Her chest tightened as memories of that meeting in her father's solar flooded back. "My father was callous. My only regret is that I shall never see my brother again … or my maid, Orla." It was true. Bran, although he did his best to hide it, was a big-hearted lad who'd been as oppressed as she had been by their father's expectations, while Orla was a kind woman who'd treated Tara like a daughter. She hoped both her brother and her maid would forgive her one day.

Jack's smile faded. "I shouldn't have let ye return there."

She shook her head. "Ye had to."

"But ye've suffered so much." His face twisted. "And all because of me."

Tara sighed. "Not *all* because of ye." Her finger traced his full lower lip. "Although, ye did put me through a great deal, Jack Maclean … who'd have thought I'd fall so madly and desperately in love with ye?"

His gaze darkened. "Perhaps ye like a man with an edge to him," he replied, his voice roughening. He was still buried inside her, but she felt his shaft harden once more. "A man who challenges ye."

"Maybe I do," she admitted as heat pooled in her lower belly. He'd just taken her in a storm of wild passion, yet her hunger for him was not sated. Not at all. She rolled her hips, gasping as pleasure fluttered through her loins. "Now, why don't ye stop talking," she breathed, "and *challenge* me, again."

EPILOGUE: ALL FOR LOVE

A fortnight later ...

TARA WATCHED HER husband take his men through drills.

It was too cramped in the barmkin for him to train them there, especially since he had nearly fifty men under his command, so Jack had led the Guard outside the castle walls, to the gently sloping ground west of Dounarwyse.

And Tara had a direct view of them from her window atop the guard tower.

Perched upon a stool at the open window, a cushion she was embroidering for their new home upon her knee, she kept glancing out at where the men wrestled, fought with practice swords and daggers, and shot arrows into targets.

It was quite a display.

And Jack was amongst them all, overseeing his warriors as they sparred, and even stepping in at times to show them how it was done.

They responded well to him, enjoying his easy smiles, yet wary of crossing him, for Jack had a fiery temper that would flare if any of them took his relaxed manner for weakness.

In the two weeks since they'd come to live at Dounarwyse, she'd watched Jack blossom in his new role.

It was as if he'd been born to captain the Dounarwsye Guard. His days were long and tiring, yet he was always in good humor when he climbed the stairs to join Tara. While he washed and changed, they'd chat about the day's events before joining Rae and Donalda for supper in the hall, along with the large host of warriors that now resided here too. The hall barely fitted everyone in, and the cooks and servants had to work hard to accommodate them.

A rich, savory aroma roused Tara from her vigil at the window. Tearing her gaze from where Jack was instructing two of the lads who were sparring with wooden practice swords, she went to the fire and lifted the lid on the iron pot. Aye, it looked as if the venison stew she'd put on a few hours earlier was finally ready. Taking protective leather gloves from the mantelpiece, she used them to lift the pot off the flames, placing it upon a slab of wood she'd set on the table. Once the stew had cooled a little, she'd carry it downstairs to the kitchen, to add to the food the cooks were preparing for the noon meal.

Tara had taken to making something to contribute every day—a gesture the cooks seemed to appreciate, for fifty warriors ate heartily, and it was a struggle to fill their bellies.

While she waited for the stew to cool off, Tara returned to her seat by the window.

Jack had moved over to where a line of men stood with longbows and arrows. Taking a longbow from one of the youngest lads, Jack showed him the proper stance. He then notched an arrow and drew the bowstring taut—all while he continued to instruct the lad—before loosing the arrow.

It struck the center of the target, bullseye.

Around him, men cheered.

Grinning, Jack handed the longbow back to the young warrior.

Tara shook her head. The man was incorrigible. Glancing down at her cushion, she made a few more neat stitches. She was embroidering a field of buttercups on

this one and was nearly done. Her attention shifted then
to the seats by the fire, where two cushions she'd already
finished—one with a castle perched on a green hill with
daffodils in bloom beneath it, the other of a sleek birlinn
with a pine-green sail and an eagle prow cutting through
the waves—sat. Thanks to Orla's patience and instruction
over the years, Tara had some skill with embroidery and
weaving.

Thinking of her former maid gave Tara a pang, and
she put aside her sewing.

Orla would be wondering where she was, and if she
was safe. The poor woman would have kittens if she
knew Tara was wed to Jack Maclean and living at
Dounarwyse Castle.

It was strange how life unraveled. If someone had
told her a month earlier that this would have soon been
her fate, she'd have reacted with rage and panic.

No foul Maclean man would ever touch her.

She would never disappoint her father.

But life had a way of molding a person, of rubbing
away all the sharp edges. In reality, she'd been
prejudiced and cut off from the truth of who she really
was.

Jack had allowed her to blossom. She was sometimes
sad about her family. The bridge she'd burned behind
her could never be rebuilt, yet she knew that this was the
path meant for her.

Peering out the window, Tara noted the sun was
almost directly above. Noon wasn't far off, and she
should get the stew down to the kitchen.

Rising to her feet, she put on the leather gloves once
more, picked up the heavy pot, and gingerly made her
way down the spiraling stone stairwell that descended to
the barmkin. There, she greeted the lads mucking out the
stables and nodded to a lass throwing grain to fowl.

They responded with shy smiles.

Some of the folk here were wary of her, yet that was
to be expected. For the most part though, they were
curious about the lady who'd given up her social
standing and defied her father. All for love.

Tara's mouth curved as she crossed to the kitchen, a low building next to the tower house. Aye, she must have been the subject of many conversations since her arrival.

As always, the Dounarwyse kitchen was chaotic and smoky. Cooks bellowed, and assistants scurried.

Greeting those she met, and narrowly avoiding a few collisions, Tara carried the pot to one of the long scrubbed oak tables and hefted it onto the surface. She then met the eye of the older woman rolling pieces of dough. "There ye go, Milly," she greeted her. "More venison stew to go with yer dumplings."

"Thank ye, lass," Milly replied, wiping her sweaty brow with the back of her hand and leaving a streak of flour behind. "That'll be a great help."

"The men will be hungrier than usual, I'd wager," Tara said then, her mouth quirking. "Since it's such a bonnie day, Jack's working them hard."

Milly pulled a face. "Don't tell me that ... I swear, they already eat like gannets."

Grinning, Tara left the kitchen—gloves tucked into her apron—emerging into bright sunlight once more.

Indeed, it was a glorious spring morning. The air had a sweetness to it today, announcing that summer was on its way. Tara sighed then. It was far too beautiful a day to be shut away indoors.

Instead of returning to her tower chamber to continue her work, she wandered out, under the portcullis and down the causeway to where Rae had joined Jack and the others. To her surprise, the brothers had both stripped off their lèines and were giving a wrestling demonstration to the men.

The guards gathered around, shouting encouragement as Jack and Rae slammed into each other, locking their arms together and circling. Their bare feet dug into the trampled grass as each tried to gain the advantage.

They were well-matched though—both of a similar size and strength.

Rae's torso and arms were just as muscular as Jack's.

Their grunts filtered up into the warm air, sweat gleaming on their naked backs as they circled in one direction and then the other.

For a few moments, it looked as if Rae would best his younger brother—but then Jack hooked a leg around Rae's and sent him topping sideways.

Cheers and heckling erupted from the sidelines.

Rae rolled to his feet while Jack pushed himself up and flashed the laird a grin. "Do ye want to go again?"

Rae snorted. "Not if ye are going to resort to cheating."

"That move is allowed." Jack's gaze glinted then. "It was the only way I was going to beat ye."

"I suppose I should take that as a compliment," Rae grumbled.

"Aye." Jack slapped him on the back. "It was *ye* who taught me to fight dirty years ago, after all."

A few men laughed at this, and Tara found herself smiling as well. Although they looked alike, Rae and Jack were very different men. Rae was serious and restrained, while Jack was emotional and liked nothing better than to tease.

Tara could see why they'd been estranged following their father's death, yet they also complemented each other well. And during the past fortnight, trust had slowly been re-established between them.

It warmed her to witness it, for she could see that mending things with his elder brother meant a lot to Jack.

Jack spied her amongst the crowd then, his face softening with that look he reserved only for her. Taking a drying cloth from one of his men, he toweled himself off before sauntering over to Tara.

Watching his approach, her belly fluttered. Jack always had that effect on her.

"Enjoying the show, wife?" he teased.

"Aye," she admitted. "Although I thought Rae was going to trounce ye."

Rae muttered something under his breath at this, although Jack merely shrugged. "He's good, I'll admit."

He stopped before Tara then, smiling down at her. "What brings ye outdoors at this hour?"

"The sunshine," she replied pertly, "and I came downstairs to bring a pot of stew to the kitchens."

He inclined his head. "I hope they appreciate the effort ye go to."

Her lips tugged into a half-smile. "And *I* hope yer men appreciate my cooking."

"Aye, well … none of them have complained of an aching belly … yet."

Tara gave him a playful slap at this, and Jack pulled her against him, his mouth slanting over hers for a hard, lusty kiss.

Around them, Jack's men hooted, although he paid them no mind. Eventually releasing Tara, he stroked her cheek with the back of his hand. His expression sobered then, his gaze shadowing.

"What is it?" she asked, her brow furrowing.

Jack pulled a face. "Just worries creeping in."

"Worries?"

"It's been a fortnight, lass … and yer father has gone quiet. I can't help but think he's up to something."

Tara gave a soft snort. "Of course, he is, my love. Take it from me … Kendric Mackinnon should never be trusted."

"Surely, the MacDonalds of Sleat have abandoned him though?"

She inclined her head. "I'd imagine so. The MacDonald clan-chief made it clear that unless his son wed me, there would be no alliance."

Jack nodded, although his expression was still a trifle strained. Their gazes fused then before he murmured, "Are ye happy here, Tara?"

"Of course," she replied, surprised by the question. "Don't I seem so?"

"Aye." He pulled a face then. "Yet ye were pampered in yer old life … and treated like the lady ye are."

"That's all behind me now," Tara replied with a shake of her head. She paused then, marshaling her thoughts.

"And in truth, I like being useful. It gives me a sense of ... belonging."

"Didn't ye feel like ye belonged at Dùn Ara?"

"I thought I did ... but that was before ye stole me away and showed me what belonging truly means." She caught his hand then, bringing his palm to her lips and kissing it. Jack's gaze hooded at this intimate gesture, and suddenly she wished they were alone in their tower room so they could take things further. "I don't think I've ever been happier than I am now," she admitted softly.

Jack's gaze turned limpid, and he stepped close, cupping her face with his hands. "And neither have I," he whispered back.

The End

HISTORICAL NOTES

Many locations on the Isle of Mull feature in this novel. I take you on an exciting tour of the island … these include:

Tobermory: a seaside fishing port located on the northeast coast of Mull. The name Tobermory is derived from the Gaelic "Tobar Mhoire", meaning "Mary's well", which refers to a well located nearby that was dedicated in ancient times to the Virgin Mary.

Ben More: the highest mountain and only Munro on the Isle of Mull, Scotland. It is also the highest peak in the Scottish Isles—and the only Munro—apart from those on the Isle of Skye. The mountain is situated close to the center of the island, above the shores of Loch na Keal.

Fionnphort: this is the principal port of the Ross of Mull, and the second largest settlement in the area. The village's name is the anglicized pronunciation of the Gaelic for 'White Port'.

The Carsaig Arches: these are natural arch cliff formations on the Ross of Mull in the south of the Isle of Mull. They are situated below Malcolm's Point, at the base of the Rudha Fhaoilean cliffs.

Lochbuie Standing Stones: this is a small and well-preserved stone circle overlooked by spectacular Ben Buie. Find out more about this mysterious location here: https://www.ancient-scotland.co.uk/site/loch-buie-stone-circle

Duart Castle: this magnificent fortress still stands today. Dating back to the 13th century, it's the seat of clan Maclean. The castle's position was a strategic one, for it sits upon a high crag at the end of a peninsula jutting into the Sound of Mull, where it guards the channel between Mull and the mainland. The 14th-century keep was built by Chief Lachlan Lubanach Maclean. On the vulnerable landward side, the walls are 29 feet (9m) high

and 10 feet (3m) thick, while the walls facing the sea are thinner, ranging from 5 to 9 feet (1.8m to 2.4m). The castle fell into ruin from the 18th century, until it was completely refurbished in 1911 by Sir Fitzroy Maclean.
Dùn Ara Castle: today, this is a medieval ruin sited 8 km northwest of Tobermory. It occupies the summit of one of several prominent rocky outcrops that lie scattered along the northern shore. It was traditionally the Mackinnon seat of Mull.
Dounarwyse Castle: known today as Aros Castle, this is a ruined 13th-century castle near Salen on the Isle of Mull. The castle overlooks the Sound of Mull.

The clan conflicts that take place in this series are based on real feuds between the Macleans of Duart and the Mackinnons of Dùn Ara. Traditionally, the Macleans of Duart were allies of the Macleods of Skye, and the Mackinnons of Dùn Ara were allied to the MacDonalds of Sleat on the Isle of Skye. It's always fun, and far more authentic, to anchor my stories on real history!

The Headless Horseman of Mull, who was mentioned in the previous book, also appears in this story. There are many tales from around the world of such a ghost, yet the most prominent Scottish one comes from the Isle of Mull. It concerns a man named Ewan of the Little Head (Eoghann a'Chinn Bhig), decapitated in a clan battle at Glen Cainnir on the Isle of Mull. The battle denied him any chance to be a chieftain.

But Ewan's ghost is unable to rest in peace, and ever since that day, the specter of a headless rider on a black horse is reported to ride through Glen More between dusk and dawn. In particular, it is believed that his appearance to one of the Maclean clan, or the sound of his horses' hooves galloping around the clan seat at Moy by Lochbuie, is an omen that a member of that family is about to die.
https://en.wikipedia.org/wiki/Headless_Horseman

https://thehazeltree.co.uk/2015/05/16/glen-more-and-the-headless-horseman/

In Chapter Eighteen our hero and heroine share some riddles. Riddling was a popular pastime in the Middle Ages. Jack and Tara's riddle game uses three sources:
https://www.medievalists.net/2023/07/riddles-medieval-of-aldhelm/
https://www.abdn.ac.uk/sll/disciplines/english/beowulf/riddle.htm
https://www.ranker.com/list/medieval-riddles-puzzling/melissa-sartore

As always, I hope these notes give you an insight into the research I do, and into the rich culture and history my novels anchor themselves on.

DIVE INTO MY BACKLIST!

Check out my printable reading order list on my website: https://www.jaynecastel.com/printable-reading-list

ABOUT THE AUTHOR

Multi-award-winning author Jayne Castel writes epic Historical and Fantasy Romance. Her vibrant characters, richly researched historical settings, and action-packed adventure romance transport readers to forgotten times and imaginary worlds.

Jayne is the author of a number of best-selling series. A hopeless romantic in love with all things Scottish, she writes romances set in both Dark Ages and Medieval Scotland.

When she's not writing, Jayne is reading (and re-reading) her favorite authors, cooking Italian feasts, and going on long walks with her husband. She's from New Zealand but now lives in Edinburgh, Scotland.

Connect with Jayne online:
www.jaynecastel.com
www.facebook.com/JayneCastelRomance
https://www.instagram.com/jaynecastelauthor/
Email: contact@jaynecastel.com

Visit Jayne's shop and buy exclusive short stories:
https://www.jaynecastel.com/shop

www.ingramcontent.com/pod-product-compliance
Lightning Source LLC
Chambersburg PA
CBHW032237310726
48973CB00008B/2174